LETHAL LEGACY

Robin C Birch

Copyright © 2024 Robin C Birch

All rights reserved

The characters and events portrayed in this book are fictitious. Any similarity to real persons, living or dead, is coincidental and not intended by the author.

No part of this book may be reproduced, or stored in a retrieval system, or transmitted in any form or by any means, electronic, mechanical, photocopying, recording, or otherwise, without express written permission of the publisher

ISBN-13: 9798344345833

Cover design by: RCTB

Chapter 1
Kwazaland 1967

The narrow dust road to Lewis Bodell's farm climbs awkwardly up from the plains below. It doubles back on itself three times, as it ascends. The long-wheel-base police Landrover ground slowly upwards over the rough, sunbaked surface. The stainless-steel body box, strapped on the roof, together with the three members of the deceased's kraal in the rear, made the truck cumbersome to handle. There is little to stop an unwary driver from sliding over the edge, down the steep boulder strewn hillside, to the bushveld, nine hundred feet below. Conscious of the unguarded drop, Lucas Darke, having visited the farm several times in the past, managed the hairpin bends with cautious skill.

Mount Muzindi tobacco farm stands beside tall gum trees, three hundred yards back from the escarpment, that marks the beginning of the foothills of Kwazaland's Eastern Highlands. The range of blue grey hills form a backdrop to the farm. They gradually rear up to the mountain from which it takes its name. Mount Muzindi, standing at ten thousand feet, is Kwazania's highest mountain. The eastern border with the Republic of Nambria, marked by the Olulopo River, lies immediately beyond the mountain range. At certain times of the day, the tall thatched roof and shaded verandas give the long bungalow a mildly brooding appearance. But from the farmhouse the views to the west, are breathtakingly panoramic. The farm's location is acknowledged to be one of the finest in the Eastern Province.

As the road topped out, the broad dwelling, with its well-watered lawn, came into view. Darke negotiated the long drive before drawing to a halt in a cloud of dust, between a Mercedes Benz saloon and a dark green Landrover. A white Peugeot 404 pickup completed the row of vehicles parked in the scented shade of the tall gums. The elevation and eucalyptus trees made the air so much fresher and cooler than that of the veld below.

It was a pleasant relief to cross the lawn and step onto the veranda, out of the sun, after the four-hour drive. The sound of his boots on the boards echoed through the open doors.

He called, 'Hello, the house,' loudly but no one answered. He knocked and was about to call again, when a dark-haired girl of, he guessed, eighteen years, dressed in riding breeches, brown leather riding boots and a crisp white open neck blouse, appeared at the far end of the veranda.

She looked at him. 'Yes?' she queried, managing to mix boredom with a haughty air, in a single word.

'Miss Bodell?' he asked. Lew Bodell had talked of his daughter, but Darke had never met her. She was normally abroad he knew, at a finishing school in France, or was it Switzerland?

'That's right', she drawled the words, 'and you are?' She looked him over, clearly unimpressed by the dust-dulled shine on his military tan boots, leather leggings and the creased state of his normally, well pressed khaki uniform.

'Lucas Darke. We've been up country. We're on our way back to Fort Albert. There's a man, apparently one of your workers, we would like your father to identify.'

'I can see you must have had a long journey,' she spoke in a crisp English southern counties accent, full of apparent distain, at his less than pristine appearance.

'A rather dusty one I'm afraid,' he said ruefully, looking down at himself.

'Quite so. Well, there is no need to bother my father with such a trifling matter.' She was obviously a young woman testing her wings in the adult world. Wiping the floor with Darke was proving an interesting interlude in an otherwise uninteresting day.

He was naturally good natured and slow to take offence, but he was no fool. He was twenty-three and had been in the district police for five years. He knew how to deal with difficult people, it was part of the job. He preferred to give them as much rope as possible. In the meantime, he would appear to miss the innuendos.

'Is Mister Bodell available? It might be better … .'

She cut him off, saying, 'He's a busy man. I'm sure I can help you without the need to bother my father. Where is this man?'

'If you're sure?' he seemed doubtful.

His seeming uncertainty encouraged her. 'Of course, however I don't have all day to stand around, Sub Inspector.'

He wondered if they had lessons in rudeness at the exclusive school she attended. Or was she deliberately doing the reverse of everything she had been taught? He waved his hand vaguely, almost helplessly, in the direction of the Landrover. 'He's apparently one of your farm's long-term employees. It would be better if your father...... .'

She interrupted, 'Oh, for heaven's sake. Where is he? In the Landrover?'

Before he could reply she was off down the veranda steps, leading the way to the pale grey police vehicle standing in the shade. As she strode ahead of him, he could see that Sergeant Kufanu had untied the elongated metal box from the roof and had it placed on the drive beside the truck in readiness. She came to the vehicle not realising the significance of the gleaming casket.

He came up beside her and said solicitously, 'Look here Miss Bodell, I think it would be better ....'

She cut him off, enjoying her new-found role, 'The sooner I see him, the sooner we can all get about our business, Sub Inspector.'

Kufanu began to unlock the lid.

Darke smiled. 'Just a moment Sergeant.'

Sergeant Elias Kufanu stopped what he was doing, his face studiously impassive. He stood back from the box and waited.

'Miss Bodell,' Darke continued. He touched her arm to gain her attention. She immediately bridled at his action and pulled away. Before she could say anything, he continued firmly, 'The person we want identified is in that box.'

She looked down at the stainless-steel coffin, then up at him as realisation slowly dawned on her. 'You mean......?' her words trailed away as her eyes, growing wider, reluctantly panned back to the casket in horrified fascination. 'You mean.......there's a body in there?' She paused briefly before saying, 'Ah yes…' She shuddered and backed off, the colour in her face draining away, under her slight tan. 'I'll...er...I'll call my father. I don't know all our workers, you see...., difficult.' She glanced at him. His face was expressionless. She turned away, then regaining her composure, turned back. 'That was hateful, you did it on purpose…. you tricked me.'

He kept a straight face. Her comments were not entirely fair, but she was attempting to save face, 'I'm sorry, Miss Bodell, but you gave me little chance to explain.'

At this point Lewis Bodell strode round the corner of the house. He waved and came towards them. He was dressed in working cloths: a wide brimmed, khaki bush hat, sweat stained and battered sat slightly askew on his head, a washed-out pink t-shirt hung loosely over his crumpled and faded grey shorts. scuffed, suede bush boots and long fawn socks, pushed down to his ankles, completed his sartorial ensemble. Pale dust clung to the sun-bleached hairs on his copper tanned arms and legs. He was just short of six feet tall, in a thickset frame. He carried with him the tang of the tobacco barn.

'Hi doll,' he called to his daughter, oblivious to her irritation. She flounced away. He acknowledge the six-foot-six-inch Sergeant Kufanu with a wave, before turning to Darke and holding out his hand. 'Luke, it's good to see you.' They shook hands. Looking over Darke's shoulder he espied the steel coffin. 'One of mine?' he asked.

'I believe so, we found him up north in the Hundi Valley.'

They moved towards the body box. The Sergeant unfastened the lid. Bodell quickly confirmed it was Petrol Mugwani, one of his employees, he had been missing for some days. 'Pity". He shook his head sadly. "A good man. Never had a lot to say for himself. He'd worked on building sites. Could turn his hand to all sorts of odd jobs around the place. What happened?'

'Looks like suicide. Hanged himself from a tree, not far from his kraal.'

Sergeant Kufanu sealed the box once more and strapped it onto the roof rack. He took the truck with the occupants, to locate Hanna Mugwani, the deceased's wife, at the farm compound. Darke joined Bodell on the veranda for a cool beer. As he suspected, the farmer could add little more to the background of the deceased man. He had worked at Mount Muzindi farm for three years and had been a good employee. There was no reason Bodell could think of why anyone would want to kill him, or why he would kill himself. They chatted idly for a while, waiting for Sergeant Kufanu to return.

From their first meeting they had got on well as they quickly discovered a shared interest. Although of different ages both had flown gliders in England, in their younger days. Whenever they met, they enjoyed swapping stories of their cross-country exploits and comparing the performance of different sailplanes. After Darke had slaked his thirst, the farmer called for the housemaid to fetch his daughter, only to be told she had left the house to ride over to a neighbouring farm.

'Oh well,' he said, 'she's always popping off somewhere or other. Can't be much fun for a young girl cooped up with me all day. You met her, what do you think of her?'

'Very attractive,' Darke replied, surprising himself. Having been on the receiving end of her sharp tongue, he had not consciously given her looks much favourable thought. On reflection he realised she was attractive. Maybe her off-hand attitude had influenced his initial opinion of her. He almost said, "Pity", out loud, but stopped himself in time.

He looked at Lewis Bodell and wondered how this rough, blunt, but easy-going character could be father to the slim, feisty girl he had met for the first time that day. For all his simple bluff exterior, Darke had come to realise that Bodell was a complex person. He was easy company, yet he often preferred to keep himself to himself. Also, Lewis Bodell had a past!

His first foray into tobacco farming in the early nineteen fifties had failed. He had been under capitalised. Following the death of his wife, after a long illness and a bad season, he had been unable to satisfy the bank, consequently they had foreclosed on him. With what little money he salvaged, after the sale of all his assets, he sent his motherless daughter to stay with his spinster sister in England, whilst he moved from one job to another. He became a train driver on the railways, up north, in Katanga, a Province, of the Belgian Congo. By nineteen sixty he had become a manager. In July of that year, five days after independence, the soldiers of the Force Publique mutinied in Leopoldville and civil order broke down. The whole country erupted into murderous violence. Widespread chaos ensued. Within four days the mutiny had reached Katanga. There was total lawlessness, with bands of armed mutineers roaming the streets: looting, raping, torturing; killing Africans and Europeans at will.

Bodell and Sandy Leitch, the Senior Maintenance Foreman, realised they no longer had a future in Katanga and their lives were at risk if they stayed. They hatched a plot which, they hoped, might give them each a fortune: if it came to fruition. Under cover of darkness, they entered the deserted goods yards and fired up a locomotive. They did not have to break into the administration building, the doors had been left unlocked when the staff abandoned their jobs. Inside they began altering the documentation relating to two trainloads of copper ore, standing in the goods yard. The ore was due to be sent for export, through the port of Beira in Mozambique. Each wagon, along the length of the train, was carefully re-labelled and re-addressed to both of them in the Portuguese East African port. The corresponding office documentation was altered, to conform to the new consignees.

As groups of marauding rebels began infiltrating the goods yards, Leitch and Bodell boarded their getaway vehicle: a 1907 Garratt locomotive, with steam up. They departed the town by rail, the only route that bypassed all the roadblocks manned by the trigger-happy, drunken mutineers. The occasional marauding group, who half-heartedly challenged them, were powerless to stop the big engine with their small arms fire. Only once did they come across a significant attempt to block their progress. A single decker bus had been quickly driven across the tracks, as they approached. The armed men were waving them down with torches. Lewis Bodell opened the regulator; unencumbered by wagons, the powerful engine rapidly increased speed. Both men ducked down and braced themselves. The cowcatcher on the front swept the bus aside, with ease. They hardly heard the gunfire aimed at them, as they sped past the drunken mob. Thereafter it was a straight run to a point close to the Northern Rhodesian border, where they had previously left Bodell's car. Together they made their way through Northern and

Southern Rhodesia, to eventually arrived in the Portuguese East African capital of Lourenco Marques, five days later.

Following Katanga's secession from the Congo and with the formation of the Katangese Gendarmerie, into a viable paramilitary force, some semblance of order began to return to the breakaway Congolese province. Strenuous efforts were made to restart the machinery of government, albeit with skeleton staff levels, as many of the experienced personnel had fled the country or been killed. It proved to be a painfully slow, almost impossible task, to efficiently breathe life back into the collapsed infrastructure. On the railways the two trains loaded with eight hundred tons of copper ore apiece, were ready to go. As all the documentation was complete, they were dispatched without a second glance, to clear the yard and begin the process of normalising the system.

It was with considerable relief to Bodell and Leitch when they were notified that the ore wagons had arrived in Mozambique. Bodell dealt with a commodities broker, who quickly found a Japanese buyer, more than interested in handling eight hundred tons of copper ore, at a competitive price. Payment was made into two Swiss Bank accounts less a sum of one hundred thousand U S dollars for each of them. These sums were deposited in their individual accounts with the Commissioner Street branch of The Standard Charter Bank in Johannesburg, South Africa.

When they reached the Transvaal, Bodell and Leitch parted company and went their separate ways. Leitch invested his money in drugs. For a while he did well smuggling heroin from the Asia into Europe, almost trebling his capital. Bodell toured southern Africa, north of the Limpopo and finally found what he wanted, a tobacco farm in Kwazaland, unburdened by any loans from a bank, that he and his daughter could call home. It was his dream. He was a competent, hardworking farmer. For the following seven years he laboured successfully, to bring the farm to its present level of productivity.

Darke knew of Bodell's background from police files. It was considered prudent to keep a check on the tobacco farmer, because of his Katangan escapade. It was a curious legal tangle; because the two men had not physically stolen the copper in Katanga, the only offence they could be charged with, in the Congo, was falsifying railway documentation. Even if an extradition treaty existed, that would not have been an extraditable offence. As far as Mozambique was concerned the two men had taken possession of goods, that were properly addressed and delivered to them, by the Katangan authorities. No persons in Mozambique had been deprived of their property. Therefore, no crime had been committed in that country.

Personally, Darke did not condone their actions, but he found the story intriguing. As long as Bodell did not indulge in any criminal activity in Kwazaland, he was free to do as he liked. Besides he was now a wealthy farmer, who had worked hard and led a blameless life for the past seven years. It was unlikely he was going to foul his own nest by needlessly indulging in crime. He was, as the law would agree, innocent until proved guilty. Darke enjoyed the company of the older man but did not intend to develop their acquaintance further.

Sergeant Kufanu brought the Landrover to the house and reported to Darke. Hanna, the distraught deceased's wife had identified the body of her husband, she was accompanying it to the mortuary. Sergeant Kufanu had interviewed her; she stated she could think of no reason why her husband would take his own life. She knew that he had been worried about something, which he had not been willing to talk about. The burly sergeant told Darke he felt there was something else she was not telling.

They were about to depart when a wiry, well-tanned, man of medium height came round the corner of the house. He broke his stride momentarily as he saw them, almost as though he wanted to turn back, but realising he had little option, he came on. Darke noted his sinewy muscles. He recognised that the man may lack inches and appear slim, but he was no weakling.

Bodell called out, 'Come and meet the local police, Sandy.'

Intrigued Darke quickly realised this must be Sandy Leitch, Bodell's co-conspirator from his Katanga days. They were introduced and shook hands, Darke had the impression of a ruthless street fighter, his thin nose, dominated his features. It had been broken at least once and left misshapen. He was probably a good man to have on your side, but not against you.

Darke said, 'You're on holiday Mister Leitch?'

'A mixture of business and pleasure, until Lew gets fed up wi' ma company.' His speech still retained his Glaswegian accent, particularly the raising of the voice at the end of the sentence.

'Sandy's using Muzindi as his base whilst he explores the country,' Bodell added.

Darke nodded. 'You've come out from the UK?'

'Not directly, I was up North for a while and came on doon from there.'

He was wary and not giving much away. His twitchy, bird-like, movements accentuating his discomfort at being questioned. Darke did not want to make him needlessly suspicious, so he wished Leitch a pleasant stay and bade both men farewell.

Chapter 2

A week later Lucas Darke was sitting in his office at Sissengeri District Police Station twenty-five miles north of the provincial capital, Fort Albert. He was second-in-command of the thirteen-man police post. Having attended the post mortem of Petrol Mugwane the day before, in Fort Albert, he was finalising the sudden death file. The pathologist had confirmed the injuries were consistent with suicide by hanging, with nothing to indicate to the contrary. The body had been found suspended from an acacia tree in an area of remote bush. The deceased's tracks to the tree were clear to see in the dust; his homemade knife was embedded in a baobab tree close by. A strip of the strong flexible bark, three inches wide and seven feet long, had been carefully stripped from the trunk to be used for the noose. No other tracks were visible.

In spite of Sergeant Kufanu's belief that Hanna Mugwani knew more than she was admitting, it was clear all the evidence indicated suicide. As Darke closed the file and placed it in his out tray, he noticed a white Peugeot 404 pickup, entering the camp square. The police post was formed on three sides by whitewashed, red corrugated-iron-roofed, buildings. The fourth side consisted of a shoulder high hedge, behind which lay the lines of single and married quarters for the complement of ten African police.

The vehicle followed the track around a small neat square of grass, with the flagstaff at its centre, flying the Kwazaland flag. The pickup drove past the Charge office to pull up in front of Dark's office, on the opposite side to the hedge. In the rear Darke could see a simple wooden coffin, lashed in place, with two of Bodell's farm workers on either side to steady it. The body of Petrol Mugwani was being returned to his kraal for burial. The two men climbed stiffly over the side and made for the nearest shade. Lewis Bodell slid slowly from the driver's seat, on the far side of the cab, perspiring heavily.

It was late October and the rains were overdue. Throughout the month the daily heat and humidity had increased their oppressive reign. Darke greeted him at the door and waved him into his office. The building was fifty years old, with a steeply pitched corrugated iron roof, lined with wood. The design allowed air to circulate keeping the interior comparatively cool.

Bodell was not his usual bluff, hearty self. He clearly had something on his mind. Darke talked generally, until the other man had recovered enough from his hot, dusty drive. He had driven from the farm up to Umbaka Airport, where he had seen his daughter off on her flight back to the UK. On his return journey he had collected the body of Petrol Mugwani from the Fort Albert mortuary. He was returning it to Mount Muzindi, for onward transmission to the deceased's kraal, in the remote Hundi Valley. After a reasonable time, Darke allowed the conversation to peter out. The other man took the cue.

'Lucas, I have to tell you, I'm in a bit of a spot.' He raised his hands in a gesture that managed to convey both resignation and frustration. 'Mostly of my own making, I suppose.' He stopped to drop his hat into his lap and to wipe his brow and neck with a large, damp handkerchief. 'You met Sandy Leitch the other day.' Darke nodded. 'He's an old friend, but he's changed. Not the man he used to be and I'm concerned.' He paused, took a deep breath, sighed and began to recount the story of the stolen Katangan copper ore. When he had finished, he gave the Sub Inspector a long look and remarked, 'You don't seem at all surprised, Luke?'

'There have been rumours.' Darke smiled non-committedly, he was not going to reveal details of the exchange of information between police forces.

'I see.' Bodell smiled wryly, 'Well, I suppose that's Africa for you, the bush telegraph and all that. I consulted a lawyer who assures me there is no case to answer in Kwazaland. Is that how you see it?'

'Unless it is a case, which is the subject of an extradition treaty, we are only directly concerned with contraventions of Kwazaland's laws, so,' he said lightly, 'don't do anything illegal, be a responsible, upstanding citizen and you'll be okay.'

'So, I'm a free man? That's a relief,' he said with a chuckle. He was becoming more like his old self. 'My reason for baring my soul in this way, is due to Sandy Leitch's visit. When he and I went our separate ways after the copper business, we lost touch until he turned up, out of the blue, recently. He's no longer the man I knew. He's edgy, unpredictable and dangerous. He may even be on drugs. I don't know how, but all his money has gone. I don't mind helping out up to a point, but he's hinting at a large sum for a deal he's putting together. I have no desire to get involved in that. As the days have gone by, he's being less subtle: almost desperate. I think he might start making threats.'

'What kind of threats?' asked Darke, whilst making notes.

'I think more in the form of blackmail: threatening to tell neighbours, or the press, or even you fellows, if I don't help him out.'

'Do you think he would carry out the threats?'

'Now that I know I haven't broken any laws in this country, I'm not worried. Virginia knows nothing, of course. If it comes to it and the truth were to come out, I'd prefer to tell her myself, rather than have her hear of the Katanga business from someone else.' He paused and screwed his face into a grimace. 'It's not the blackmail really. His behaviour, as I mentioned, at times is not rational. I have a feeling that he could lose control of himself and do something silly. It's just an impression.' He took a deep breath before continuing, 'He's not the Sandy Leitch I knew.'

'What sort of 'silly' thing do you think he's capable of?'

'Oh, I don't know. You have to see him sometimes. He'd been drinking the other night. He talked of a partner in the South of France, who had, he said, cheated on him. He'd used a knife on him and although he didn't actually say it, he left me with the feeling he'd killed the man. That came as a shock.'

'Leitch murdered him?'

'Sounds dramatic, but that's the impression he gave.'

'Did he say who it was, or where, or when it happened?' Darke, knowing the dangers of drug trafficking, did not disbelieve the tobacco farmer's story.

'No, I did try asking, but he ignored me. He just mumbled and sank into a kind of stupor and said no more about it.' Bodell changed the subject. 'Look, I know the police would need much more evidence to do anything about it. I'm sure I can handle Sandy. I think he still trusts me. At the end of the day, I may give him a hundred or two to help him out, but I'm not going to underwrite some illegal deal.'

'Obviously if you did, it would make you an accessory to whatever he was involved in.' The other man nodded, understanding the implications. 'If you feel you can't handle him then I suggest you tell him to leave. Under the circumstances a police officer could be present and escort him from your property. In the meantime, I'll check if there is anything in our files. There may be an international arrest warrant out for him.'

'Thanks for the offer, but I'm sure I can handle him.'

'You mentioned a possible deal he was putting together. Any idea of what it is and where it might be?'

'No, if I find out any further information, I'll let you know.' As he stood up the chair creaked under his solid weight. He shook Darke's hand. They walked to the door together and out under a hot, brooding sky. The rains were coming. Tall, slate-grey clouds were unfolding above, and the evening sunlight, cast long slanting shadows across the camp, washing the white walls of the buildings with a warm, golden hue.

The rains held off for five more days. The clouds threatened, yet nothing happened. The heat and humidity continued to plague humans and animals alike. Early on the fifth day, Darke was called out to Kalagan 'B', a company owned farm, forty-five miles north of the outpost of Sissengeri. The manager, John Warren, had gone missing and blood had been found on the veranda of his quarters. The report said bursts of gunfire had been heard during the night. Russian and Chinese backed terrorist groups had not operated in the area for more than a year. Darke hoped this night's work did not presage a new wave of attacks, to intimidate the local African population. As usual the farm workers had sensibly locked themselves in their huts, to await daybreak. Sergeant Kufanu took the call. The informant was instructed to keep everyone well away from the Manager's house until the police arrived. As it was likely to be a terrorist act, Toby Brenner, Darke's superior, called Provincial Headquarters, in Fort Albert, to notify Special Branch and request the Dog Section to attend the scene.

It took one-and-a-half hours, under a darkening sky, over corrugated dust roads to reach the farm. Darke kept his foot to the floor as he raced down the deserted bush roads, dragging a dense plume of dust behind, which quickly obscured the view through the rear door of the truck: coating it with a thickening layer of fine red powder. A farm worker met them at the roadside, by the open entrance gate. He climbed into the back of the police vehicle to guide them to the company Manager's house. As they drove up the track, the sky to the west, was separated vertically into azure blue sky on the left and a gunmetal grey curtain to the right. Heavy rain was sweeping towards them. Darke thought for a moment the storm would pass them by, but soon occasional large spots of rain fell, leaving miniature dark craters in the dust. They were in for their first deluge of the rainy season. He stopped the Landrover fifty yards from the single-story house, to avoid contaminating any evidence that may have been left on the drive.

Two African constables alighted and donned their khaki rain capes. Darke put his cap and police trench coat on leaving it unbuttoned with the belt hanging. The atmosphere was clammy. Sergeant Kufanu instructed the house staff and other employees, standing around the vehicle, to stay away from the building. He stationed one constable beside the Landrover, to guard the rack of firearms and another to patrol in a wide circle around the house, to keep any curious sightseers at bay. The Sergeant, carrying a self-loading rifle, carefully picked his way toward the rear of the building, scouring the area with his eyes as he went.

Darke loosened the Smith and Wesson revolver, in its deep leather holster, as he moved slowly forward, carefully inspecting the rain-pocked ground as he went. The chance of any hostile elements, still lingering in the vicinity, was remote. He felt self-conscious about approaching the house, waving a revolver around. Too much display of guns by the police always upset the local population. They were unused to the police with drawn weapons. The best way of defusing the situation was to return to an appearance of normality, as quickly as possible.

There were a number of fragile tyre marks and footprints in the dust. All were indistinct: the dust was too dry and fine to retain a detailed impression. The coming rain would obliterate any traces in a moment and it was seconds away. He made his way carefully onto the stoep as the curtain of water swept over the house, heralded by a rush of wind. The sheer volume of rain made a loud hissing noise which changed when it hit the corrugated iron roof of the house. It became a wild discordant drumbeat.

He looked back, the light grey police Landrover, with its dark blue lettering, was almost invisible behind an equally grey, swaying screen of falling water. The ground had gone too. The rain had quickly washed the dust from the sun hardened earth, huge droplets were bubbling and bouncing off the surface to a height of nine inches. It looked as though a seething; panic-stricken shoal of fish had been caught in the shallows.

The coming of the rain brought a cooling breeze, which rapidly dropped the air temperature by ten degrees. Near the top of the steps was a pool of blood, still vaguely red in the centre, but dried to near black at the edges. It was a large pool. The surface of the stoep was polished concrete. There was nothing to soak up the spillage and lessen the impression of quantity. Darke reminded himself that often blood spills look worse than they really are. 'But maybe not in this case,' he thought to himself. He moved on methodically.

The roof overhung the stoep, keeping the rain off the blood-spill. Apart from the rain, all was still. The rhythmless drumming on the roof continued to deafen, providing an accompaniment to his growing fears. One of the wicker veranda chairs lay on its side. The double screen doors to the sitting room, with their dark green frames, were half open. Inside he could see the room had been ransacked, the contents of cupboards and drawers scattered indiscriminately. The plaster walls were chipped and scarred by gunfire. No one was in the room. He did not venture in. Using the open front door, he found the dining room and bathroom were untouched. He passed down the passage to the kitchen. Blood was splashed everywhere; it told a story. Shots had been fired and the victim had fallen against the wall. The body had been dragged away. A smeared trail of dried blood led along the hallway to the first bedroom. He followed, stepping carefully.

The door was ajar, his hand was raised to push it open when Sergeant Kufanu's deep voice, in clear tones called out, above the beating rain, 'MISTER DARKE DO NOT OPEN THE BEDROOM DOOR. THERE IS A GRENADE ATTACHED TO IT!'

Darke's outstretched hand froze, midway to the door handle. He stared at it for a moment judging the distance. It needed to travel barely six inches to the door knob, to trigger the trap. 'OKAY SERGEANT, I HEAR YOU,' he yelled back, expelling air slowly between his teeth, before retreating to the front door.

He made his way round to the rear of the building. As soon as he left the shelter of the house the rain soaked the grey fabric of his police trench coat. Sergeant Elias Kufanu stood by the bedroom window, partially protected by the eaves, the rain was cascading from his khaki plastic cape. His drab green uniform cap was soaked a darker hue by the rain. Water was steadily dripping from the peak.

'Thank you, Sergeant.' He took a deep breath, realising the narrowness of his escape. 'That was too close for comfort.'

Kufanu said, 'It's a nasty set up, sir. There's a man lying on the floor. I think he's dead. The body', he continued, 'is beside the bed. A grenade is attached to the chair. There are no identifiable footprints outside the window.'

The Sergeant was a big man, standing six feet six inches tall, five inches taller than Darke and five years older. He possessed an open, easy manner and was highly intelligent. Like his father before him, he had been a school teacher before joining the force. Darke knew that if it had been anyone else at the back of the house, other than Sergeant Kufanu, he would have been dead, or seriously injured by this time. In his three years' service he had gained his sergeant's stripes in record time and was marked for rapid promotion when the colony gained its imminent independence,

Darke looked through the mesh fly screen into the shaded interior. The window itself was raised. It was not so easy to make out the form on the floor, let alone the booby trap. He gave a low whistle and said, 'Well spotted.' He realised how near he had been to being seriously injured. 'I owe you,' he added, in recognition of the Kufanu's contribution to his continued existence.

A rod had been taped to the door knob. It looked like a broom handle. It extended out to rest on the back of a wooden chair. The booby trap was an olive green smooth-shelled hand grenade. It was taped to the chair, with the pin almost removed and attached to the rod end, by a paper clip, bent into a hook. The first inward movement of the door would push the rod, release the pin and trigger the device. A quarter of a pound of exploding TNT, would have caused extensive damage to the building, killing or maiming anyone coming through the door.

Using his penknife Darke levered the corner of the wood frame and pulled. It moved easily, the entire mesh frame coming away in his hands. It was clear that whoever planted the grenade could not have left by the internal door, once the trap had been set. He must have left by the window, pushing the screen back into place before he departed. Darke handled it by its edges, as it might yet yield fingerprints.

He half jumped and half pushed himself up through the aperture. Using exaggerated care, he crossed to the chair. He gingerly took hold of the top of the grenade and pushed the pin firmly back into position. Next, he disengaged the bent paper clip, from the ring of metal, to make it safe. He left the rod resting on the back of the chair beside the taped grenade. The Scenes of Crime Unit would want everything left as close to how it had been found as possible. The African male beside the bed was dead. No one with that many gunshot wounds and the amount of blood loss, could have survived. Darke noted the distinct metallic scent that often accompanies death.

The rain abated and the sun returned to draw myriad wisps of moisture from the sodden ground. Torrents of surface water had washed gullies across the bare earth on their way to lower levels. The Special Branch team, from Fort Albert, took longer than expected to arrive, held up by the rain storm. They looked like fish out of water, with their suits creased and dampened by their journey. It was not common for CID or Special Branch to operate in the district areas. Uniform branch investigated most crimes, the exception being acts of terrorism. As this attack and murder of the African servant had all the hallmarks of terrorism, together with disappearance of John Warren, it required Special Branch to attend the scene and take over the investigation.

Darke knew the plain-clothes investigating officer. They chatted briefly as Darke gave him his report.

The other man said, 'Could be KPDC, but more likely KAPU, as it's a Russian hand grenade. We haven't had terrorist activity in this area for some months. I'm surprised we've had no warning of possible infiltration.'

The Special Branch officer had cancelled the request for the dog section, as the heavy downpour had ruined any chance of a scent. Also, he had radioed to Fort Albert for Geoff Otterly to attend the scene. He was the mining explosives and ex-army bomb disposal expert, who acted as advisor to the police in the province. Until he had rendered the hand grenade safe and checked the rest of the house for booby-traps, the team would not be able to enter the bedroom. Having completed his hand-over Darke returned to the truck.

'Sissengeri Mobile, Sissengeri, over,' Toby Brenner's voice, only slightly distorted with static, came over the Philips radio, on the passenger's side of the instrument panel.

Darke retrieved the handset from the radio on the passenger side of the dashboard and answered, 'Sissengeri, this is mobile. Strength five, over.'

'Luke, there's been a report of an accident on the approach road to Mount Muzindi farm, two occupants believed dead. An ambulance is on its way. Can you get over there, when you're through with the S B boys? Over.'

'Roger Toby, wilco. Have just finished here. I'll head that way now. Out.' Darke was thinking of the paperwork the two events would be generating. He wondered with some concern, who and what he would find when he reached Mount Muzindi Farm. It would have been raining there also, which would complicate his investigation. Then there would be the two bodies. 'A policeman's lot is not always a happy one,' he thought.

The road, half way up the climb to Mount Muzindi farm, was partially blocked by storm debris. Lewis Bodell's Mercedes had left the narrow road above, then slewed and rolled its way down, onto and over the lower road, as it doubled back on itself. It had left a trail of torn earth, stones, brush and vehicle parts in its wake. The final resting place of the limousine was just below the level of the lower road, where it had burst into flames. Bodell's body had been flung clear at the final moment. It lay awkwardly face down against a large rock, some twelve feet from the car. He had sustained multiple injuries. His head was resting at an unnatural angle.

The accident might have occurred just before the rainstorm, but more likely after it had begun. It had rained heavily since the accident. Bodell's body was half buried in the ground. The rain rushing down-hill, had heaped silt up and around his inert form, partially covering the body and head and burying one hand. The clothing was damp and ingrained with gravel. The back of Bodell's head was visible. His hair was matted. A large open wound was clearly visible on the back of his head. Any blood had been washed away by the rain leaving the gash, down to the skull, grimly bloodless. It was contaminated with grit and hair. Darke needed no doctor to know he was dead. In that position, even if the neck had not been broken, he would have suffocated, half buried face down in the silt, as he was.

The Mercedes was a burnt, twisted wreck, with the remains of the passenger still located in the nearside seat. The heat of the fire had the usual effect on the body. The charred remains were drawn up into a semi-foetal position as the body's tendons had contracted with the fierce heat. The extremities of the limbs were down to charred stumps with curled talons where the fingers had been. The rain had done nothing to quell the effect of the burning fuel. The intensity of the heat had reduced everything else to blackened metal or cinders. The stale smell of smoke lingered. Both front doors had been ripped from their hinges, the driver's door stood almost upright leaning against a broken tree trunk, immediately above the wreck of the saloon. The other lay, partially buried, fifteen feet to the left side of car's final resting-place.

Sergeant Kufanu and Darke measured the scene. Darke drew a map for future reference. He began photographing as much as possible with his camera. Whilst taking a shot of the front passenger door access, he noticed the finger for the first time. It was clear of the vehicle and partially hidden from view. It was a complete unburned little finger from a left hand, severed at the bottom joint. He photographed it. A quick check showed that Bodell's fingers were all complete. The charred remains in the vehicle, on closer examination, had no remnant of a little finger on the left hand. Beneath the passenger's body the remains of two items caught Darke's eye: a penknife and a cigarette lighter. Adhering to the charred wrist was what was left of a watch, with the leather strap burnt away. More photographs. He placed the finger in an evidence bag and the penknife in an envelope, along with the watch and cigarette lighter. The lighter must have exploded in the heat, bursting along a seam, but the engraved initials "A L" could be discerned on the side.

'Alexander Leitch and Lewis Bodell, partners in crime and partners in death,' he mused out loud.

He posted a constable to guard the scene. Higher up the hillside, where the vehicle had left the road, there was nothing of significance to see. The drenching rain had swept away the graded surface of the road, on its way down the escarpment, leaving deep, pebble-lined gullies, angled across the road. If the cause of the accident had been a blown tyre there was no evidence, such as skid marks, remaining. The tyres themselves had been reduced to black dust, all the wheels had been damaged as the vehicle careered down the rock-strewn slope.

After the deluge a normal road vehicle would have problems safely negotiating the road up to the farm, until the surface had been re-graded. The Police Landrover in low range, four-wheel drive, slowly swayed and bucked its way to the top. The farmstead was abandoned. Darke went through the house. Everything appeared normal. Leitch's room, redolent of stale whisky, was not tidy. All his possessions were scattered about, as though he had intended to stay a while longer. A search of the room revealed nothing untoward. There were no letters or an address book, to give an indication of contacts, just packets of cigarettes and his passport: in it the section relating to next of kin had been left blank.

In Lewis Bodell's study, one wall was lined with books, with a section filled with variously labelled arch lever files, indicating that the study doubled as the farm office. Everything was neatly arranged. The large dark oak desk, with red leather blotter, facing the window, was devoid of papers. A telephone, brass desk lamp, pen stand, and two photographs in frames were neatly arranged. One coloured photograph was recent, showing Virginia Bodell in riding attire. The other was older, in black and white, it portrayed a girl, not much older than Virginia, with similar features. He assumed this to be Virginia's mother. Bodell's address book lay in the top left-hand drawer. His spinster sister's address in England was there under "B". He took a note of it.

Chapter 3

Three days after the accident, a letter arrived from Lewis Bodell addressed to Darke. It was dated two days before the accident; it read:

Mount Muzindi Farm,
Fort Albert Province,
Kwazaland.
8th November 1967

Dear Luke,

I think I've been wrong about Sandy Leitch; he's changed. He's become even more introverted and sullen. I didn't tell you the other day, that after we were paid for the ore in LM, we both decided to set aside one hundred thousand U S dollars each, in separate safety deposit boxes, with the bank. This was in the way of an escape fund, in case we needed to disappear quickly, at any time. My fund has never been touched and has recently been transferred into krugerrands, but I gather Sandy has long since used his.

We were talking the other evening and brushed on the topic of these funds. Foolishly I let slip that I had transferred my fund into gold coins, thereby indicating my fund was still intact. Ever since that time he has badgered, and all but threatened me to lend it to him, saying it was an investment and would be repaid twice over. I was fed up and said 'No'. I think he realises I meant what I said. He did not like it. Anyway, ever since then his attitude has changed. He is less than friendly and, when he's had a few drinks, sullen and antagonistic.

If something does happen to me at his hands, I have written a letter to Virginia explaining the Katanga business, which will be held by my solicitors: Blexell, Landon, and Tanwick, 12 -14 Hackett's Walk (near Lincoln's Inn Field), London. If the whole truth is likely to come out, I would like the chance to explain everything to Virginia first, in my way, rather than have her hear it second-hand from less sympathetic sources, such as the newspapers.

As time may be running out, I have taken the liberty of giving them your name. I have asked them only to release the letter to Virginia on your instructions, or if at any time my involvement in the ore business is likely to become public knowledge. Obviously, you are most likely to know before anyone else. Therefore, your authorisation will allow more time for Virginia to come to terms with her father's dubious past!

I am sorry to put this on your shoulders, but you are the only person who knows my situation. As I sit here, I feel a little foolish re-reading the above. On the other hand, matters may be coming to a head and my time limited. So, if something should happen to me, please contact my solicitors, as early as possible and instruct them to give Virginia the letter. She is the best thing that ever happened in my life.

Thanks for your help.

Best regards,

It was signed *"Lew"*

Saddened Darke placed the letter on his desk, leaned back in his chair, closed his eyes and ran over the circumstances of the accident in his mind. He had attended the post mortem of both men the day before, however it was the picture of Bodell's body face down on the hillside, half buried in the silt, he kept recalling. 'Poor Bastard,' he thought.

There was absolutely nothing to suggest murder, particularly as the Police in the Congolese Republic had confirmed that the print from the little finger, recovered at the scene, was that of Sandy Leitch. Prints recovered from the bedroom, used by Leitch, at Mount Muzindi Farm, also matched. They had died together and there was nothing to suggest foul play. The story of their Katangan escapade was not likely to come out under these circumstances. As such, there was no requirement, according to the terms of Bodell's letter, to contact his solicitors in London.

Lew Bodell's funeral took place a week later. Darke felt slightly awkward attending the ceremony. He had only known him for eighteen months, since his transfer to Sissengeri District Police station, but they had always got on well together. The admission about the Katangan copper ore theft, coupled with the letter Bodell had written to him, induced him to feel an obligation to the dead tobacco farmer. He was not religious and it did not make much sense, but he knew he wanted to go. He only had the one suit, fortunately it was dark grey in colour. His wardrobe, other than his uniforms, consisted of several pairs of shorts, a pair of grey flannel trousers, blazer, dinner jacket and the suit. Mostly he wore uniform. Even at the country club, of an evening, he would often be on call and therefore in uniform. If off duty then shorts and casual shirt was his usual dress. The suit and dinner jacket were reserved for dances and parties.

Darke's off-white Volvo Amazon crested the escarpment and turned for the house. The road had been regraded in time for the funeral. The farmstead looked no different from all the other occasions he had visited, but he knew it would never be quite the same again. He was surprised by the number of vehicles already parked in the shade of the eucalyptus trees. The veranda and interior of the house were full of sombrely dressed couples. The men of the local farming community were awkwardly buttoned into suits from a past era, bought for a more youthful version of themselves. Even their highly polished shoes appeared to hurt, used as they were to wearing the comfortable suede bush boots, favoured by most of them. Slicked down hair added to their discomfort. Their conversation was respectfully hushed. Occasionally a farmer would spot another individual, not seen for a time, across the heads of the crowd. Natural bonhomie and healthy exuberance would well up to a hearty greeting, only to be checked, in time, and changed to a cautious wave and a few mouthed words of enquiry. The womenfolk on the other hand were pictures of decorum, clearly enjoying the occasion. Their respectful and modulated chatter in no way inhibiting their all-seeing eyes.

As he climbed the steps to the veranda people greeted him. It was his job to know them, they were his "parish", so to speak. He visited them regularly on patrol and all, but a few, were members of the Kwazaland Auxiliary Police Service, which provided a backup to the regular police in emergencies. Whilst the men patrolled, the women took turns to operate the radio network and feed those coming off duty.

The hearse, a majestic 1933 Rolls Royce Phantom II, appeared to glide silently, at walking pace, to the front of the house, halting just forward of the steps. Inside, the coffin rested amid a display of exotic blooms. The crowd on the veranda parted, allowing the chief mourners to file out from within. They took their positions behind the gleaming black vehicle. Darke recognised the tall veiled figure of Virginia Bodell, dressed all in black, her head bowed in grief. She stood with an older, shorter woman, whom Darke assumed to be Lewis Bodell's sister, both were newly arrived from the UK. They were accompanied by Casius Mchingwa, Mount Muzindi farm's manager.

The veranda emptied as the last mourners left to take up their positions further behind the coffin. The cortege began to move. Virginia Bodell raised her head and followed the hearse, her eyes never wavering from the coffin. It was not a long journey, less than a quarter of a mile from the house to a knoll, overlooking the plain below. The View was spectacular across the veld to the far horizon. It had been a favourite spot of Bodell's and he had made it clear it was his wish to be buried close by. He had placed stone seats, sheltered in the lee of an overhang of rock, beside a narrow cave. The cave contained well-preserved bushman paintings, depicting lions, elephants, elands and kudu, as well as Muzindi Mountain itself and other less identifiable geographical features. Darke recalled that framed watercolour copies of these paintings, competently copied by Lewis Bodell, hanging in the sitting room of the farmhouse.

Darke had once before visited the spot with the tobacco farmer. He had been on patrol in the area and, as was often the custom, Bodell offered him a bed for the night. It was more comfortable than camping. In return the farmer had company for the evening. They had strolled up to the knoll in the late afternoon to watch the sunset. The terrain below them was clearly picked out in detail by the strong light and long shadows of the lowering sun. In that light it felt as though one could reach out and touch the ridges and folds on the plain below. Darke gave a low whistle of appreciation.

'Not a bad place to be planted, eh?' Bodell had said, explaining it was his intention to be buried there.

The visitors filed out to one side of the open grave. The farm's workers lined up respectfully on the other. Darke kept to the back of the graveside gathering. He was not religious. It was something that had never featured in his life, outside school. The service was unfamiliar to him. As Geordie Cooper, the Presbyterian minister, gave the service, he felt vaguely like an imposter, bowing his head along with the others. Yet, not to have done so would have been disrespectful to Virginia Bodell and her aunt.

After the ceremony the farm workers gave a series of chants, stamps and roars, in unison, as a farewell to their employer, then filed back to their compound, where food and drink awaited them. The other mourners split in two; some wandered back to the house whilst others lingered at the graveside. Darke moved towards the house, chatting with various acquaintances as he went. On the veranda stood Virginia Bodell, side by side with her aunt, greeting everyone as they passed into the cool interior, for refreshments. Most, with the exception of the farm's nearest neighbours, were unknown to her, as she had spent only her holidays in Africa. When he came up to her, she showed no sign of recognition. Which was not surprising. She would have remembered him more for his police uniform. He was near the end of the queuing guests. The occasion had been an ordeal for her, yet she remained composed. Her pale features and mature demeanour impressed him. She was no longer the headstrong, frivolous girl. Her bereavement had transformed her into a grieving woman. She shook his hand firmly.

'This is a sad loss for you Miss Bodell. Your father talked of you often, when you were away,' Darke sympathised.

She politely acknowledged his words. She must have heard much the same from the other mourners.

'It might help you to know your father wrote to me recently, that you were the best thing that had happened in his life.'

'Thank you for reminding me,' she said, looking at him intently for a moment, her hand still clasped in his, until a tear formed and ran down her cheek. She quickly brushed it away. 'I had forgotten that he had used the same phrase to me several years ago.' She withdrew her hand. 'It's a comfort. I'll not forget his words again.'

She was not at her best, but the smile she gave him was bewitching. He realised again that he had been right to tell Bodell that his daughter was very attractive.

Chapter 4
Ten years later

Aviemore in October hosts the four-day annual Scottish Highlands and Islands Gift Fair. It is based at the ice rink, suitably floored over for the occasion. The event marks the end of the tourist season for the year, in Scotland. It is the first opportunity for the trade to buy for the following year. Most buyers use it as something of a social occasion. The hotels are full, with many people spending three or four days to do what could comfortably be done in two. The atmosphere is convivial and the buyers and exhibitors alike are relaxed, winding down at the end of a hectic season. The weather at this time of year is almost invariably crisp, cold, with raw, clean, pine scented air. The surrounding woods and forest are at their autumnal best, shrouded in red, copper and gold mixed with evergreen, set against a backdrop of snow-capped mountains. It is a pleasant occasion to relax after a busy season, meet old friends, renew acquaintances within the trade and catch up on the gossip.

The ice rink exhibition is mainly restricted to individuals and companies located in the highland region. It severely limits the number of potential exhibitors. The population of the highlands is small. The majority of the manufacturers and wholesalers to the Scottish gift trade are based elsewhere in the British Isles. To cater for these other, perhaps more commercial elements another gift exhibition is held, simultaneously, in the nearby Coylumbridge Hotel, at Rothiemurchus. These two exhibitions feed off each other. It ensures that almost everyone, associated with the Scottish gift industry, will be in Aviemore at some time during the four-day duration of the shows.

Lucas Darke led the way through the early throng of buyers and headed for the far side of the ice rink. He preferred not to start visiting the stands nearest the entrance, as this was where everyone else began, causing inevitable bottlenecks. By heading for the farthest away corner, He and Alison Falkener were able to work their way back, to the main entrance, relatively unhindered. By the time they met the tide of buyers coming towards them, the crowd had spread out to a more manageable level. Alison followed him along the aisles of stands, occasionally tapping his arm to point out an item of interest on display, or a face they knew. Alison was the manager of his five shops.

Since leaving the Royal Kwazanian Police six years earlier, following the death of his uncle, his only living relative, he had used his uncle's inheritance to open gift shops in Scotland. Alison managed all five, ensuring their smooth day-to-day running, visiting each one at least once a week. She was a tall, athletic girl, a natural organiser. Even in tweeds and very little makeup she was strikingly attractive. She carried herself well, and exuded unconscious sex appeal. In the early days together, Darke had been tempted to develop their friendship, but it was as if both of them realised that it would ultimately jeopardise their business relationship. They became close friends, respecting the others talents and abilities. Both aware of the unspoken boundaries necessary to maintain a sensible business atmosphere.

Darke had his key suppliers marked on the stand layout in the show brochure. They moved methodically between them, keeping their eyes open for anything of interest. By mid-morning they decided to have a coffee, to review the morning's business. They found a seat in the refreshment area, located in the centre of the ice rink. They chatted about the show for some minutes, when, through the general hubbub, a man's voice jarred his memory, causing him to swing round involuntarily.

The man he thought to see was not there. He could not be of course, for Sandy Leitch was dead. The man with the Glaswegian accent was on the edge of a large exhibition stand, thirty feet away, with his back partially to him. Although approximately the same height, his build was heavier than Darke remembered, also his profile was different. His nose was smaller and straighter, nothing like the wreck of a nose that Leitch had, when they had met at Mount Muzindi farm.

Alison had struck up a conversation with a woman at the next table. Darke idly continued watching the man who briefly turned in his direction. According to the plastic badge he wore, clipped to the breast pocket of his tweed jacket, he was an exhibitor. He had not the manner of a salesman; he appeared slightly uncomfortable discussing the products. The two other men on the stand, taking orders from buyers, seemed to defer to him and even seemed wary of him, when he spoke. "The Great Glen Trading Company", according to his Buyers' Guide, was *"A wholesale importer, of selected items ideally suited to the Scottish gift market"*. They were the agent for the *'Sutherland Celtic Jewellery Company'*. The postal address of the firm was shown as Glasgow, with an agent in Inverness. Darke rose and sauntered towards the stand to mingle with a group of American buyers, as they wandered past.

He came within a few feet of the man as he answered a query from a passer-by, 'Orkney, hand carved,' the man nodded his thanks and moved on.

It was the double of Leitch's voice. It made the hairs on the back of Darke's neck stand on end. It was uncanny. As he passed by the stand Darke noted the name on the man's plastic exhibitor's badge. It read, *"Trevor Yarrick, Chairman*" followed by the company name. As Darke moved away with the crowd, he saw Yarrick turn and speak conspiratorially to a tall, square faced man with broad shoulders, who had just arrived on the stand. He glanced at his wrist watch, the movement clearly showed Darke that the little finger on his left hand was missing. A strange numbness clutched at Darke's chest.

A few steps took him back to the table. Alison's new found friend was gone. Darke told her to continue the tour of the exhibition by herself. He had complete confidence in her buying judgement, and he needed time to think. She looked at him curiously. He seemed distracted and not his usual relaxed self.

He noted her expression of concern. 'My past life catching up with me,' he confided, with a wink.

'Tell me.'

'All in good time.'

She raised her eyes to the ceiling of the ice rink, picked up her handbag and the exhibition carrier bag, partly filled with brochures. With a wave of her hand, she disappeared in the direction of the next row of stands. She was intrigued, she wanted to know what was going on, she had never seen him so concerned and mysterious before. He would tell her in his own time. So, irritatingly she would have to wait.

When she had gone, he sat down and reviewed the facts. Yarrick did not look much like Leitch, but appearances could be altered. His height was the same and that is difficult to change. He was more heavily built, but then Darke was a few pounds heavier than he had been, ten years before. The voice was the same and the little finger was missing. Had Leitch faked his own death? Had he removed his little finger, leaving it at the scene, together with his penknife and cigarette lighter, to persuade the police that the charred body, in the front passenger's seat, was his. It was a gruesome thought, but not impossible. Who was it who had actually died in the accident with Lewis Bodell? If it was not Leitch, then who was it? Had Leitch murdered someone, cut off that person's little finger disposed of it, severed his own to leave as evidence, then crashed the car down the hillside, with the two men inside. He would have to have deliberately set fire to the car, if it had not caught fire by itself. It would have been necessary to disguise the identity of the passenger, so the body could be mistaken for him.

It was circumstantial evidence and insufficient to take to the authorities. He did not entirely believe the evidence himself. Besides the police file, pertaining to the accident, may not necessarily still be in existence; Kwazaland had become the independent Kingdom of Kwazania five years before. Nonetheless, if the man Yarrick was Leitch, then it was likely he had cold bloodedly murdered Lewis Bodell, and another, unknown person and got away with it. And he, Lucas Darke, had been the investigating officer at the scene.

Two days later, he sat alone in his study. His old diaries from his police days lay in the glow of the brass, green shaded desk lamp. Mrs MacGriff had gone, reminding him his dinner was in the oven. The tape machine was playing late night jazz. The ice clinked around the heavy cut glass tumbler, as absentmindedly, he sipped at his brandy and ginger. His eyes moved between his notes and the diaries, refreshing his memory of the events from ten years before. It had been some years since he had even glanced at them. The memories came back, vividly into that darkened room, lit by the single lamp and the log fire. The visions, with remembered scents and sounds of Africa, so different from Britain, that he had missed through the years. He had pushed the memories back, compartmentalised them, and closed the door on them. It had been better that way, Africa was a different world, they had been good days, but it was time to move on. Africa was changing, but however you tried you could not forget. Something would act as a trigger and the memories would return unbidden, to grip your heart and call you back, even if in mind only, to that raw exciting continent. He smiled and sighed wistfully, as he fought back the nostalgia.

Since returning from Aviemore he had considered the problem of Yarrick. He was almost sure in his own mind that Leitch and Yarrick were one and the same person. For his own peace of mind, he needed to take the matter further, not least because he had probably been duped ten years before. He needed to resolve the matter one way or the other. First, he needed to know more about Yarrick and his Great Glen Trading Company. Was it used as a legitimate front, to disguise his criminal activities?

During the next few months, he spent time gathering information. The address of the company was listed in the Aviemore Gift Show Buyers' Guide, as Greville Street in Glasgow. By questioning a number of gift trade associates, over a period of time, he ascertained that Yarrick rarely visited the offices, generally only appearing for the regular monthly board meetings. Information, available from Companies House, Edinburgh, showed the registered address of Trevor Yarrick, Chairman, as flat one, Aberavon Lodge, Leven Terrace, Bearsden, Glasgow. Further inquiries showed this to be a two-bedroom apartment in a renovated Victorian mansion, originally built by one of Glasgow's shipping magnates. It was an attractive location, but rarely visited by Yarrick. He might stay perhaps six times a year, but was often abroad in Africa, according to the caretaker. Other people would call regularly to pick up the mail, on his behalf.

To find where Yarrick mainly lived, when in Scotland, was going to take time. On the date of the March board meeting of The Great Glen Trading Company, Darke parked his hired Ford Cortina in Greville Street, where he could comfortably note the comings and goings of all who entered the building. A quick foray on foot revealed that the front door opened into a well-lit hall, occupied by two small lifts, serving four floors and housing six organisations. There was a rear entrance that led through an alley, to the street behind, accessed by a fire door. Darke could see no reason Yarrick would not use the front entrance. He had no doubt the company was legitimate. If his suspicions were correct, it was a respectable front for Leitch's criminal activities; assuming he had not mended his ways in the intervening years.

Half an hour before the appointed time of the board meeting, a silver Audi Quattro dropped Yarrick, dressed in a black leather coat, at the door and drove off. Three dull hours passed, in which he fed money into the parking meter four times and dodged the traffic wardens twice. Eventually he saw the Audi return, double park in front of the building, on the opposite side of the road, facing towards him. He started the Ford Cortina and manoeuvred it in readiness. Yarrick came from the building and slid in beside the driver. The Audi pulled away and passed him heading in the opposite direction. Darke noted the time. With little room to spare he swung the Cortina around and headed after the other car.

The Audi was driven well, at a steady pace through Glasgow, up the high street and out of town, on the Stirling Road. There was plenty of cover from other vehicles. Deliberately he was driving one of the most common cars on the road. The Audi could have left him standing. However, it maintained a legal speed all the way to and through the centre of Stirling. From there it continued on through Bridge of Allan to Dunblane. In Dunblane it turned onto the Doune road, briefly, before pulling into the car park, on the opposite side of the railway lines, to the station. Yarrick left the vehicle smartly and crossed the footbridge, to the far side and disappeared behind the station building. Without drawing attention, Darke circled round to head back the way he had come. He turned left over the railway bridge and left again for the station. As he suspected, by the time he drove into the station car park, Yarrick was gone. He had covered his tracks and disappeared. A classic method of shaking off a tail. Darke knew it was unlikely that Yarrick had realised he was being followed. It was more a precaution he performed each time he came to Glasgow. He had melted away. It was most likely that another car had been waiting for him. Anyone following him across the footbridge, besides giving themselves away, would have been left stranded, without immediate transport to continue the tail. It was an indication Yarrick had something to hide.

The same pattern of events took place after the board meeting the following month. Darke was prepared on entering Dunblane to head for the station building, to wait for Yarrick to cross the footbridge and pick up his car. It was not to be. When the Audi entered Stirling, it made for the railway station. Judging the time perfectly, Yarrick leapt from the passenger seat to make his way onto the platform and board the train, moments before it departed. He had obviously acquired a ticket in advance, making it almost impossible for anyone to follow. Darke drove quickly out of the station and headed for Dunblane as fast as he could. It was just possible that Yarrick would leave the train there and pick up a car as before.

It was the only option he had. He guessed the train would be in Dunblane long before he could arrive by car, but it was the only thing he could think to do. The alternative was to give up, go home and wait another month. He took the shortest route to Dunblane, following the river to Bridge of Allan. He was almost through the village heading for Dunblane when he spotted Yarrick, driving a Jaguar, waiting to pull out of the road from Bridge of Allan station.

It was a stroke of luck for Darke. Yarrick was not heading for Dunblane after all, he clearly had no intention of repeating any part of his pattern from the previous month. Instead, he had left the train and picked up his car in Bridge of Allan. When the Ford reached the Doune turnoff, Darke took it and almost immediately turned into the wide, prestigious entrance before the gates of the Keir Estate. He swung the car in an arc that brought him back facing onto the road, before coming to a stop. His road map lay on the seat beside him with his binoculars. In a moment he placed the map on the steering wheel, in the typical pose of someone checking his route. Either Yarrick would take the Doune turnoff or continue on the A9. From his position Darke would see which way he went and quickly follow.

Moments later, the dark green Jaguar, Yarrick was driving came into view, indicating for Doune, He swept past the Cortina without a glance. Assuming that Yarrick would continue to drive well within the speed limit, as had been done on all previous occasions, Darke allowed moments to pass before following. There were few places to go before reaching Doune itself, so allowing the other man a head start would alleviate any suspicions of a tail. He could catch up on the outskirts of the village. He nearly miss-timed it, but as he entered Doune, he just caught sight of the Jaguar in the distance, at the cross, bearing right for Callander. Darke kept falling back when he knew it was relatively safe to do so, then catching up at the last moment.

The Jaguar followed the A84 through Callander, on to Strathyre and Lochearnhead. After this the road rose up through Glen Ogle and down into the Campbell country of Breadalbane. Having gift shops at various locations around Scotland, Darke was familiar with these roads. He was able to keep in contact with the other car without coming too close, or making himself obvious. These roads ran through some of the most beautiful scenery; the wooded glens and lochs of the Trossachs, to the more sparsely covered but majestic terrain, further north. As the afternoon wore on the daylight began to fade, Darke switched on his sidelights, then headlights. At this point he decided to pass the Jaguar to make for the hotel car park at Kinorchy, which would give him a view of the next major junction.

It had not been a bad afternoon's work, all in all. He was feeling pleased with himself. Although it is less easy to identify a tailing vehicle, with the onset of nightfall, it was also correspondingly more difficult to maintain accurate contact from behind. He would be able to confirm the identity of the car and see where it was heading, from the comfort of the hotel car park. He increased his speed as much as possible, to get well ahead of Yarrick. He had only just parked the Ford, in a position overlooking the road, when the Jaguar came into view. To his surprise it indicated left, pulled off the road and entered the hotel grounds. It pulled to a stop less than thirty feet from him. Yarrick stepped out, locked the door and disappeared into the hotel.

'And what happened then?' Alison asked.

'I hung around for a time watching the Jaguar, the car park and the hotel. I thought I'd lost him. I was unsure what to do. Then a man, similar in build and dressed like Yarrick in a black leather coat, came out and drove off in the Jaguar, but it definitely wasn't him. I assumed this was another cut-out in the system. Eventually Yarrick appeared with three other men. He was now dressed in tweed shooting jacket and deerstalker. Yarrick and one man climbed into a Landrover and the other two drove a Landrover each. The three vehicles left with Yarrick in the lead. They were well-spaced out over a quarter of a mile, and travelling at forty miles an hour. They took the right fork. The only thing I could do was follow, then pass them. To have tailed at their speed and kept Yarrick in sight would have made them instantly suspicious. I continued on at sixty miles an hour for about six miles, until I found a farm track in some trees. I parked there out of sight, but they never came past.'

'What are you going to do?'

'The only thing I can do. Wait until next month.'

'Why doesn't he use a light aircraft, or helicopter, it would be quicker and easier?'

'Nothing to stop him, but I guess he knows it would be easy for the authorities to track him. They can follow an aircraft with radar or soon work out its route, even if it was flying low. Aircraft make a lot of noise and it's not easy to hide one, or a landing strip. He's far more anonymous and difficult to follow using cars and trains.' Darke was absorbed, almost mesmerised, by the flames of the fire in his study. He sat in his leather chair, gently swirling the ice in his brandy and ginger.

Alison was curled up on the green leather chesterfield, her chin rested on her hands, as they rested, in turn, on its high studded arm. She gazed across at Darke. He intrigued her. It was the first time he had spoken, in depth, of his years in the police in Africa. He had given her the background story of Sandy Leitch, alias Trevor Yarrick, assuming they were one and the same person. It was a different world, she was amazed at the responsibility for handling serious crimes, given to young men, as a matter of course, when only in their early twenties. It gave her an insight into the man. It added a new dimension to her picture of him.

She knew him as a competent businessman. He often saw opportunities before other people. Retailing is not an easy game. Too many see it as a way to get out of the rat race: buy a shop and semi-retire. If you are lucky, fine and good, but people often have their fingers burnt. A successful retail business, like any other business, depends on a large number of factors, which have to be identified and understood. It is often a constantly changing environment and, in extreme cases, it is a question of knowing when to cut your losses and get out of a particular location. She knew Darke to be astute, there was no doubt about that. He had built up a chain of shops in a changing market. He had the ability to identify the most relevant factors in a business decision. However, his heart was not always in it. She had been aware of that early on in their relationship. She saw her role as taking care of the day-to-day running of the business, leaving Darke to plan and develop its future. He had a fine analytical brain, but it was necessary to keep it pointing in the right direction. His fault, if it was a fault, was an ability to do most things well. It became a fault when he failed to concentrate on his business, because he was distracted by something else. To be fair, he knew himself well enough, so when she 'blew the whistle', demanding that he concentrate on the business, he would take heed and do what was necessary. A wave of affection for him swept over her. He needed a wife. That's it, she thought, she would find him a wife. That would give him the direction he needed in his life.

Had Darke been aware of the thoughts fermenting in the head of his friend and manager, he would have been astonished, appalled and instantly wary, but he did not know and she knew better than to give him a hint. He thought she was concentrating on the problem in hand. There had been several occasions in the past when Alison had contrived to introduce him to nubile young women, but all ended, after a few months, in disappointment. This time she would have to be far more subtle.

'I think', he mused, 'we have tailed him to the last leg of his journey. The nearer we get to his hideaway, the more intricate the screen has become. The fact that there were three Landrovers in the convoy is significant. They will have branched off onto rougher roads and gone across country. The question is, north or south of the road to the west?'

Chapter 5

The variometer needle, on the sailplane's instrument panel, was indicating a six-knot climb. Darke repositioned the glider, almost invisible from the ground three and a half thousand feet below, in the expanding core of the rapidly rising thermal. He switched on the artificial horizon. The gyroscope would take several minutes to reach the required twenty-four thousand revolutions-per-minute, to power the instrument accurately. The heavily shaded underside of the cloud above was coming ominously close and the lift was increasing. The thermal was strengthening. He was circling and climbing at a very respectable eight knots per hour. Darke closed the small Perspex direct vision window, to reduce the wind noise. He needed to concentrate fully on his instruments, once in the cloud. The air temperature was dropping as the sunlight disappeared.

The slate grey cloud base was domed above his head, a good indication of the strength of the thermal. He felt the increasing surge of power that drew him skyward, into the misty core of the cumulus cloud. The variometer signal was bleeping furiously. He dialled down the volume to a moderate level. The needle was off the dial: he was now climbing at more than ten knots. Darke, flying by instruments, was circling at fifty-five knots per hour, keeping the glider in a rate one turn. His compass was swinging wildly. The core of the cloud was a darkening, swirling, unfocussed mass of tumbling grey vapour. The soaring machine was winding itself upward, with nature's helping hand.

On occasions the turbulent cloud attempted to eject him from its core. His quick reactions always brought the, seven-hundred-and-seventy-pound, sailplane back under control. In his experience, time seemed to slow down when cloud flying. After what seemed like twenty, but was more like ten minutes the lift lessened and the pewter shroud around him became infused with increasing light, until suddenly he topped out into brilliant sunlight. The transition was stark. It was one of his favourite sensations. The introverted rough and tumble of cloud flying with its concentration on the instruments, to the exclusion of everything else: compared with the sudden transition to relative calm, amid brilliant sunlight and the dazzling glare of white capped clouds.

Darke brought the wings level and eased the glider's nose down to increase speed. He banked until he was heading for Kinorchy. Below and around columns of plump clouds were obscuring half the terrain. He sped over the snow-white shoulder of a neighbouring cloud and kept going. There were no other aircraft to be seen. The altimeter indicated a climb of five thousand five hundred feet from cloud base. He was still climbing at between one and two knots, but it was time to push forward, trading height for speed, aided by a light breeze, to reach a position above Kinorchy and wait for Yarrick. He checked his watch, it was 3.15pm and the train was due at the village station at 3.30pm.

Earlier that day he had towed the glider in its trailer, by road across to the gliding club at Glenning, where he had arranged to meet Nat Poldowski. Nat was a friend and fellow glider pilot. He also owned a Tiger Moth adapted for towing gliders. Before Nat arrived Darke had rigged and inspected his machine: a German built Glassflugel Libelle, a fifteen-meter wingspan glider. It was parked carefully at the eastern end of the runway. Everything was loaded and ready to go. He was seated outside the clubhouse, with a sandwich and a flask of coffee, when he identified the distant, happy sound of the Tiger Moth's Gypsy Major engine. Nat was on time.

At twenty past One o'clock, a telephone call came through from Alison. Yarrick had left the board meeting of the Great Glen Trading Company. The chauffeur had taken him to Glasgow Central station, where he boarded a train for the Northwest. That was all she knew. She would head north and meet him at the airfield. Also, Alison said he owed her for a parking ticket.

The information had thrown Darke slightly. It was the first time Yarrick had used the railway from Glasgow. He could leave the train at a number of stations, through to Daldrummie or Kinorchy. He might even continue on to the end of the line, on the West Coast. He conferred with Nat. Within ten minutes they were airborne, heading east, in the refuelled, silver painted Tiger Moth. Twenty minutes later they were circling Daldrummie station, but there was nothing significant to see. Disappointed, he instructed Nat over the intercom, to head for Kinorchy. Ten minutes flying north brought them above the centre of the village. They circled the small station car park once, at eighteen hundred feet. Darke could see a dark green Jaguar clearly visible, parked beside the fence. He hoped this was the same Jaguar used previously by Yarrick.

Assuming the train was not late, they could now estimate Yarrick's possible arrival at Kinorchy. Within twenty minutes of landing back at Glenning airfield, Darke was being launched in the Libelle, behind the Tiger Moth. As they approached cloudbase of a developing cumulous cloud he felt the surge of lift. In response he pulled the yellow knob, on the left of the instrument panel, to release the tow rope a hundred feet beneath the dark base of the cloud. He climbed of to the left. He radioed Nat and thanked him for his help, wishing him a safe flight home before settling into the thermal. It was 2.45pm.

The care that Yarrick had taken, to avoid being tailed, convinced Darke that he would be too wary to be tracked from the air, by powered aircraft. It would take a moment to stop, switch off the vehicle's engine, and listen for the sound of an aeroplane. If one were heard then it would be a question of not proceeding until it had gone. A glider on the other hand is silent and above three thousand feet, not so easy to see from the ground, even if you know it's in the vicinity. On a good day, gliders cross the country all the time, but are rarely noticed from the ground. Even their radar image is small.

A crackle of static came through the radio, mixed in with Nat's voice. He was north of Daldrummie, heading for his home airfield near Loch Leven. He had deviated from his course to check on the train from Glasgow, which he now had in view. It looked, he said, as though it was on time. Darke acknowledged and thanked him for the information. He checked his watch. It was 3.20pm.

Five minutes later he had descended to two thousand feet to windward of Kinorchy station. Darke was circling in a thermal, using it just to maintain his height. The train drew alongside the platform. As it pulled away three people exited the station building. One of the tiny figures climbed into the Jaguar. The dark green left the car park heading west. He could not be certain, but had to assume this was Yarrick. His binoculars showed the Jaguar moving along the road to the west. Now it was just a question of staying aloft and following. His only concern was Yarrick swapping to a vehicle he had not seen before. In that case he might easily lose him. He would not be able to maintain a constant watch, as he needed to keep a safe lookout for other aircraft and monitor his instruments. Within half a mile, the Jaguar pulled into a lay-by, partly obscured by trees. Less than five minutes later it turned round and retraced its steps towards Kinorchy. Almost immediately three Landrovers pulled on to the road heading west for the coast.

Once more he had to assume Leitch had swapped and was in the three-vehicle convoy. As before they spread out. Three miles further on the leading vehicle turned north, onto a narrow single-track road. The others followed. Looking down from above, it was difficult to assess the terrain over which they were travelling. His air navigation map indicated they were heading for a plateau, known as Craigdallon Moor. They seemed to reach a highpoint on the edge of the moor, where the lead vehicle halted and waited for the other two to draw alongside. All the drivers climbed out. They carefully scanned the landscape, with binoculars, in the direction they had come. Once satisfied, the two leading Landrovers drove off along a narrow track, leaving the third to continue the vigil. Darke took a mental note of the position of the vehicles and their heading, then turned his attention for five minutes to regain height to three thousand five hundred feet.

Without any lift the Libelle's glide angle is thirty-two to one. In other words, one thousand feet of spare height should allow the sailplane to glide for six miles. It would obviously be less into wind and more than that with a tail behind. Under the good thermal conditions he was experiencing, it was relatively easy for Darke to top up with, or stay in lift as necessary. If the conditions prevailed, there was no reason why he could not stay aloft until sunset. Under good conditions it is not uncommon for a glider flight to last eight or ten hours or more. He refreshed himself with orange juice from a flask. It was important to avoid dehydration. It was warm in the tiny cockpit with the Perspex canopy shielding him from the elements, but acting like a green house.

Visibility was becoming a problem, as the cumulus clouds were developing and obscuring his view, forcing him to descend to keep track of the two four-wheel-drive vehicles. They continued slowly across Craigdallon Moor for almost five miles, stopping occasionally to check the road behind. At the western edge of the moor, defined by sheer cliffs running for some twelve miles, from north to south, Darke became aware of a Victorian pile, marked on his map as Rasguneon Castle. It was built on top of a six-hundred-foot sheer rock face, looking towards the picturesque village of Craigdallon, five miles to the west. It commanded a view of the upper reaches of Loch Craigie, a sea loch, that wound its way some nine miles inland from the coast.

Slowly the Landrovers ground their way across the moor to within a mile-and-a-half of the castle. Here they stopped, beside a small six wheeled, all-terrain-vehicle. One man left the leading truck, to join the driver of the waiting buggy. It immediately rotated in its length, before heading off towards the castle. The Landrovers turned and drove off, in the direction they had come. Ten minutes later the all-terrain vehicle entered the castle courtyard and disappeared from view. Yarrick had come to Rasguneon Castle by the back door. It was an effective, if complicated way, to ensure he was not followed.

The Libelle was down to two thousand two hundred feet, as it crossed the west-facing cliffs. During the afternoon the wind had strengthened and backed, to become more westerly, putting the rugged line of cliffs almost at a right angle to the wind. Just forward of the rock face, he banked the glider round to the south to fly parallel to the ridge. Half a mile from the castle the escarpment rose to nine hundred feet, where he began to feel the power of the ridge lift, carrying the sailplane upwards. He followed the line of lift continuing to rise. After several miles and a climb to three thousand feet, he turned and headed back towards the castle. His camera was locked into a bracket, in such a way as to point along the starboard wing. By swooping down, at one hundred knots, then climbing and pulling the glider round in a tight right-hand turn, over the castellated turrets, it was possible to take a plan view photograph of the castle with its surrounding grounds. He noted that the ridge fell away to meet the sea loch, just to the north of the castle.

Chapter 6

It was gratifying to have traced Yarrick to his lair. However, Darke needed more information on him and his activities before he could prove, beyond doubt, his belief that Yarrick and Leitch were the same person. Over the next few months, he spent frequent weekends at the Loch Craigie Hotel, in Craigdallon, becoming a familiar face in the village. Alison Falkener was fascinated by what she saw as an adventure. She accompanied him on several occasions, against his better judgement. Darke tried to impress upon her that if Yarrick was Leitch, then he was a very dangerous man, who would not hesitate to use extreme violence. She was undaunted and insisted on becoming involved. A natural communicator, she enjoyed talking with people. Darke tended to be more reserved, it did not come naturally for him to pass the time of day talking with strangers. He managed it by planning ahead, drawing up a mental list of topics, to fill the lulls in the conversation.

He had learnt from an early age that people enjoyed talking about themselves, or being the "expert", able to impart their knowledge on a subject. By encouraging people to talk about themselves, their hobbies or locality, it was easy to sit back, listen and allow the conversation to flow, nudging it now and again in the right direction. Between them they were able to compile a picture of Rasguneon Castle and its occupants.

The new Laird, it was confirmed, was Trevor Yarrick, a bachelor, who kept himself very much to himself. "New money from Glasgow", it was said. He was rarely seen in the village. His staff were not local people. This had caused much resentment five years previously, when the castle had been sold and six locals had lost their jobs to 'incomers'. It was not difficult to meet up with these former castle employees in the hotel bar and draw information from them. Some said there were strange 'goings on' up there. Fishing boats and launches, had been seen going up to the castle jetty, at odd hours. It was the first information Darke had of an easy access to the sea, from the castle. Such a facility would serve Yarrick well, if he was still involved in drug smuggling, as Leitch had been.

The jetty, they discovered, was six hundred feet below the castle, in its own bay, set into the cliff wall. There were steps cut down the cliff face, to connect to the bay, but were said to be in poor condition in parts. In late Victorian times a lift had been installed. Apparently, the entrance to the bay was well-hidden, unless you knew where to look. Darke was determined to see the jetty for himself. Forays up to the castle by road had revealed that the main entrance was guarded by tall wrought iron gates. High walls surrounded the property.

It was a simple task to hire a boat, to explore the upper reaches of the sea loch, without exciting suspicion. It was something the owner of the local boatyard would do, on request, during the tourist season. It made a fine day out for Darke and Alison, with a picnic provided for them by the hotel. By the end of the trip Darke had located the entrance to the castle jetty and familiarised the approach to it. It was set back and flanked by two daunting rock formations. At the entrance a large freshly painted, notice board, bolted to the rock, proclaimed:

RASGUNEON CASTLE
KEEP OUT
PRIVATE PROPERTY

Paradoxically, without knowing exactly where it was, it would have been difficult to spot without the aid of the notice. On their return to the yard Darke spotted a clinker-built boat, lying beached and covered with an ancient tarpaulin. It looked abandoned, in need of some attention. It was the size of a whaler, except for a transom stern, with a partially enclosed cabin, well forward. The name could be deciphered with difficulty. It read, "Pelican" in faded white letters. Marty Kettles, the boatyard owner, said it was for sale, together with an old but reliable, outboard motor. He agreed to give it a coat of paint and the deal was done.

Three weeks later the two of them returned to Craigdallon to pick up Pelican. They parked the car in the late morning, and launched their craft to set off for the head of the loch. They spent the day pleasantly familiarising themselves with the new acquisition. They explored, more intimately, the upper reaches of the sea loch. It was evening before they turned back heading for Craigdallon, into a lowering sun. They were motoring against a strong flood tide, as they came level with the entrance to the castle's bay. With Darke's encouragement the engine began spluttering intermittently. it cut out completely, as they passed the entrance. Quickly switching to the oars, he worked hard to row against the current to enter the bay.

The day's outing and the remains of a picnic in the hamper would serve to support their story. They could claim the engine had stopped and they had to sought refuge in the castle's small bay, against the strong incoming tide. Once the boat was past the rock bastions, that marked the entrance, the effect of the tide subsided. The bay was larger than one might have expected from the outside: it was as wide as it was long, about a hundred-and-fifty yards in each direction. Two craft were moored to buoys in the bay away from the jetty. One was a fishing boat, the other a powerful seagoing cabin cruiser.

At the jetty long lines moored a rowing boat fore and aft, which allowed it to rise and fall with the tide. Their little charade was not necessary, as the bay area was deserted. It was surrounded by almost sheer rock walls and was out of sight of the castle. The only access to it from the landward side was via the man-made steps, leading up from the bay at the far end of the concrete quay. The steps quickly disappeared through a cleft in the rock, thirty feet above the jetty. The whole scene was blanketed in silence, save for the slapping of the water around the boats' hulls. Even the seagulls, in the dying light, had fallen silent. Darkness was being hastened by gathering rain clouds, giving the bay a sombre atmosphere.

Alison shuddered in the cool evening air; she was less sure of her spirit of adventure now. She took a deep breath and smiled across at Darke.

'So far so good,' she said, more for the want of something to say than anything else. It helped her to dispel the feeling of loneliness that swept over her.

Darke grinned back and guided the craft between the two moored vessels towards the concrete structure. No one appeared. They had twenty minutes before the tide slackened and they could quietly exit the bay, using the oars, to head back safely to the boatyard. Sunset was not far off as they came alongside a set of stone steps up to the jetty. He shipped his oars at the last moment and glided the remaining few yards.

'Okay?' he asked.

She nodded and said, 'Of course,' as she took his place between the oars.

He stepped onto the jetty, stretched his legs and asked, 'You'll be alright?'

She nodded again and resisted the temptation to say, 'be careful.' Instead, she pushed off, unshipped the oars and pulled away, round to the far end of the jetty, where she would not be seen by anyone entering, or descending to the bay.

He waved encouragingly before heading for the steps at the opposite end. He did not expect a guard on the jetty, but assumed someone could be on guard between it and the castle above. It made sense, he thought, that a lookout would be stationed to discourage intruders. As he ascended the steps a fine drizzle began to fall. At the fissure he stopped, waved back to Alison, who was standing in Pelican watching his progress, before cautiously looking round the corner of the rock and continuing his climb.

Darke mounted the steps. They twisted and turned, before disappearing through the mouth of a small cave a hundred feet higher, to reappear thirty feet higher, well below the lower stage of the lift. The antiquated lift system was guarded by ironwork gates. The cab or car was absent. It appeared to travel on a single rail, that ran not quite vertically up the rock face, hauled by a cable, running up to the ramparts high above. As he could see no motor at the bottom, he assumed the drive mechanism to be located at the top. The system was a fine example of Victorian over-engineering. It was clearly still serving its purpose efficiently. The giant pulley and steel cable, were well greased and obviously in regular use. He continued up the steps. It would be a long climb so he paced himself. It was clear that the steps, above the lower lift station, were in varying states of disrepair and little used. In the fading light he had to take great care. He was confident now that no guard would be encountered before he reached the castle.

His confidence was confirmed when he eventually came to the base of the castle walls, built on the solid rock. The parapet was fifty feet above. Here the steps had dangerously crumbled away in a rockslide, close by the lift system. In their place a set of three rain washed, aluminium retractable ladders, recently bolted to the parapet wall, could be lowered to a point where the steps were undamaged. The lowest rung of the ladder hung twenty feet above his head. The ladders were obviously retracted for security. It would need a long hook, or rope, to pull the ladders down to their full extent. He could climb no further. Disappointed, he began to retrace his steps to the bay as daylight faded.

He descended with more confidence than he had ascended, also with less caution. He had just passed the lower lift station, when he saw a torch beam moving upwards in the cave. There was no time to retrace his steps without being seen. He had no choice, but to scramble up the rock near the lift cage. He flattened himself on a narrow ledge eight feet above the steps, just as the first of three men exited the cave. Two men followed carrying a large hold-all, in each hand.

The increasing darkness and rain helped to give him cover. His position was uncomfortably exposed. From where he clung, facing the damp rock, he could look one way down in the direction of the bay and the other at the lower stage of the lift. A flash of a torch beam, in his direction, would be enough to light up his form, clinging to the rock. He was eight feet above, and less than ten feet from them. He dared not move. The chill rain began to trickle down his neck and a breeze ruffled his jacket. All three had their backs to him, hunched against the weather. The first man, tall with broad shoulders, pressed the red button for the lift to descend.

Immediately an inquiring voice came through an intercom from above, 'Yeah?'

'It's Brogan. Delivery for Mister Yarrick,' the first man replied. His two companions sniggered, at what was obviously a feeble joke.

'Okay, coming down,' the voice answered from above.

The machinery hissed into life as the motor high above set the well-greased cable travelling round the pulleys. Darke's heart was thumping in his chest. His hands were white in the darkness so he pulled on the cuffs of his jacket to hide them and covered his face with his arms. He judged he would give himself away by unzipping his hood from the collar of his sailing jacket, so he left it alone. He only glanced at the men from time to time.

He recalled an old hunter he had met, in the African bush, who had given him a piece of advice, 'Never', the lean, fit, older man had advised, 'stare at your prey for any length of time. There is an instinct in some animals that tells them when they are being watched. They will turn and look in your direction, not necessarily knowing why they are doing so. It puts them subconsciously on their guard and that's not what you want'. He had gone on to say that some humans would do the same.

Darke was not about to test the theory with these three, so he kept his eyes moving around the scene before him. Soon from above he could make out a cage descending. He transferred his gaze from the men to the cage, watching it, until it came to rest.

The tall leader, who had called himself Brogan, opened the two concertina gates with a rattle and a crash. The three men entered and turned to face in his direction. This was the moment of maximum danger. The interior of the cage had a dim light under the covered roof. He hoped it was sufficient to disturb their night vision. The torch beam swung in his direction, passing across him several times, before it was switched off. If the men had been concentrating, they would have seen him, but they were talking. Their eyes were focused within the cage, as it started its upward journey. He waited until the lift had climbed, on its angled track, for fifty feet before stirring. With great relief and tortured limbs, he gingerly lowered himself down to the path, before stiffly making his way, thoughtfully, to the little harbour. It occurred to him that the lift appeared to be controlled from the upper station only, which made sense from a security perspective.

Alison had been lying down in the bottom of Pelican, below the level of the jetty, when the boat with the three men entered the bay. She had begun to imagine all kind of terrible fates, that could have befallen Darke. When he arrived, she was pacing the jetty, in the darkness. She met his return with obvious relief.

Confident the falling rain would blanket any sound, he started the engine and headed for the entrance. The three men had arrived in, what looked like, an ex-naval fast motorboat. An ideal seagoing craft, Darke thought, for carrying drugs and for liaising out at sea. Once out of the bay they headed down river for Craigdallon boatyard.

As the year wore on Alison and Darke accumulated more material on Rasguneon Castle and its occupants. They spotted Yarrick on two of his rare trips through the village. On one occasion an, ex-castle, employee pointed him out, and confirmed he was Laird of the Castle.

Research in the local library had unearthed original plans of the castle. Alison excelled at gathering information on the up-to-date layout, from previous members of the household. It was not a huge building; it was more the size of a large country house. It had five public rooms, eight bedrooms, with staff quarters in the attic. The kitchen occupied the most northerly part of the ground floor. In the courtyard, to the south of the building, the stables had been converted to garages and a workshop. Turrets and castellations enhanced the impression of size. Its broad terrace ran the length of the building, along the cliff edge, with magnificent views westward, over the sea loch to the distant coast.

Despite rumours of craft moving up the loch to the castle, at odd hours, Darke had never seen anything suspicious himself, other than the fast motor boat in the bay of the castle. His watches had been limited to the odd night at weekends, without success.

As summer faded to autumn, he decided to attempt to positively identify Yarrick as Leitch, during the October Aviemore Highland Gift Fair. He assumed his prey would be there. He would be using such public occasions to underpin his cover as the Chairman of The Great Glen Trading Company. An invaluable and legitimate front for his nefarious drug activities. Darke had no doubt now, from his behaviour, that the person known as Yarrick, was involved in some serious form of criminality.

Chapter 7

It had been a successful year for tourism in Scotland, which always encourages buyers to place early orders with greater confidence, for the following season. In spite of the cold winds Aviemore was busier than normal for the Gift Shows. There was a real sense of optimism among the buyers, on the first day of the show. Something that Darke felt had been lacking for several years. He spent time looking and ordering for the following season, waiting for the throng of buyers to reach Yarrick's stand. Once they had arrived, he and Alison stopped at the refreshment area for a coffee and a sandwich.

The stand of the Great Glen Trading Company was close by, in the same position as the previous year. It was busy with buyers either engaged in placing orders, or waiting for attention. Darke carefully watched Yarrick. He and two other men were busily engaged with customers. It was obvious that Yarrick was still no more familiar with the stock. Preferring to stand back, unless all his representatives were occupied, he kept interrupting the other salesmen when unable to answer a question. Darke finished his coffee and suggested that Alison continued buying by herself. She was reluctant to go. After all the visits to Craigdallon, she was intrigued to be able to study Yarrick more closely.

'It's not a good idea for the two of us to be here together,' he told her.

'Why not, he doesn't know us?'

'There's twice as much chance of being recognised again, if we are both here together.' He stood up and gently took her arm and steered her away from the refreshment area.

'Oh, come on Luke, surely not, with all these people milling around?' She grinned at him. 'You're up to something.'

'You are tall, blonde and not unattractive. People look at you and at the lucky man you are with. That is not what we want at this moment. So, please go and spend some of my money.'

Alison was pleased with the compliment. He rarely said anything of the sort. So, with a brief wave of her hand and a dazzling smile, she headed off down the nearest aisle. She was correct, he was up to something. He moved back to the vicinity of the stand. He checked that Yarrick and all three employees were occupied, before stepping onto the raised display area. He casually looked around, picked up products here and there, checking the price labels, before retiring out of sight, without drawing attention to himself. Carefully held by its base, between his thumb and forefinger, was a small pewter quaich he had purloined. It was one that Yarrick had lifted to check its price. Satisfied his crime had gone undetected, he set out to track Alison down.

Eventually he found her, on the stand of one of his regular suppliers of Celtic silverware. He was greeted warmly. After a brief exchange of pleasantries, Darke asked for and was given a box and a plastic bag, for the pewter bowl. Also, he begged a large brown envelope, big enough to take the boxed item. He placed the package inside the envelope, sealed it and signed across the flap. He asked Alison to do the same. He next dated it, with the time and place.

As they left the stand Alison felt herself being guided by the arm, back along the aisles they had already covered.

'Where are we going?'

'I want you to make a telephone call for me.'

'Why can't you do it?'

'I will be elsewhere.'

'Is this to do with Yarrick?' she asked, as they came to a public telephone at one side of the ice rink.

'That's right, I want to see his reaction,' he went on, 'All you have to do is ring the exhibition office. The number is on this card. Ask them to announce what's written here.' He handed her the card with the details on it.

'Why can't I go up to the office and ask them personally, or is that a silly question?'

'Because the call must be untraceable. It must appear to come from outside the hall.' He paused for emphasis before saying, 'Wait for five minutes after I've gone, then 'phone.'

'I see,' she replied, not really seeing at all.

'If anyone asks for your name, make one up. Anything but your real name. I don't want the call to be traced. Okay?'

'All right, but I don't understand why you're being so secretive.' She gave him a long-suffering look.

'Good girl. I'll explain it all later. I'll meet you back here in fifteen minutes.'

Within three minutes he had reached a position from where he could view the stand of The Great Glen Trading Company. Yarrick was nowhere to be seen, but shortly he appeared from behind a display unit. He was almost facing Darke, when the public address system overwhelmed the general hubbub in the hall, to announce, with a metallic click, "THERE IS AN URGENT TELEPHONE CALL FOR MISTER SANDY LEITCH, FROM KATANGA, AT THE EXHIBITION RECEPTION DESK. MISTER SANDY LEITCH, CONTACT THE RECEPTION DESK, PLEASE".

The message was repeated several times, but Darke's attention was on Yarrick. His head jerked up, towards the nearest loudspeaker, at the sound of the name. He froze briefly, then looked around sharply before resuming a more natural attitude, but it was clear he was unnerved. His movements were stiffly self-conscious. His mind was obviously racing, to grasp the full implications of what he had heard and to work out what he should do. He seemed to make up his mind. Turning, he left the stand to join the throng of slowly moving buyers. A few feet from the stand he stopped, disrupting the movement of people in the narrow aisle.

His movements made it plain that he was thinking, 'Am I being watched?' He glanced in all directions without identifying Darke, who was well hidden, observing him, through a narrow gap, between display units. Yarrick returned to the Great Glen stand to resume his position, amongst his stock items. He began to relax. Once more the message came, causing his head to jerk round involuntarily, but otherwise he remained still. One of the exhibition staff walked past. Yarrick stepped away from the stand to call to him. A brief conversation followed, then the man indicated towards the side of the hall. Yarrick moved off in that direction.

The crowded exhibition hall gave Darke all the cover he needed to follow the other man's movements. In the aisle, closest to the side of the hall, Yarrick crossed to an internal telephone, picked it up and dialled once. Darke could not hear the conversation from where he stood, but he was now in no doubt in his own mind, that he was watching Sandy Leitch. So, who was it who had died in the crash, along with Lew Bodell, to enable Leitch to fake his own death? The implications were enormous; it meant the man he was watching, was most probably a double murderer.

Chapter 8

Three days later Darke stood brooding over the facts. He looked down the length of the loch from his first floor sitting room window, undecided as to what course of action to take. The bleakness of the view matched his mood. The cloud base was down to three hundred feet above the grey, wind-swept water. A fine, soaking rain had been falling for hours. Five minutes previously he had placed the telephone back in its cradle, having spoken at some length, to a Colonial Office civil servant. His former employers were not interested in a ten-year-old murder in a post-independent Kwazania. Their slimmed down ministry was hard pressed to carry out their diminishing role, without complicating the situation with a possible unsolved murder from a decade ago.

A call to the Kwazanian embassy was equally unhelpful. The Under Secretary he spoke with sounded bored with the whole idea of an unsubstantiated murder allegation, which had been satisfactorily dealt with, as a road accident ten years before. Darke could understand his point of view. When the man suggested he set it all down in writing and they would review the case, it was apparent he was getting nowhere.

He decided on a walk. Armed with a stout stick and dressed warmly in a wool crew neck pullover, waxed jacket, thorn-proof trousers, boots and cap, he set out. He walked purposefully westward, on a track that led along the glen, above the south side of the loch. It felt good to be moving through the cold air and gentle rain. From all about him came the sound of water, gurgling and trickling in rivulets, rushing in burns, cascading in falls. The hillside was like a sponge, able to absorb copious quantities of water, before releasing it gently over three or four days, into the loch below.

Soon his mind turned back to Leitch and the murder of two men. If the relevant government office in

London and the Kwazanian embassy were not interested, then others, most likely, would be of the same mind. He stopped and realised, if the probable double murder of Lew Bodell and some person unknown was to be taken seriously, he must return to Africa. He looked over the loch. The cloud base hung like a ceiling not twenty feet above his head. In either direction he could see the mist clinging to the brown heather as the terrain rose steeply from the loch side.

The scene around was desolate. He liked it that way. He was alone, save for two men on the path behind. There was nothing unusual in that, except, even at a quarter of a mile distance, he could make out their inappropriate attire. One wore a fashionable dark trench coat, the other a light-coloured knee-length car coat. The first was short and stocky, the other taller, wide shouldered, with an athletic build. They wore no hats. The way they were walking reinforced the impression that they were shod in lightweight footwear, unsuited to the rough terrain. They would not have looked out of place in a city, but here on a drenched hillside, amongst the brown heather, they stood out incongruously. They were making heavy going of it.

Amused at their slow progress, he continued his upward journey, determined to keep an eye on the two, to ensure they did not get into too much trouble. It was no place to be stranded if the mist came down. It was doubtful whether they even had a compass. He was familiar with the hills around, but it was all too easy to get lost if the weather worsened, as it often did.

He was enjoying the exercise and strode out. The path led upwards, into the mist, so he chose a sheep track that branched, at a slight angle, to his right. It continued horizontally along a ridge, just below the ceiling of mist. He splashed his way through puddles sweeping aside the coarse fronds of heather, clutching at his legs. The track had narrowed so much in places, making it hard to follow. It was nothing more than a dark wavering line in the heather before him. The men had dropped further behind. Twenty minutes later, he had almost forgotten them, when the mist suddenly swept down the hillside. He stopped to enjoy the sensation of being engulfed in the swirling vapour. He could not see more than a few yards; the mist had turned the walk into much more of a private experience.

It was him versus nature, an exercise in navigation. It was time to backtrack and check on the two "townies". It was not a simple task to follow the line of the trail. Without the mist he could look ahead, to see the general direction of the track. However, with visibility cut to a few yards, it was possible to become side-tracked, to only discover the error when it petered out. The problem then was to find the point at which you had left the original track. The secret here was to look for your boot prints previously made in the peat. They were not obvious to the eye, as the overhanging heather frequently hid them from view. It took him time to make his way back along the overgrown track. He reaffirmed his position, when he saw the form of a rock lined gully, appear through the mist. He had crossed it a short time before. Using his stick and free hand he gingerly climbed his way down to the gushing stream that had, over the centuries, carved this watercourse down the hillside to the loch below.

Just downstream of his crossing point there were rocks, below that the slope fell away vertically. The rock formation at this point pinched the water flow to half its width causing it to shoot out from the hillside, as though poured from a spout, down into a pool eighty feet below. It was known locally as the "Mare's Tail".

'Mister Darke?' the question came from the taller of the two men. The man in the light-coloured car coat, standing above him on the opposite side of the gully.

'Yes?' He looked up. The man was thirty feet away and twelve feet higher. He levelled his arm and Darke saw the gun. He heard the report and saw the flash of flame as he ducked and flung himself to his right, behind a buttress of rock. He was aware that the second man was coming round from behind his partner as he fired. Darke used two hands on his stick, wielding it like a paddle to drive it, haphazardly, into the rocks and shale to give him purchase; to propel himself up the steep, narrow gully. Fear drove him on. One glance behind showed the shapes of the two men through the mist, just by the rock, behind which he had taken cover.

The taller man looked as though he had just slid, feet first, down the side of the gully. He was lying awkwardly on his back, blocking the movement of the second man. The man in the trench coat was leaning awkwardly round the rock, waving his pistol in Darke's direction. He fired two shots. Darke instinctively ducked at the noise of the double crack. The shots were not well aimed and went wide, smacking into granite to his left. He pushed himself behind another rock and heaved upwards. His lungs were drawing in huge draughts of moist air from fear and exhaustion.

The mist had swallowed him. He cleared the side of the gully and moved out into the sodden heather to climb higher, above the barely visible path. His breath was coming in great gasps. He stopped. There was no sound of a pursuit, he sat down facing the way he had come. The blood pounded in his ears, as he gulped for air and tried to steady the drubbing of his heart, that racked his body. He reckoned he was pretty safe, as the visibility was no more than five or six yards. If he lay still his followers would almost have to fall over him to find him.

The bigger man he had instantly recognised when he called his name. He was the tall, square headed man Yarrick had been speaking to on the exhibition stand, when Darke had spotted Yarrick's missing little finger. Also, the man he had seen in the castle lift, who had identified himself as Brogan. They were after him. This was no case of mistaken identity.

'Stupid, stupid, stupid fool,' he said to himself almost under his breath. He should never have put out the call on the public address. It had seemed such a neat idea at the time; a way of forcing Leitch to give himself away, but it had also made Leitch aware that someone was onto him.

'Fool,' he whispered again. He had not looked at the situation from the other man's point of view. What would he have done in Leitch's place? It was obviously a ploy to see his reaction and he must have known he had given himself away. So, who was spying on him? It stood to reason that it was most likely to be someone in the gift trade. How difficult would it be, in the small world of the Scottish gift industry, to ask around about anyone who had lived and worked in Africa? A number of his acquaintances in the gift trade, were aware of his police background. Even if Leitch did not remember his name, it would be sufficient to make him investigate further. They had found him and now he was in trouble. He must get away, but first he must gain time to get back to the house, to gather the necessary items he would need. Not least of which would be money and his passport. Now he needed to draw them further to the west to give him time to return to the house.

He was used to stalking deer when photographing them, now he would stalk these men. If he could get them lost, he would have time to make good his escape. His brief rest had quietened his breathing and reinvigorated his aching muscles. He stood and cautiously made his way downhill, angling away from the gully. It was not long before he came across the sheep trail. He would have missed it if he had not known it was thereabout. It was one thing to follow it when walking along the line of it, but far more difficult to identify it when crossing at an angle. He could also hear the rush of water as it swept through the rock outlet to form the Mare's Tail. He dropped down to the trail, keeping well away from the gully's edge. He moved cautiously, straining his eyes to catch any movement through the blanket of mist. Shortly he heard their voices above the rush of water. He sank to his haunches in the heather.

The fog made it difficult to work out the direction of the sound. Eventually he decided they were still in the vicinity of the gully. There was sound of their voices and smell of tobacco smoke drifting up towards him. The tumbling water covered any slight sound he made through the grass and heather. He crawled forward to look over the edge. The shorter man had the collar of his dark trench coat pulled up. A damp cigarette hung limply from his lips, it jumped up and down as he hopped from foot to foot, in a vain attempt to keep warm. The taller man sat on a rock massaging his right ankle. He was drawing hard on his cigarette and cursing the weather and his ankle in equal measure.

Darke withdrew, retracing his way back along the track, to a point fifty yards from the gully, where there was a rock outcrop. He loosened a boulder, almost too big to lift, until he was satisfied, he could move it away from its companions. Next, he took his handkerchief from his pocket. Holding the cloth in his palm he brushed it over the rough grass, beside the rocks, until it was soaked. He took out his penknife and tested the point. With a grimace he nicked the end of his left thumb, drawing blood. He had cut deeper than he had intended and the blood welled up in rich red beads. He caught each drop in the centre of the handkerchief, ensuring it created a widening stain on the damp, white linen. When he was satisfied, he placed the bloodstained handkerchief in the open, beside the trail on the lower side of the track, as though it had been dropped. He rolled the loosened rock and, letting out an agonised yell, allowed it to slide down a fellow rock and thump onto another below. It was left where it fell across the line of the sheep trail. He moved westward up the hillside away from the outcrop and took a prone position amongst some grassy tufts, from where he could look back and just make out the formation of rocks.

The shorter man in the black trench coat appeared first. Slightly hunched against the cold, he moved around the fallen stone, and continued along the track. Darke could make out his silhouette, he carried a pistol in his hand. The shadowy figure moved on from the fallen rock. He gave a grunt as he discovered the bloodstained handkerchief.

'Hey Big Man', he called to his companion. A shadow limped into view. The two men conferred in lower tones. Before moving on towards the west.

Pleased with himself, Darke kept parallel with them, but out of sight in the mist. They were clumsy in their movements and voluble in their condemnation of anything that smacked of the countryside. Their lack of vocabulary was supplemented by much cursing. Eventually Darke was confident enough to increase his pace and draw ahead of them. He guessed by now they had walked beyond the western end of the loch. It was time for more theatrics. He could no longer hear the two men talking. They had either run out of spare breath, or realised they could be heard and in turn would not be able to hear any sound he might make.

Confident that he was well ahead of them, he swung down the slope to cross their line of walk. He kept going for fifty yards, before turning and listening. There was nothing to be heard through the mist. He hoped they had not given up.

'Help,' he cried in a desperately hoarse voice, 'Help,' and again, 'Help'. He moved back up the hill further to the west, assuming that if they were going to respond they would move down at an angle and not bump into him. He lay down and waited. Soon he heard movement, but was unsure of its direction.

'Where are yer?' The cry rang out not thirty feet away.

Cautiously he lifted his head and spied two misty figures, above him and to his left. He turned his face to the heather, his heart beating. He was no longer confident in his ability to remain unseen. The swish of feet through the rough growth warned him they were on the move. They passed by him at a distance of no more than twenty feet. He raised his head and watched them go. They called again as the mist closed around them. Relieved, Darke rose quickly to climb, once more, to the almost invisible sheep trail. He was confident they would have difficulty retracing their steps and identifying the way back to the east end of the loch. If they continued in the direction they were going, they would not meet the loch. They were well beyond its western end, which should add to their confusion. He hoped to return to his house with a minimum of twenty minutes to spare.

He needed to find their car. It was likely that they had parked close by, but not in sight of the house, which stands alone in an acre of ground. There were only two possibilities: the lay-by at the loch end or the old farm track beyond the house. He did not want to walk into a trap, should there be one, as they had made it all too clear they meant to kill him. One near miss was all he needed to take the hint. If he had had any remaining doubts about Leitch, he now had none. This afternoon's adventure had served to show how serious his situation had become. He was no longer an observer of events; he had become a player, inextricably involved. He was in a weak position and he needed time to think everything through, but that would have to wait until later.

The mist was thinning as he approached the house. He approached it from a high angle to avoid being seen from the sitting room windows, should any of Leitch's men have entered the house. He moved beyond his walled garden, before descending the short distance to the road. There was no car to be seen in the lay-by. Its damp, black asphalt surface, dully reflected a slightly lighter ash coloured sky. It was occupied only by an overflowing litter bin. Darke kept off the road, behind the high stone wall marking the boundary of his property and out of sight of his house. Trees from the garden threw branches low over the wall, giving him shelter from the drizzle and cover from prying eyes.

Having skirted his property, he could see a metallic grey Volvo estate, parked well into the farm lane, amongst the trees. It was the same colour as the Volvo estate he had seen Yarrick driving through Craigdallon. The lane itself was overgrown, the undergrowth easily shielding the car from any casual passer-by on the road. Darke entered the wood on the far side of the lane and stealthily moved towards the vehicle. It was empty, with nothing of interest inside. He wondered if the two he had left on the hill were the only ones to have come in the car, or were there others? Time was running out, he needed to get into the house, to get away before they returned. Also, he needed to know whether there were others watching out for him. If so, they would most likely be in the house, or watching it.

From the cover of the wood, he checked as much of the area as he could, but saw nothing suspicious. He returned to the Volvo and moving slowly, circled it, checking the ground. He assumed the number plates were false, to make it hard to trace. The grass by all four doors was trampled. Longer strands by the nearside rear door had been trapped when the door was closed. It could indicate that at least three people had left the vehicle. It could also mean, of course, that two only had arrived then opened the rear doors to collect items from the rear seats. The signs strengthened his belief, it would be safer to assume that he had four men to deal with. If there were two others, one might be watching the front and the other the back of the house.

Knowing the terrain, he was able to move about keeping himself well hidden. He checked all the obvious vantage points from good cover, without seeing anyone. It was possible they were inside the house, waiting for him. The more time passed the more he believed this to be so. He decided against calling the police. He was not entirely certain there was anyone in the house. Anyway Callum Sanderson, the local bobby, would not constitute much of a threat to these thugs. They were armed: he would be just one more person to shoot. He decided to allow Callum the opportunity to live a little longer and not call on his services. He could walk away from the house and make good his escape, but if he was going to sort this mess out, beat Leitch and his thugs, he needed to begin the process in Africa. To do that he needed his passport and money, and that meant getting inside the house. He made his mind up.

The wall by the stone outbuildings stood six feet tall and out of sight of the main windows. He slid over the top and silently landed amongst the shrubs bordering the garden. He was facing the gable end and side door of the house. The stone outbuildings housed his workshop and garage. The workshop was not locked, he entered and closed the door behind him and propped his stick against the end of the bench, keeping clear of the window. Darke hunted for anything useful. The first item he found was an old French clasp knife that could be locked open, by turning a metal collar at one end of the varnished wooden handle. He slipped it into his pocket. It would have to do. He then noticed his old epee from his school fencing days. The cumbersome, bowl-like, aluminium guard was slightly oxidised. The surface was dulled, with a myriad of scratches, from numerous long forgotten bouts. The maroon, leather-bound handle was flecked with specks of sage green mould. He carefully withdrew it from among the bamboo canes and abandoned walking sticks, standing in an ancient umbrella stand.

He wiped the mould from the handle and wafted the blade experimentally through the air. The small flattened disc-shaped end, had broken off years before, leaving a jagged point approximately an inch shorter than the standard vee-shaped steel blade. It was dull with rust, but the balance was good; improved by its shortened length. The weighted chrome pommel unscrewed with difficulty. He withdrew the handle and removed the aluminium guard before replacing the handle and screwing the pommel back into position. He was not likely to come up against a swordsman, therefore the guard was an unnecessary encumbrance and bright enough to draw attention. He took a rag and drew the blade through it. He repeated the process three times before he was satisfied that most of the loose rust was removed. It might not perform well against a gun, but it gave him some degree of comfort. He had done only a modest amount of fencing in recent years. It was all mostly electric these days, which was not quite the same. The balance of the weapons is different which encourages different tactics.

It took a few sweeps with a file to bring the jagged end to a useful point. Even the low rasp of the two metal surfaces working together, made the hairs on the back of his neck stand on end. He was conscious that he still had no idea whether there was anyone in the house, let alone their location if they were inside. He needed to hurry. There was no movement outside, as far as he could see from the workshop window. The key was in his hand as he made his way to the side door of the house. The sound of the key turning in the lock would travel in a silent house. He took his time to turn it in the lock, holding the door tightly closed as he did so. Eventually it had rotated fully. With a shaking hand he removed and pocketed the key. The door handle slowly turned until it would move no further. With slight forward pressure, the door opened quietly. He stepped inside, closing the door behind him. He stood to one side, among wellington boots, overcoats, hats, caps and other outdoor paraphernalia. He listened carefully but could hear nothing. The door to the passage was closed. Carefully, he removed his wet wax jacket, hiding it amongst the hanging items. His boots he put behind the others. He took rags from a cardboard box, and using them to squeeze out most of the moisture from his sodden trouser legs. When he was sure he would not leave a tell-tale trail of water wherever he went, he slipped on an old pair of shoes he kept for the garden and crossed to the door to the passage. It came open painfully slowly. It was, thankfully, Mrs Mcgriff's day off.

The corridor led past the kitchen door and on to the entrance hall. No sound came as he moved through the shadows of the unlit passage. The door to the kitchen was open, spilling light across his path. A glance inside told him everything was in order. He moved on keeping the epee blade ahead of him. There was no hint of movement or sound of voices. Only the familiar tick tock of the grandfather clock. Watching the head of the carved wooden staircase he crossed the oak panelled entrance hall and slipped, quietly, through the open door to the study. The place had been ransacked; drawers emptied; their contents strewn across the floor. The drawers themselves were lying abandoned among the debris. The contents of his bookshelves had been swept onto the floor, the empty dark oak shelves looking stark and undressed, denuded of their contents. His decanter of whisky was gone, together with two matching crystal glasses. The glass door to the garden had been forced.

So, they had been inside. If they were still in the house, he expected them to be in the sitting room on the first floor. The house had been built in the previous century, to take advantage of the view along the loch, with big bay windows facing down the glen. From there they would have a view of their returning companions, who had followed him onto the hill. The mist and the return route he had followed had kept him hidden from their view. He re-entered the hall. The dining room door was situated on the opposite side of the cavernous open fireplace, to the study. It was empty and untouched. As he re-entered the hall, he heard a muffled laugh and caught the low hum of voices, from the sitting room above. He retraced his steps, past the kitchen and took the narrow stairs, at the opposite end of the house, which provided an alternative route to the landing above.

He knew the oak stairs creaked, so he deliberately placed his feet to the side of each step. Once only the tip of the epee tapped the plaster wall as he climbed. He froze instantly, but nothing disturbed the silence. When his heartbeat returned to normal, he stealthily continued his ascent. He reached the upper landing and slipped across it, into his bedroom. They had been here. The bedroom and his dressing room beyond, had been roughly searched. Much of his belongings were scattered about where they had been thrown. However, they had not discovered the safe behind a panel in the dressing room. It took him a moment to enter the combination and open the heavy door. He withdrew the sealed buff envelope containing the quaich, a file, his passport and two thousand pounds, in two bundles of Bank of England ten-pound notes. Lewis Bodell's letter, still in its yellowing envelope, caught his attention. He put it in his pocket. His empty suitcases had been opened, and thrown on the floor. He picked the medium sized case, in brown leather. Into it he bundled a range of items: a suit, socks, shirts and shoes, as well as casual items. As long as he had enough to travel in without standing out in a crowd, he could buy any other items he needed later.

As he closed the case, he felt a wave of pessimism engulf him. His chances of getting away without being detected, were almost nil. He stopped and took several deep breaths, before deciding to take one step at a time. He moved quickly, stopping only to listen and check the bedroom beyond. It took an effort of will to move out from the dressing room and across the bedroom to the door. Listening intently revealed no sound. He had the suitcase and epee in one hand leaving his right hand free. He was about to slip out of the room, when he heard voices raised in the sitting room at the far end of the passage. The next moment he heard two men moving down the main stairs and across the hall. There came the sound of the front door opening. The distant crunch of their feet on the gravel drive gave him all the incentive he needed: he darted down the back stairs to the corridor below. Pushing the suitcase and epee ahead of him, he turned in the direction of the side door, through which he had originally entered the house.

'Hold it right there,' ordered a voice with a strong Birmingham accent.

Darke felt a bolt of fear run through his body. He turned his head. In the semi-darkness of the passageway, he saw over his shoulder, a figure of a man of average height, standing in the light from the open kitchen door. In his right hand he held a pistol.

"There were five of them," the thought went through Darke's mind. He cursed himself for his ill luck. The man was six feet behind him.

'Turn round slowly. Very slowly.'

Darke was slightly stooped forward, away from the man, he took hold of the thin bladed sword with his right hand, leaving the case in his left. He straightened up and turned slowly round to his left, covering the sword with his body as he did so. The rusted blade was dull, not easily seen in the half-light of the passage. He carefully turned towards the man with the gun. He held the case forward and let it drop. Instinctively the man's eyes flickered, he looked down as the case hit the floor. In that moment Darke whipped the epee blade round and upwards. He held the handle lightly, between thumb and forefinger, with the thumb on top. The other three fingers relaxed, to allow the Pommel end of the handle to swing outwards, free of the palm. As the blade moved up level with the gun, he snapped the three fingers closed on the handle, whipping the tip of the unseen blade hard into the hand holding the gun, deflecting it sideways.

Years of fencing took over and without conscious thought, the parry, in a fluid movement, became an attack. The smallest correction by the fingers, brought the point of the blade on target, as Darke's arm straightened into a lunge sending the ragged point through the man's bicep. The man dropped the pistol, looking stunned. He made no sound as the blade penetrated his flesh. In truth he felt it more like a punch, than a stab. He only realised he had been run through, when he looked down to see the thin blade protruding from his upper arm. Darke twisted and pulled.

This action his victim did feel. With a gasp of pain, he clutched at the wound before the blade had been fully withdrawn. The rough blade ripped the web of skin between the first and second finger of his left hand. This seemed to cause him more instant pain than the arm wound. He slumped against the wall, cursing loudly. Darke swung the weighted pommel of the epee, hard into the side of the man's head. Soundlessly and in slow motion, he slid down the wall and lay still. Darke picked up the fallen pistol and rapidly checked it. It was an FN Browning, nine-millimetre, semi-automatic. It was cocked and ready to fire. He released the hammer and applied the safety catch. The magazine held ten rounds with another loaded in the breech, A quick search of the fallen man's jacket pockets resulted in another full magazine and a silencer. He pocketed both items, retrieved his case and retraced his steps out to the workshop, collecting his car keys from the boot room as he went. Adrenalin was coursing through his veins.

Once inside, he crossed to the connecting door to the garage, returning the epee to the old umbrella stand, as he passed. He felt more confident now that he had the Browning in his pocket. He placed the suitcase in the car. He knew what he had to do. From the inside he unbolted the garage doors, but left them unopened. It was his intention to wait until those outside the house had returned inside. Otherwise, he would have little or no chance of making his getaway, as he must drive past the front of the house, turn right down the long drive. It was a fair assumption that the two men had left the house on seeing their two companions returning from the hill. He doubted the hill walkers were in the best shape.

His Rover 3500 was parked in full view in front of the house, but in the garage was his pride and joy: a nineteen thirty-eight, four-and-a-half litre Bentley open tourer, painted in a deep green with fine gold coach lines. His Uncle had had it restored to perfection and he had inherited it. The previous day had been one of those perfect autumn days, mild, dry and sunny. He had driven the car for two hours, just for pleasure and to clear his mind. Returning in the late afternoon, he had reversed it into its garage. It always gave him pleasure to open the garage doors to see that Bentley radiator between large Marchal headlights, ready to head for the open road.

It was imperative not to forewarn Leitch's men of his whereabouts, until the last possible moment. Using the starter motor would be noisy and not an option. The ground was flat and unsuited to an easy "bump" start, for such a heavy car. Using the starting handle was less noisy, but still might generate enough noise to be heard in the house. However, he had a party trick which might serve him well.

From the garage he surveyed the front of the house. Within five minutes he spied the four men: the two returning from the hill and the other two from the house. They made for the main door. Brogan, the taller man of the two, was being assisted by both men from the house, whilst 'Trench coat' limped along with head held low: his breath was condensing as he struggled to keep up with the others. The bigger man was obviously giving the others an account of events. He did not seem too happy.

Darke moved back to the open door of the Bentley and slid into the driver's seat. He switched the ignition on and juggled the advance and retard lever. With the merest vibration the engine came to life. The sound was no more than a deep rhythmic burble. The Rolls Royce built, four-and-a-half litre engine was so perfectly engineered and balanced that after twenty-four hours, the mixture in the six cylinders was still under compression. Just switching on the ignition and upsetting the balance, by oscillating the advance and retard lever, was sufficient to rotate and fire the engine into life. He had done it many times before to the amazement of a number of his friends, but this time it had a practical use. It could make the difference for a successful escape.

He left the big engine running almost silently and slipped back to the doors. Through the high windows he was able to see the men entering the house. As soon as they disappeared Darke swung the doors wide and ran to the open driver's door. Once in the seat he closed the car door gently, using the outside handle. He released the long handbrake lever with his right hand, engaged second gear and eased the clutch out. The eighteen-inch wheels began to turn, slowly, effortlessly. He took the Browning in his right hand and cocked it. The large tyres on the gravel drive, made the most noise.

He accelerated as he came level with the nearest corner of the house. The front door opened as he drew abreast of it. A bemused figure appeared gun in hand, curious to investigate the sound. He was obviously surprised to see a car driving past. Darke fired two rapid shots at the feet of the man, causing him to leap back through the doorway. The Bentley surged forward, swung right at the far end of the house and accelerated down the long curving drive toward the road. As he neared the stone pillars marking the entrance, there was a loud report from the direction of the house and a bullet dug a groove in the righthand stone column. He accelerated again, as he turned right onto the single-track road, hidden now by the stone wall before a second shot could be fired. He gripped the large four-spoked steering wheel with both hands, as his whole body began to shake with nervous reaction. He laughed out loud in relief. There had been a moment or two in the house when he had thought he would never get away.

The Bentley's long bonnet dropped before him as he crested the hill at the end of the Glen. He swung the car left onto a forestry track to park out of sight off the road, among the fir trees. He took a pair of binoculars from the glove compartment and returned to the edge of the woodland, from where he could view the road he had just left. Yarrick's men would not stay at the house now that he had gone, but he wanted to be certain they had left before leaving the Glen.

Fifteen minutes later the grey Volvo estate made its way down the deserted road, at speed. The noise of its tyres on the wet tarmac increasing as it came on. All five men could be seen inside as it passed by. It was five more minutes of rain drenched silence, with no other traffic, before he started the Bentley and drove back to the road. He was uncertain whether to follow the other car or return and check the house. For all the time it would take he decided to retrace his steps. He turned in the direction of the house, to make sure it was secure. It was his intention to be away for some time. He was as sure as he could be that all the men were gone. There was no point in any of them staying behind, as it was likely he would summon the police, which would not be to their liking, particularly as there was only one road out of the glen.

A dark shadow caught his attention as he drove towards the house. With a sickening realisation he could see, in the direction of his home, a column of smoke rising and spreading out, as it mingled with the low cloud base. When the house came into view, tongues of flames were flickering behind the windows. He turned the car through the gates and halted. It was pointless to drive further. His home was engulfed in smoke and flames along its length. As he watched with sickening awe, flames began to penetrate through the tiles of the roof.

They must, he realised, have torched a number of the rooms for the fire to have spread so rapidly throughout the building. Even if the retained firemen of the local brigade were called, he knew there was nothing they could save. By the time he reached a telephone and made the emergency call it would be all over. The men would have to leave their jobs, make their way to the fire station, in Kilpicton, man the tender, before heading the five miles to the house to fight the fire. It would take thirty minutes at least.

Darke watched as the roof collapsed in on itself with a roar and a massive eruption. Sparks flew skywards to be quenched by the low hanging clouds. The first floor quickly became a burning shell. He was numb, he felt detached from the sight. He backed the Bentley onto the road and with a final glance at his burning home, headed along the road for Kilpicton. He was now determined to exact revenge and nothing would deter him.

Chapter 9

The picturesque village of Kilpicton nestles between the river Muire and the heavily wooded slopes of Ben Dhu. The police station is situated on the outskirts, set back from the road. Sergeant Callum Sanderson, a portly forty-year-old, was puffing in his tight uniform, as he put a call though to the Fire Master. He replaced the receiver before settling his large girth back into a more comfortable position, the better to hear Darke's narrative. Twenty-five minutes later Darke was heading for the row of detached, stone built, Victorian villas, at the far end of the village, which was the home of Alison Falkener. He was unsure of her movements, but, if she was not at home, he would leave her a message. As his manager, he knew there was a chance she might be in danger from Yarrick, particularly if he had discovered her involvement in their inquiries into his background.

He turned the Bentley into the drive and saw, with relief, her Mini parked close by the front porch. She had clearly just returned, as the door of the house was ajar and the door of her car was open. He stopped beside the red mini and walked to the house. As he looked back to the car her handbag caught his eye. The tan leather bag lay open, beside the driver's door with most of its contents strewn on the gravel drive. Fear gripped him as he realised what must have happened. He called her name several times. He spotted the gouged tyre marks in the gravel, where a large car had accelerated hard, spinning its wheels, as it took off.

They had taken Alison. His mind was full of questions. These people were killers. Why had they not killed her straightaway, as they had tried to do with him? Maybe to get at him, or get information from her about him. After they had finished with her and extracted the information they wanted, he knew they would kill her. He had to find her and quickly. Their most likely destination had to be Rasguneon Castle.

Three hours later, as light was beginning to fade, Darke entered Loch Craigie boatyard. The Bentley's dipped headlights caught the small craft paraphernalia of ropes, fenders, oars, spars and launch dollies. He had locked Alison's house and car. As an afterthought he had opened the garage doors. The house belonged to Alison's parents, who spent most of the year in France. The contents of the garage were mainly those of Ewan Falkener, Alison's father, a retired major of a highland regiment. He was well known locally for his prowess as a fisherman. A rack of his rods hung on the wall. The longest Darke guessed was for sea fishing. He took it down complete with line and reel. What he needed most was rope. He picked a coil of nylon cord he knew had been used during the summer, for lopping and lowering of branches from trees in the garden. An old rubber quoit also caught his attention. He partially dismantled the rod and with the quoit, placed it on the floor of the car, in front of the passenger seat. He had filled the car with petrol in Kilpicton and set off westward.

The roads to the West Coast are broad and well maintained with sweeping curves ideal for the Bentley's long stride. Best of all they were mostly free of traffic, allowing him to make good time. Darke had no plan beyond getting into Rasguneon Castle. Once inside he would have to play it by ear. The element of surprise was on his side, as Yarrick was unaware that Darke knew of his castle hideaway. They had gathered sufficient information about the castle to know its layout. His reconnaissance trips with Alison had shown that men were on watch around the castle, but they were not dedicated or trained for the job. Most of all they would not be expecting trouble. He hoped it would not prove difficult to gain access to the building. That could present a problem, he realised, as time would not be on his side. He needed to rescue Alison before they had finished with her. He knew how ruthless Yarrick could be, particularly when his whole future was at stake.

The Pelican, helped by a flood tide and a freshening westerly wind, made good time up the sea loch. He wore his dark blue sailing anorak, kept for the purpose in the locker beneath the seat. In the left pocket was his torch. As he steered with his arm hooked over the tiller, he checked the Browning pistol. There were eight rounds in the magazine and one in the breech. He worked the mechanism to clear the round, before loading it back into the magazine. Next, he swapped it for the full one and slid it into the butt of the gun. He pocketed the spare, partially filled, magazine. The weapon appeared to be clean and working properly. There was a safety catch at the top of the butt, on the left side. He switched it to the safe position. Next, he took out and screwed on the silencer and tucked the gun into his righthand jacket pocket. The last thing he wanted was to fire the thing, but it was comforting to have it available. He knew he would have to use the weapon if necessary.

Only as he entered the bay, feeling the wind subside, did he throttle back on the engine, to allow the boat to coast across to the concrete jetty. As previously there was no one about, the two boats were moored in the bay as before, plus the fast motor boat. He had just enough light to draw alongside, to moor close to the concrete steps, with the bows facing back the way he had come. He made fast with a bow and stern line secured for a quick getaway.

It took a moment for him to unload rod and quoit onto the jetty and pull himself stiffly onto the rough surface. It had been colder out on the water than he had expected. He quickly retrieved the items at his feet and walked the length of the jetty to the steps. He was aware of the mixture of apprehension and excitement that had been building within him, since he left the boatyard. It was good to be on dry land and closing in on the castle. No sign of life was discernible. His prior knowledge of the route was invaluable in the darkness. The moon was barely visible, filtered by an even layer of moderate cloud. The wind whipped his hair as he climbed and the stiffness in his limbs faded with the exercise. He used the torch sparingly, with most of the light hidden by the bottom of his anorak, leaving only a narrow shaft, sufficient to pick out the worn steps. Every so often he stopped and listened for perhaps ten or fifteen seconds to check for possible danger. Nothing occurred to impede his ascent to the badly damaged steps at the foot of the castle walls.

The dank ramparts above stood out against the paler moon-tinted clouds. The retractable ladders glinted dully as they reflected the muted lunar light. He could hear nothing untoward, as he assembled the rod and tied the quoit to the end of the line. Attempting to swing the rod to throw the rubber ring over the lowest rung was not as straightforward as he had hoped. It took a number of awkward swings and precious time before he began to master the technique. He needed to drop the rod out, away from the wall, steady it momentarily, then swing upwards, releasing the line as the quoit took off under its own weight. Three minutes of effort was rewarded: the quoit slid over the lower rung of the ladder and dropped at his feet, bringing the fine line with it. Within a minute he had cut the quoit free and fastened the cord to the line. It took no time to reel the heavier nylon rope up and over the lowest rung and back down to his outstretched hand.

Holding both lines of cord, Darke gingerly pulled down, increasing the pressure a little at a time. The ladder gave slightly and he instantly stopped. There had been no sound. With a pounding heart he altered his grip higher and tried again, pulling gently but firmly. He felt movement in the cord, accompanied by a muffled squeak. He continued to pull downwards. Once the counterbalanced ladders began to move, it took little effort to keep them coming. The ladders gave a sharp click half way down, which sounded shockingly loud, but after that it unfolded soundlessly. He slotted the lower rung under two stanchions, located for the purpose, to stop it from springing back up the wall. He secured it into position with the locking lever provided.

On his drive from Kilpicton he had gone through a rough plan in his head. It was unlikely, once he had rescued Alison, that they would get away without a chase. He guessed, in the absence of evidence to the contrary, they would assume he had entered the castle, through the main entrance or over the walls, on the east side of the house, away from the terrace. It would not do to give them any reason to suspect he had used the jetty. He dismantled the rod and coiled the cord, placing the items out of sight, close to the foot of the ladder, ready for collection later.

The Browning slipped easily from his pocket. It took a moment to release the safety catch and gently work the mechanism, to feed a round into the breach. He left the hammer uncocked with the safety catch on, before pulling on a pair of unlined leather gloves and beginning the climb. Six hundred feet above the loch the wind was significantly stronger. He felt its cool claws tugging at his clothing as he silently climbed. Once he reached the point where the retracted ladders were usually located, he was surround by hoops of aluminium, two feet apart, which made it almost impossible to fall, even if he slipped. It was thirty feet to the parapet.

He ceased climbing before his head protruded above the castellated wall. All was in darkness. The wind whipped round his head. To his left, twelve feet away, sat the metal cage at the top station of the ancient lift system. Occasionally gusts drew eerie whistles from the contraption as it shredded its way through the ornate Victorian ironwork. Cautiously he raised his head above the parapet until he could make out the terrace, in deep shadow before him. It measured, he guessed, one hundred and twenty feet long by thirty feet wide. The castle, slightly to his left, was shrouded in darkness, save for a shaft of light towards the far end of the building, which cast a distorted rectangle of light onto the flagstones of the terrace. As he watched, a tiny red glow swung up in a narrow arc, at the farthest end, close to the ramparts. It glowed much brighter as the smoker drew the tobacco fumes into his lungs. He could just make the man out. The red glow flicked upwards at a forty-five-degree angle, as the butt of the cigarette arced out over the parapet, to disappear into the black void below.

The dim silhouette started to move slowly towards him. As the man came nearer Darke was able to hear him whistling quietly through his teeth. Then came a tattoo, slapped out with the flat of both hands, on the breast-high stonework, finishing with a sideways kick at the wall, with the edge of his left shoe. Apparently pleased with his newfound musical talent, he tried it again, a few paces later. A bored guard idly filling in his time; certainly not the sign of someone expecting trouble.

It would be a serious problem if the man was stationed on the terrace for his entire watch. It would make an unobserved entry to the castle almost impossible. The man drew nearer and Darke shrank down below the level of the parapet, merging into the shadows as much as he could. To his relief the guard broke off before reaching his position. He moved diagonally across the terrace, to the nearest corner of the castle. Engulfed by the shadows, he was lost from view. Darke could make out nothing until a gate creaked open, revealing a narrow courtyard, palely lit from a faint source within the castle. The guard let the gate close behind him, with a rusty squeal. The darkness returned.

At least if the man came back the noise of the gate would give warning. It was likely the he was patrolling a continuous route, around the castle, without backtracking. With a surge of excitement Lucas Darke rose from his position to step onto the terrace. Cautiously, without a sound, he jogged across the flagstones towards the deeper shadows.

A dozen strides took him to the shelter of the northwest corner of the building. The west wall of the castle consisted of three sets of tall bay windows. Each bay had a set of French windows giving the rooms access to the terrace. He moved along, towards the slash of light. As he passed the first two bays, he gently tried the door handles without success. The shaft of light, he was heading for, came from the third and final bay. The curtains had been hastily drawn and were not fully closed. He glanced through the glass and immediately saw Alison, sitting in a wooden chair, at the far end of the long room.

The creak of the gate echoed the length of the terrace, sending an unnerving shock through him, jerking him away from the lit window. Momentarily blinded by the light, he swung round nearly blundering into a muddle of tables and chairs, roughly stacked against the wall, between the last two bays. Feeling his way, he backed into the shadows, dropped to one knee and removed the silenced Browning pistol from his pocket. The whistling watchman wandered into view, slapping and tapping his way along the parapet. His musical accompaniment ceased, when he drew abreast of the shaft of light. Curiosity overcame him, he moved down the light beam towards the window.

Darke's police training caused him to reflect on his intentions. He was only too well aware that his actions were not those expected of an ex-police inspector, which would weigh heavily against him in a court of law. Carrying a firearm, intending to break and enter into a property, are serious offences that would be difficult to justify. He would need to prove that by contacting the police and telling them what he knew, would have resulted in too great a delay, to save Alison. He would have to prove that Leitch and his gang were killers. Although he had personal proof of their murderous intent, that very morning, he had no witnesses. He was sure that Leitch had killed Lew Bodell, but, as far as everyone else was concerned, his death was the result of a road accident. Until he had spied Alison inside the room, even he had no positive proof of her whereabouts. He was there on supposition alone. Now that he had seen her, everything had changed. His actions may not be entirely legally justified, but as far as he was concerned, they were morally right. Previously, he might have been wary of using excessive force, now it was different. He felt free to use whatever force was required, to release her from the clutches of these people. They were killers, they had more than demonstrated that. Once they had finished with Alison, they would kill her. Sentimentality and chivalry did not exist in their book, they would only be interested in covering their tracks, with the easiest and most obvious solution.

The guard looked through the French window, clearly intrigued by what he saw. Silently Darke unwound himself from his crouched position. He knew that the night vision of the other man would now be completely impaired by the light from the room. As long as he made no sound Darke knew he would not be visible to the other's peripheral vision. The butt of the pistol slammed into the back of the man's head. The impact sounded loud to Darke. He realised his heightened senses exaggerated the sound. He searched the slumped form, removing a short-barrelled revolver, from a holster on the man's trouser belt. He emptied the six cartridges before throwing it far out over the balustrade, to land six hundred feet below. By the heavy sound of his breathing, he guessed the guard would be drumming tattoos on the parapets of dreamland, until dawn. The dead weight of the man was awkward to drag. Darke half pulled and half rolled him into the space, beside the tables and chairs, between the bays. Back at the French windows he was able to scan the scene in the room inside.

He knew from the plans they had of the castle that this was the library, which was confirmed by the rows of glass doors protecting shelves upon shelves of leather-bound volumes, many in matching sets. Alison was facing the window at the far end of the room, there was a trickle of blood from her lip. She sat defiantly watching Leitch who was talking. He was half sitting on the far side of a heavy broad-topped desk, swinging a leg. Two other men were present. The figure standing in front of Alison, as though guarding her, he recognised as Brogan: the tall, broad-shouldered man who had shot at him on the hill that morning. Another bald headed, villainous looking character, to Leitch's right, was sitting, shin across one knee, in a maroon leather club chair. A door was located on the far wall and another midway along the left-hand wall, leading into the next room.

The thought of them hitting Alison made Darke furious. He checked himself; this was no time to allow his emotions to get the better of him. He suppressed the anger and deliberately cleared his head, the better to think rationally. Moving away from the lighted windows, he made for the south end of the terrace. Around the corner of the building, he came to an unlocked half-glazed door, that opened inwards. A loom of a light shone dimly from around the far corner, at the end of the corridor. All was quiet. He moved quickly over the stone floor.

Time was not on his side; he knew someone sooner or later, would miss the guard. Around the corner, beyond a second half-glazed door, a lamp stood upon an oak table, illuminating an imposing hallway. It was clad in pale stone with light wood panelling, perfectly in keeping with a Victorian castle. Darke silently entered the hall, closing the door behind him. The atmosphere and scent of the materials assailed him; reminiscent of so many ancient village churches. The table lamp stood beside a closed door that Darke judged to be the library. The Browning was cocked and ready. Through the heavy door he heard Alison give a yelp of pain.

He twisted the door knob and in one swift movement slipped inside, kicking the door shut behind him. He took a pace to his right. The three men were surprised, it took them several seconds to comprehend the evidence of their eyes. Before they could move, Darke raised the semi-automatic, pointing straight at Leitch and warned, 'Not a word or movement. Having been shot at twice today I will happily shoot to kill.'

'Lucas!' Alison spun round in her seat, amazement and relief showing on her face. He kept his eyes on the men.

'Mister bloody busybody Darke......,' Leitch's Glaswegian accent was more pronounced with the tension of the moment.

Darke cut across him in mid-sentence, 'Shut up. I meant what I said,' and they believed him.

Alison's safety had eclipsed all else since the discovery of her kidnap. But the realisation that these were also the men responsible for setting fire to his home, brought him close to the point where he could happily use the gun, with the least provocation. Leitch had half risen from the edge of the desk. He appeared to be settling back, when suddenly he threw himself to one side, behind Brogan. He pushed the taller man at Darke. Brogan, flailing his arms, stumbled, off balance, toward Darke. He wildly tried to reach out for Darke's gun, before he could shoot. It was simple to side-step the awkward attack. With the ease that comes from recent practice, Darke drove the butt of the gun into the tall man's face. He felt an inordinate degree of pleasure, as the butt crunched into thinly fleshed bone. Brogan uttered no sound. His tall athletic shape crumpled to the floor, with a dull thud, cushioned only by the ancient Persian carpet.

Leitch was diving and sliding back across his desk, feeling for the drawer on the other side, as he went. Out of the corner of his eye, Darke saw the bald-headed man, in the club chair, bringing a heavy colt automatic up to the aim. The Browning, weighted by the silencer, felt awkwardly barrel-heavy, as Darke swung it round to his left. The pistol twitched twice as he fired. It sounded as though someone had taken two strokes to beat a rug. A disconcertingly innocuous sound. Reassuringly a hole appeared close to the man's heart. The second bullet created another, six inches higher, at the base of his throat. The colt clattered noisily on the wooden floor. Darke swung his weapon back to Leitch.

The little Scot had disappeared over the desk, with a crash of splintering wood as a partially opened drawer disintegrated under his weight. With amazing alacrity his head instantly appeared, followed by his hand holding a small black pistol. For Darke the world slowed down. It was as if his brain was suddenly working at five times its normal speed. All around him was in slow motion. The effect gave him time to see everything with absolute clarity. Leitch's gun was lining up on him, as his own Browning was swinging back toward the desk. Instantly he knew that Leitch was ahead of him and would fire before he could bring his weapon to bear. In a reflex action he started to dive to his right with an agonising lack of speed. It was a forlorn attempt to avoid the inevitable.

As the black hole of Leitch's gun barrel lined up on him, he steeled himself for the impact. Alison had anticipated the danger. She threw herself forward with her left arm outstretched she swung her right arm wide, scrabbling for the old-fashioned brass upright telephone. Before Leitch could aim, her left hand struck the leather blotter which skidded into Leitch's gun arm, resting on the desk top. Her scything right arm caught the desk lamp and brass telephone, sweeping them forward over the far edge of the desk, with just sufficient weight to throw Leitch further off balance. Darke's Browning was now aimed at Leitch, but Alison's momentum was carrying her forward to obscure what little there was to see of the man. She sensed the situation and began to roll to her right. Then the light went out.

Darke dodged to one side and fired two shots in rapid succession clear of Alison, but close to where Leitch had been. In reply the roar from the two shots fired by Leitch were deafening, obviously aimed at where Lucas had been standing. The spurts of flame from the other man's pistol gave him a target. The ringing in his ears blanketed the 'phut', 'phut' of his own two answering shots. He moved back towards Alison, found her in the dark and pulled her away from the desk. His ears were ringing as he made his way towards the bay window. He wanted to move quickly, before they began to recover their hearing. There was no point in leaving by the door through which he had come. The instant it was opened they would be silhouetted against the light from the hall. Besides, Leitch's shot must have alerted the entire household. Holding Allison's arm, he moved steadily towards the bay window, sweeping his gun hand in front of him, to detect obstacles.

He came in contact with a small round-topped table. It was solid, but easy enough to lift. He swung it high, diagonally back across the room. Even with ears ringing they heard it land with a crash of glass. Two shots came from one side of the room accompanied by orange jets of flame. Darke fired double shots, where the flashes had been and moved on. The silenced weapon was perfect for the task. Deafened again by the latest shots, Leitch could not hear the minimal sound of Darke's silenced pistol. Nor could he see flames from the barrel, as the silencer acted as an anti-flash device. Darke had the advantage and Leitch knew it. The floor length curtains in the bay brought Darke to a halt with relief. A slight draft wafted from across the room. He guessed the door in that direction had been opened and Leitch was making his escape, via the unlit adjacent dining room.

Moments later the Glaswegian's voice could be heard, above the ringing in his ears, yelling furiously for assistance, 'Nobby, Bell, Dixon where the fuck are you? We've got a fucking intruder wi' a gun.'

Sweeping the curtains aside, Darke guided Alison to the French windows. Thankfully the key was in the lock. It turned and he pulled one door open, to allow them through.

The effect of an empty terrace and fresh air was exhilarating. It took a moment to close the door and check the condition of the unconscious guard. There were low groans coming from his direction, but he was obviously still far from conscious.

Keeping close to the building they sprinted along the terrace, to the north of the house, toward the lift and the aluminium ladders. Darke checked around the corner of the building, in the direction of the creaking gate, but everything was quiet. Alison responded to his touch, together they set off at an angle towards the ladders. Once on the metal platform Darke indicated for Alison to go first. She was agile and slid easily between the hoops and disappeared out of sight. Spotlights nearly blinded him as the terrace became as bright as day. He slid down the ladder as figures came running into view from the far end of the house. They stopped; the last thing he saw, as he ducked down below the level of the platform, was the two men looking round at an empty terrace. He hoped they would assume they had escaped via the courtyard on the southeast side of the castle. At the bottom of their descent Darke released the ladder, allowing it to withdraw noiselessly, back up toward the parapet. He released the magazine from the butt of the Browning and swapped it with the nearly full one from his pocket. Next, he picked up the rod, cord and quoit, before leading Alison down the many steps to the bay.

Chapter 10

It was an overcast autumn day in London. Rain drenched gold and copper leaves were sticking to the damp cobbles that paved Hacketts Walk. The ancient thoroughfare is situated within a stone's throw of Lincoln's Inn Field. The period buildings, that made up the cobbled pedestrian way, represented a variety of architectural styles from several earlier centuries. All were carefully maintained. The only thing these disparate structures shared was the absence of a straight line, or level surface: roofs dipped and rose, walls sloped, windows bowed and doors leant. Even the panes of glass were dimpled or rippled with age.

The offices of Blexell, Landon, and Tanwick, Solicitors, occupied numbers twelve to fourteen, two of the larger buildings forming this ancient London lane. Situated in a first-floor office, to the front of the building, sat Mister Charles Tanwick. He was a tall, thin, balding man in his early fifties, dressed in pinstripe trousers, a black jacket and waistcoat. He was the epitome of a solicitor. The room was large and square. Lamps with amber shades were situated in all four corners to assist the light from the tall, small-paned windows. Along one wall were shelves fully occupied with many buff files, tied with pink ribbon. More documents occupied one corner of Tanwick's spacious desk.

'I have here', he looked up from the file open before him and confided, in a measured tone, 'the letter to which you refer. On receipt of the covering letter, I remember I was concerned by the state of mind it seemed to convey.' He glanced down at the letter, choosing his words with care before he continued, 'I inferred from its contents that the letter was written in haste and with perhaps some agitation. Sadly, there was never an opportunity to confirm his wishes, as written, for by the time we received the letter, Mister Bodell had already, tragically, passed away in a car accident.'

The grey light from the lattice windows was reflecting dully off Tanwick's pink, entirely bald pate, as he diligently scrutinized Darke's passport. He carefully closed and returned it to the former colonial policeman, together with the letter Bodell had written to Darke.

'That seems quite in order, Mister Darke. I can see from the contents of his letter to you, the reason for his state of mind. His obvious wish to forewarn and prepare his daughter is understandable. Particularly the details of his earlier exploit in Katanga. I was not familiar with Mister Bodell's activities, prior to the time he bought the tobacco farm in Kwazaland. It appears they could be described as of a criminal nature?'

Darke nodded and replied, 'Technically it was only a minor offence of falsifying documents in Katanga. The receipt of the ore took place in Mozambique, sent with the unintentional cooperation of the Katangan railway authorities. As far as Mozambique was concerned, the two men received goods, legitimately addressed and sent to them, so no law was contravened there. Mister Bodell broke no laws in Kwazaland. So, as long as he behaved as an upstanding citizen, he was free to go about his business.'

'What I don't understand is why there is a need, at this point in time, to activate Mister Bodell's wish to notify his daughter. The man Leitch, who was the reason for writing the two letters, died alongside Mister Bodell in the road accident.'

'I have recently discovered that Leitch did not die in that accident. He, it now appears, put someone else in the car in his place. He planted his own wristwatch, cigarette lighter and little finger, from his left hand, to make everyone believe it was his body in the car.'

Tanwick grimaced. 'Surely the police...?' he started.

'I was the Investigating Officer, Mister Tanwick. I was the man he fooled. I had the fingerprint, of the finger we found next to the vehicle, checked at the time. It was confirmed as belonging to Leitch, but I have seen Leitch recently, minus a little finger, and there is no doubt that he is alive. It is a reasonable assumption that he murdered Bodell, and someone else, to stage the accident.'

The Solicitor gazed upon Darke with eyebrows raised. He was not a criminal lawyer and as such he was not used to such revelations. He took the information calmly; it was his duty not to be perturbed in pursuing the interests of his client. He had represented Lewis Bodell and thereafter his daughter for seventeen years. It was of paramount importance, that if a potentially life changing step was to be taken, which affected his client, it must be done with the utmost care and scrutiny.

He leaned forward. 'Can you prove this, Mister Darke?'

'I have a set of fingerprints of the man I have recently seen, which I am taking to Kwazania to have checked.'

'Why not send them?'

'There is a reluctance at the Colonial Office, and the Kwazanian embassy, to consider reopening the case. I can see no alternative other than to go to Kwazania myself, to present the evidence directly to the police, in Fort Albert.'

Tanwick nodded thoughtfully, 'And if they are reluctant to act?'

'I have no choice, but to keep going. I have been shot at several times, in the past few days. Leitch and his henchmen have burnt my home to the ground. My manager, Miss Falkener and I are a threat to him. As a start we must persuade the authorities to reopen the case and issue a warrant for his arrest. If we can do that, hopefully, it will make life more difficult for him. If I go to the police here in the UK I doubt they will be able to move quickly enough to catch him, or protect us. He will have gone to ground by now, I doubt anyone will find him easily, so we would be forced into hiding ourselves, for an indefinite period.'

'I see.' Tanwick said with furrowed brow, 'From my client's point of view. Is it necessary to confront Mrs Easterton with her father's past at this stage?'

'Once I have informed the Police in Kwazania and proved the sample of fingerprints are those of Leitch, it is likely to trigger a murder hunt. Thereafter, the newspapers may well take an interest. Lewis Bodell's past could be all over the front pages of newspapers, here and in Kwazania, at any time. It might be a matter of a few days or months. If we want to be certain of forewarning her. it had better be done sooner rather than later.'

Tanwick gave some consideration to Darke's words before replying, 'I believe you are right. Miss Bodell married Charles Easterton five years ago. Sadly, he died suddenly, of an aneurysm aged thirty, just two years ago. Mrs Easterton is presently at Mount Muzindi farm. If you intend to leave immediately for Kwazania, I would be obliged if you would take the letter with you and see that she receives it safely.'

'Of Course.' The thought of meeting Virginia Bodell, or Easterton, again was not an unpleasant one, in spite of their first meeting. The last time they had met was at her father's funeral. In the short interval between their two meetings, she had become a woman.

Darke left the solicitor's office carrying a manila envelope in his pocket, containing the letter from Bodell to his daughter, with a covering letter from Mister Tanwick. The wind was bowling menacing rain clouds over the roof tops, as he made his way the short distance to Fleet Street, where he had arranged to meet Alison for coffee.

Ten minutes later he was gazing from the first-floor window of Dunes Coffee house, at the bustle of Fleet Street below. There was rain in the east wind. It buffeted the hunched figures fighting to control angled umbrellas. Fine black cloth straining inwards, vibrating against spokes, coat tails flapped, as the huddled figures fought their way along rain swept pavements.

'So, what now?' Alison Falkener asked, stirring her coffee. Her tailored tan leather coat was open, revealing a wide-necked, cream sweater over an olive-green, calf length skirt. Tan leather high-heeled boots completed her outfit.

He turned and looked at her critically. Working together all the time, as they did, he frequently forgot how attractive she was. Her well-proportioned figure was slim without being thin. She had great legs he knew, and shapely hips. The elegant line of her neck and the way it curved up from her shoulders to the jaw line was enchanting. She had a neat nose, wide-set hazel eyes, a generous mouth, turned up at the sides, slightly swollen on the left side where she had been struck during her ordeal at the castle. Her hair varied from light to dark blonde, fell in long curves. There were ways she moved it, that conveyed her moods. Her small neat ears were revealed, only on occasions, when she swung her head quickly, or swept her long fingers energetically through it. She was extremely attractive. They worked well together. They were a good team. He felt a genuinely brotherly affection for her.

'You look great this morning,' Darke said

'Thank you, Lucas. You never usually notice.'

'That's not true, I always notice, however, I do not always mention it,' he pointed out pedantically.

She pursed her lips, 'That sounds as though it might be another compliment, but I'm not quite sure. However, you still haven't answered my question. What happens now?'

Looking at her he could not help but marvel at her resilience. She seemed to have recovered completely from her recent ordeal. His mind retreated to that night. The intense feeling of fear he had felt, had been like a blow to the stomach, when he realized she had been kidnapped. He experienced an all-consuming rage he had fought to control. Shooting the bald-headed man in the chair had brought exhilaration and some relief from that internal turmoil. The pleasure of being able to hit back, was not something he had expected to experience. A primitive feeling of success, in a dangerous situation, perhaps. It was nothing compared with the relief he had felt, when the Pelican pulled out of the bay, knowing they had escaped. A terrible threatening shadow had lifted from his shoulders; knowing Alison was safe.

She had collapsed into the bottom of the boat. Steering one-handed, he had retrieved her sailing jacket from the locker and encouraged her to put it on. Reaction had set in. She was trembling with shock and the cool of the night. He drew her up beside him and held her close. She had turned her face towards him, in the dim light from the translucent clouds, her features were hardly discernible, yet he knew there were no tears in her eyes.

'You killed him, didn't you?' she had asked, intently, as he guided the craft downstream.

'I believe so. I doubt he could have survived for long with those wounds. Either one would have killed him pretty quickly.'

'What do you think will happen now?'

He had been unsure what she meant. 'How do you mean?'

'I mean, what will the police do?'

'I don't intend to go to the police. I'm not going to hang around, waiting for the authorities to get their act together and give Leitch a chance to kill us.'

'What about the dead man?'

He could feel her breath on his chin as she leant her head back to look up at him. 'Leitch will expect us to call the police. Once he knows we've escaped, he'll want to get as far away from the castle as possible. He'll leave quickly, covering his tracks as best he can. I've no doubt he has an escape plan or two, up his sleeve. As for the dead man, I expect the body will be taken well out to sea, weighted down and dumped overboard, where no one will find it. Leitch will not want the police discovering dead bodies at the castle. As long as we say nothing, no one, other than those involved, will ever know the man is dead.'

'They would've killed me wouldn't they. They would never have let me go?'

He nodded his head. 'They're ruthless, they'll stop at nothing.' He told her briefly of the attempt on his life that morning, also of the torching of his home. 'Leitch is desperate. Since his plastic surgery he knows we are the only ones who can identify him. It makes sense to get rid of us, before we stir up the authorities and reveal his new identity. He is desperate to leave his past undisturbed.'

She shuddered at the memory of the man. He exuded evil, when he threatened her, she had not doubted him for a moment. She had felt utterly helpless, even so she had tried to face up to him. When the bald-headed man had hit her, making her lip bleed, it had made her angry, determined not to tell them anything. In reality, she knew that once the anger had subsided, she was helpless in their hands. They would make her tell them whatever they wanted to know. First, they had demanded to know where Lucas Darke was or where he might go to hide. Also, who else had knowledge of Leitch's existence.

'Thank you for coming to my rescue, Lucas, you were marvellous. It was like a wonderful dream when you burst through the door.' She stretched up and shakily kissed him on the cheek.

He grinned wryly, 'You very quickly returned the favour. Leitch would have shot me if you hadn't flung yourself across the desk and upset his aim.' He was embarrassed, he knew her praise was not really justified. All this had been his fault. If he had not had Leitch paged, over the public address system, at the Aviemore show, the man would have been unaware that he was under suspicion. He would not have sent his thugs to deal with the two of them and they would not be in their present plight. It had been a stupid blunder. It was going to take a great deal of effort, not to mention luck, to put it right. Reluctantly he explained it all to her.

She kissed his cheek again. 'I think it was an excellent idea, it certainly proved he was Leitch. You can't blame yourself, we both knew we were playing a dangerous game.'

'If I had known this would happen, I would never have involved you. It would be unforgivable if anything happened to you, particularly as a result of my stupidity.'

'You can't possibly foresee every eventuality. You're being too hard on yourself,' she added, 'It doesn't alter the fact that you came and saved me.' She settled closer into him to keep warm. 'You can be my "knight in shining armour" for a while longer.'

He grimaced at her in the darkness and noticed she was no longer shaking.

'It's not over, is it? We will have to go into hiding. We cannot carry on as normal.' She was echoing his thoughts.

'We will make a brief visit to Kilpicton to collect some clothes for you, then we must disappear.'

'For how long?'

'A week or two maybe.' He gave a slight shrug. 'As long as it takes to sort this mess out.'

Alison chuckled.

'What's funny?'

'We'll be the talk of Kilpicton. My reputation will never be the same again.'

'Why, we often go off to trade shows together?'

'Yes, but there are no trade shows at the moment, are there? Disappearing together, that's quite another thing.'

His thoughts returned to the present. A rain-filled gust swept along Fleet Street under a lowering sky, it rattled on the ancient window panes and interrupted his pattern of thought. Alison was waiting for his reply.

'Sorry,' he murmured, aware that seconds had elapsed since she had asked the question, 'I think you should come to Kwazania with me. You'll be out of Leitch's way and I can keep an eye on you.'

'Well, there's an offer I can hardly refuse,' she said, with mock sourness.

The sarcasm was not lost on Darke. 'I didn't mean it like that,' he said placatingly, 'It makes sense. I have to go to Kwazania and if you're with me, I'd know you were safe. Two birds with one stone and all that.' As soon as he said it, he knew it was a mistake.

She grimaced and spread her hands wide. 'Who said chivalry was dead? You have such a charming way with words. What girl could resist?' Her face turned to a stunning smile, as she unwound herself from her chair, 'If I was one of your string of girlfriends, Lucas Darke, no doubt I would be bowled over by your eloquence, but somehow I find myself less than persuaded.'

Pushing back his chair, he stood up, before tucking two folded one-pound notes under his saucer, to cover the bill.

'Be fair Alison, we work together. We're friends. I shouldn't have to vet every word I say to you. You know what I'm trying to say.' He was worried that she had taken umbrage at his words. Perhaps the events of the past few days had had a deeper effect on her, than he first thought.

She rested her hand on his sleeve. 'Don't worry, I'm teasing you. I've known and accepted for years that you are an insensitive, self-centred pig. As your *friend,'* she stressed the word, 'I naturally make the relevant allowances for your thoughtlessness, and I always will. That's what friends are for.' She delivered her words with saccharin sweetness and a vacant smile.

'Okay. Okay, I'm sorry.' He took a deep breath recognising her mood. He had two choices: either he could ignore her until she came round, or try to talk her out it, 'If I went to Africa and left you behind, I would constantly be worried. If you don't want to go, then I have no other option, but to stay here. Ideally, we want Leitch arrested and in prison for the rest of his life. It's the safest solution for us. Besides,' he said with a hint of sadness, 'I was hoping to show you the Kwazania I knew, before I knew you.'

She gurgled with genuine laughter, in spite of herself she was obviously pleased. 'You see you can talk your way out of anything. You *can* be considerate when you try.'

They threaded their way between the chairs of the Dickensian restaurant, down the steep, dark wooden staircase and out onto the rain-soaked street. Darke hailed a passing black cab and asked for the Royal Cadoggan Hotel. As they settled back in the seat Alison asked, against her better judgement, 'Did you mean that?'

'Mean what?'

'I knew I shouldn't have asked.'

'Of course I meant it.'

She paused looking at him earnestly, until she said, 'Alright I'll consider it, but something's going to have to change.'

'What? Why?'

'Because you treat me abominably, as a friend and even worse as an employee.' She crossed her arms to reinforce the point.

He turned his head to look at her. 'That's not a nice thing to say, I don't think of you as an employee.'

'You don't think of me as anything.'

'You'd like Africa,' he said, to change the subject.

'Yes, I've been looking forward to it since we left Scotland,' she commented, looking out of the cab, as they left The Strand, heading west.

He found his mouth gaping open and closed it quickly. She had known what he was planning all along. He should have guessed. He had never known a woman as irritatingly intuitive and quick-witted as Alison. She was, in spite of her normal uncomplicated nature, capable of teasing him unmercifully. It was a disconcerting combination. She could be tough, capable of anticipating and manipulating situations, but would do so only on rare occasions and by design, not by nature. She was a fascinating contradiction.

'You're a cunning, Machiavellian witch,' he replied, stretching his long legs in front of him, as far as the taxi's interior would allow.

She smiled sweetly as she continued to gaze out of the window at a rainswept Trafalgar Square.

Chapter 11
Kingdom of Kwazania

The Boeing 707 taxied to halt in front of the long two-storey terminal building of Umbaka International Airport. The shimmering sunlit white plaster, of the art deco structure, contrasted with the blue tinted glass of the windows. A handful of brightly dressed people waved from the first-floor balcony. The line of disembarking passengers snaked across the apron to the customs and immigration hall, shepherded by uniformed ground staff. Some passengers waved back. At the centre of the flat-topped roof hung the pale blue Kwazanian flag, it carried the emblem of a black and white cowhide war shield, with crossed spears, at its centre. It hung limply, occasionally rolling round the flagstaff, in sympathy with an almost imperceptible eddy of air.

They passed from the artificial cool of the cabin into the balmy air of tropical Africa. A faint scent of jacaranda excited Alison's senses. This was Africa. It was as she had imagined it. A small, sun-drenched airport, the heat, colourfully dressed people, the occasional European and African businessman dressed in safari suits. It was very exciting, she decided. The jet turbines whined to a halt and silence took over. Further along the concrete apron a Douglas Dakota in the colours of Pan African Airways, stood reflecting the sun off its aluminium skin. A twin-engine Dragon Rapide and a yellow painted Tiger Moth kept it company.

The airport formalities were cursory. Within the hour they were heading, in a hire car, for the capital of Kwazania's Eastern Highlands. Fort Albert lies a three-hour drive from Umbaka. Its location, at the centre of a wide fertile valley, with mountains to the north and south, makes it the most attractive of Kwazania's provincial capitals. As they came over the pass, famed and named in the early days for its population of leopards, Darke pulled the car across the opposite lane. He parked in the large specially built lay-by, which allows travellers to enjoy the view without blocking the highway. It was as he remembered it. It looked the same: the valley, with the town at its centre, spread out before him, the azure sky, peppered with small cumulus clouds, receding into the distance, as far as the eye could see. To the east glimpses of the Olulopo River glinting in the sunlight, marking the border with the Republic of Nambria. This region of Kwazania was known for its coffee, tea, tobacco and forestry plantations. Fortunately for its people, unlike so many African countries, Kwazania had not regressed following independence.

A combination of wisdom, luck and for once responsible politics, had ensured that the rate of the country's growth, had hardly slowed during the transition from a colony to an independent kingdom. Much of this success was down to a handful of hardworking, dedicated civil servants. They pushed through their ideas without much interference from United Kingdom politicians, whose attentions were distracted by the economy at home and problems elsewhere in the world. Unlike what happened to other colonies, Kwazania was not handed over to gangs of thugs, vaguely masquerading as political parties, who had terrorised their own people into supporting them, at the point of a gun. They were not to be forced to vote for a one-party state, run by people only intent on lining their own pockets. Kwazania was ninety percent populated by Kwaza people, the remaining ten percent being sub tribes, conquered and all but absorbed by the Kwaza warriors some one hundred and fifty years earlier. The country was not split on tribal lines, something that was often exploited in other African colonies.

There were political parties formed in the early nineteen sixties, to ride the African wave of independence sweeping through the continent. Initially there were two, both communist backed: the Kwaza Peoples Democratic Congress

(KPDC), equipped and trained by the USSR. The other was the Kwazanian Republican Front (KRF) which owed allegiance to Communist China. Later both parties threw off splinter paramilitary groups: the Kwaza African People's Union (KAPU), from the KPDC and the Kwazanian National Front (KNF) from the KRF. The result of their infighting eventually resulted in a loss of credibility for all of them. The King of the Kwazas was a wise, strong and charismatic chief, who condemned them all as undemocratic thugs. He refused to bow to their threats. He also shrewdly maintained a well informed and highly trained military. The result was minimal support for any of the terror groups, from the indigenous population.

King Tagaweyi, an old Harrovian and Sandhurst trained, was an enlightened monarch who wished to emulate a British style democracy. He realised his dreams would have to wait until a higher proportion, than the present twenty-five percent, of his population were educated. Following independence, he ruled with the aid of The Chamber of Members comprising a mixture of chiefs, sub chiefs, senior kraal heads and elected representatives. It was decreed that the elected members would increase, at each election, for twenty-five years, following independence. After that time the Chamber of Members would become the upper House. They would hand over the day-to-day parliamentary function and formation of the government, to a lower House of fully elected representatives.

The King had encouraged the white population to continue with their mining and farming, knowing them to be the mainstay of the economy. New farms were being developed, carved from virgin bush; trees stumped and rocks blasted, for the growing ranks of college trained African farmers. The old ruinous practice of stream bank cultivation, employed by the farmers in the tribal areas, was actively discouraged. It was important not to over cultivate; thereby turning fertile soil into barren land, as often happened with traditional methods. Instead, they were being trained in the use of irrigation systems and fertilisers. Utilising aid from Britain, the whole process was on schedule. The erstwhile colony continued to flourish.

'So, this is where you spent your youth,' Alison observed, taking in the vista. Scotland has big views but none were like this, she thought. She felt that if only she could focus a little harder, she could see forever.

'This was Provincial Headquarters. I was in the District Police and stationed mainly to the north of here on various police posts, but I did some socialising here in Fort Albert.'

'There would be girls here of course. Let me see, policemen and nurses go well together, I believe?'

He smiled, a faraway smile. 'I was young, impressionable and easily led.'

'I'm surprised you dare return. There's probably a dozen of your progeny down there,' she responded primly.

Instead of motoring down into the valley, Darke turned off, a few hundred yards along the highway, into the wide driveway of the Leopard Pass Hotel. Once settled in his room, Darke showered and changed, before putting a telephone call through to Provincial Police headquarters, in Fort Albert. His conversation with the Charge Office Inspector culminated in an appointment, the following morning at ten o'clock, with the Officer Commanding Muzindi District.

Heavy rain was falling vertically through breezeless air, from a leaden sky, when Alison, dressed in a pale-yellow linen dress, came to meet him on the wide veranda. The various sounds of rainwater on broad leafed plants, overflowing veranda drains and gutters, meant she had to raise her voice to speak. He had been standing looking out at the torrents of water. He pointed to a table, they sank down into deep cushions, on wicker armchairs, facing the downpour.

'Does it rain like this often?' she asked above the noise.

'This time of year, it generally settles down to rain between four and six in the afternoon.' As he spoke the rain ceased, the sun came out and the sound of dripping water slowly receded.

She said, in amazement, 'It stops just like that?

He nodded and breathed in the fragrances, drawn out into the humid atmosphere, by the cooling rain. Africa was in his blood. He was at home here. They watched as the wisps of clinging mist, above the surrounding bush, gradually disappeared in the warmth of a freshly washed sun. He explained the plan for the following day.

Darke entered the police station through the main entrance, carrying his briefcase, as he had so often done in the past. But it was different, he no longer belonged. It was all so familiar still, after six years, yet he was no more a part of it. He no longer wore the uniform of an Inspector. He felt a sudden nostalgic sense of loss. They had been happy, fulfilling times, but they were past. Instead of walking round the counter and into the back offices, as he would have done before, he halted at the wooden barrier. There were two constables working at separate desks. The duty Sergeant, with his back to him, was occupied at a filing cabinet. The old central fan, hanging from the high ceiling above his head, with its six feet of vertical shaft, whirred and vibrated as it always had. He would have bet it would have given up by now, yet here it was, still stirring the air. A minor miracle he thought, as the Sergeant placed the sheaf of papers on top of the cabinet, before turning to the counter. Darke gave his name and the time of his appointment.

The Sergeant nodded, lifted the barrier and politely asked him to follow. He led the way along the cool, dark wood panelled corridor, that had not changed, since Darke had last walked on its ochre tiled floor. They climbed the familiar wide stone steps and along the upper veranda that surrounded the peaceful inner courtyard, with the stone water fountain at its centre. The Sergeant stopped at the door marked 'O C - Muzindi District', knocked and entered, 'Mister Darke to see you, sir.'

Darke entered the wide room to see a giant of a man rising from his seat, 'Mister Darke, it's good to see you again.'

'Good heavens!' he said in amazement. Elias Kufanu stood before him, resplendent in a senior officer's khaki uniform, complete with blue and silver collar tabs and epaulettes. On a side table rested a baton and khaki cap, with a broad blue band, insignia and a peak trimmed with silver oak leaves. 'Superintendent Kufanu, this is a welcome surprise.'

They shook hands warmly and spent the next twenty minutes catching up on the events of each other's lives. Elias Kufanu was five years older than Lucas Darke. He had left teaching to join the Royal Kwazaland Police and soon became one of the youngest sergeants. After independence his rise had been meteoric. Within days he was promoted to inspector. Thereafter he was selected for the Police Staff College, where his outstanding abilities were recognised and developed. For the past year he had been Officer Commanding Muzindi District, Eastern Province. Eventually their conversation returned to the reason for Darke's appointment. From his briefcase he drew a slim file, which he slid across the desk.

'Before you read that let me ask whether you remember the accident at Mount Muzindi farm, when Lewis Bodell was killed?'

'Yes. Yes of course.' The bigger man's eyes were trained far away, above Darke's head, as he marshalled his memories of the case. 'That's right,' he went on, 'the other man, the burnt body in the car, was Bodell's partner in crime from his time in Katanga?'

'Correct, Sandy Leitch. That's what we thought. However, it wasn't Leitch that died in the car.'

The bigger man raised an eyebrow. 'But there was the print from the little finger. Are you saying we were misled?' Kufanu's analytical brain was grasping all the possibilities. Intrigued he smiled, saying, 'I can assume you would not have come all this way, without some form of proof?'

Lucas Darke grinned across the desk. It brought back memories of the cases they had worked on together. Their minds were so alike, they could often pre-empt each other's questions. He withdrew a bulging, sealed manila envelope from his briefcase and laid it down in front of the other man, together with a buff folder containing documents.

'In that envelope', Darke explained, 'is a quaich: a pewter bowl, I took from a display stand at a gift fair in Scotland. If you still have them on file, I believe you will find the fingerprints will match those of Alexander Leitch?'

The Superintendent looked at the envelope with its date and the signatures of Darke and Alison Falconer across both flaps. He pushed it gently to one side and opened the folder to flick through the contents. It contained amongst other things: a diary of events, Bodell's letter to Darke, together with statements from Alison and Darke, relating to the pewter bowl, sealed in the envelope.

'Before we go further, unless you have any objections, I'll call in Detective Inspector Desabi, otherwise you will have to go over everything again, with him.'

A telephone call and a wait of a few minutes brought a knock on the door. A tall, slim man, in his thirties, entered the room. He wore his light grey, well cut suit, with elegant ease. Superintendent Kufanu introduced the two men. He handed the Inspector the envelope Darke had brought, then rapidly filled in the background of the ten-year-old case. They discussed various points, before Kufanu gave the Detective Inspector the background to Darke's visit.

'Take the envelope,' he said, 'and have the bowl checked for prints. The archives downstairs, will have the Traffic Accident Report. In it should be a copy of Alexander Leitch's fingerprints.'

He looked across at Darke who nodded in agreement. The little finger found at the scene had been matched at that time, with numerous sets of prints, found in the bedroom used by Leitch, at Mount Muzindi Farm

'The date was the tenth November nineteen-sixty-seven,' added Darke.

Detective Inspector Desabi carrying the bulky envelope moved to the door and left saying, 'I'll get on to it right away, sir.'

Twenty minutes later he returned with the file, announcing. 'It looks like a good match, sir.'

He handed the set of prints, newly lifted from the bowl, to his superior, together with the copy from the file and a magnifying glass. The Superintendent held both examples fanned out, close up to his eye, looking from one set to the other, comparing the "deltas" and "whorls", one by one, through the powerful magnifying glass. Almost inaudibly he slowly counted to seven, before looking up.

'Well, on my count that would stand up in court,' he said, grinning with satisfaction, before passing everything across to Darke.

Darke went through the same exercise, then sat back. 'Thank heaven for that,' he remarked, exhaling with relief, as he did so.

It was only then did he realise how tense he had become. How so much depended on the fingerprints matching. If they had not, his problems would have been overwhelming.

'Of course, it will have to be verified by an expert, but there's no point in delaying further.' Kufanu addressed the Detective Inspector, 'Jason, you now have the pleasure of investigating a ten-year-old murder...'

'Double murder,' Darke interjected, quietly.

The older policeman looked at him and nodded, 'That's true. Who then was the unknown man?'

Simultaneously they both answered the question, 'Warren!'

'It would fit. In which case we can add the killing of the servant,' Darke added, 'That potentially makes it three murders.'

'That's right. This is becoming more complicated by the minute.' The Superintendent turned to Desabi and said, 'Jason,' the Detective Inspector was looking bemused, 'get down to Special Branch archives and look out the file for the same date, on a murder and missing person, believed kidnapped by terrorists. One John Warren, manager of Kalagan 'B' farm.'

Chapter 12

A tobacco barn had been rebuilt, but otherwise, Mount Muzindi farm remained unchanged since his last visit. Darke stood on the veranda looking out at the view, it was truly magnificent and precisely as he remembered it. A footfall on the veranda interrupted his reminiscences. He turned to meet the grey eyes of Virginia Easterton. As she introduced herself, he could see her searching her mind.

'Forgive me, but have we met before? she asked.'

He explained he had been in the Police, that he had known her father and had attended his funeral.

'Your father and I were not close friends, but we got on well together. We shared a common interest in gliding. On the occasions we met, we would talk at length about flying.'

She smiled and nodded. 'He talked of buying a glider and installing a winch here at Muzindi on more than one occasion. I think the only thing that stopped him, was the lack of sites to "land out" safely.' She changed the subject, motioning him to be seated. 'You mentioned, on the 'phone, you were carrying a letter from Blexell, Landon and Tanwick. Have you just arrived from the U K?'

'We flew out two days ago.' Darke gave the briefest account of why he and Alison had flown to Kwazania, then continued, 'Mrs Easterton, shortly before he died, your father confided in me regarding certain matters. Two days after his death I received a letter from him, written a few days prior to his accident. In it he wrote of another letter he had sent to his solicitors, in London.' He handed her the Solicitor's manila envelope. 'That letter is in here, with a covering letter from Mister Tanwick.'

He studied her, as she opened and began to read the covering letter. Her features were more distinct than he remembered them, the years and the loss of her husband had

had that affect. She was strikingly attractive, but it was a difficult attractiveness to describe. She seemed to radiate an inner calmness and strength. Her features were well formed: the eyes were set wide apart, the nose straight, the mouth generous, well defined and balanced by her firm jaw, but it was the intelligent grey eyes, that brought the face to life.

She looked up once to meet his gaze as she opened her father's last letter. Her fingers faltered; her emotion was clear to see.

'With your permission I'll take a walk, whilst you read.'

She half smiled, acknowledging his understanding of her desire to read the letter alone. He left her and walked down the veranda steps, into the afternoon sunlight. The road leading away from the farm disappeared down the escarpment, a quarter of a mile from the house. Leitch, he thought, would have taken the car and the bodies, alive or dead, down this stretch of road to set up the fake accident. Had anyone seen him? Certainly no one had come forward, at the time. When had Leitch severed his finger. It was a gruesome and drastic thing to have done: all to convince the authorities he was one of the victims. It showed the man had guts. And it had done the trick.

'Mister Darke,' Virginia Easterton called.

Her voice brought him out of his musings. He turned to see her, tall and slim, at the top of the veranda steps, still holding the letters. He walked back towards her.

'My father writes that you were aware of his past activity in Katanga?'

He nodded.

'I'm surprised the police did not pursue him.'

She was embarrassed, he could see the tenseness, in the way she held her shoulders slightly raised. He felt she was having to adjust to being the daughter of a criminal.

He explained the unusual nature of the crime. The fact that having been initiated in one country, but completed in another had create a strange legal limbo.

'He was fortunate. As he never contravened any Kwazaland laws, the police here had no reason to interfere.'

'But you knew of the theft?'

'Police forces talk to each other. Such information is filed away for future reference, if necessary. Like little pieces of a jigsaw, often they can be put together to build a picture. Your father came to Kwazaland to farm, ahead of any intelligence of his exploits in Katanga. When his background became known the police in this area were informed, as a matter of course and a regular check made on his activities.'

Gazing into the distance she said, 'It's difficult, eleven years later to have to see your father in a different light. To know that all this', she waved her arms about her, 'was built on ill-gotten gains.'

'You could always pay the money back.' She turned to look at him. He continued, 'Of course the problem then is to determine who should be repaid. The Congolese government, the breakaway Katangan government, or the Belgian mining company? All might justifiably claim the money should be theirs. Your father could also have claimed that he was, at least, entitled to something in the way of compensation, for his loss of livelihood, home and future prospects. The world is not as simple or straightforward as we sometimes care to believe.'

'You almost sound as though you're on my father's side in this,' she said, almost willing it to be true.

'I wouldn't go that far. The lack of an obvious victim, the breath-taking simplicity and swashbuckling nature of the event, makes it intriguing. Morally it has to be wrong, but who is it who has been wronged? I suspect if you made it known that you wished to make amends for your father's actions, you would immediately be involved in claims and counter claims. All sorts of organisations would contrive to present themselves as the victim, in need of recompense. Litigation could ramble on for years, costing all involved a great deal of money. Maybe more even than the original value of the ore. And may never reach a satisfactory conclusion. At the time Katanga and the rest of the Congo were in a constitutional limbo. Someone has been deprived of two train loads of copper ore, but exactly whom under the circumstances, might not be so easy to determine.'

She pondered his words for a while. 'He also said to contact you concerning the circumstances of his death, almost as though he knew he was going to die. Why would he write such a thing?'

Darke was unprepared for this, he had assumed the letter would have touched on the possibility of his potential murder. He drew breath, 'You met Sandy Leitch?' he started.

She nodded in reply.

'He was supposed to have died in the car with your father, but the authorities now have good reason to believe that it was not Leitch who was the passenger in the car.' He stopped and pointed to the chairs. 'Do you mind if we sit down?'

They both took a seat. Darke gathered his thoughts, as he looked into the distance beyond the escarpment. Patches of the distant landscape were stained a pale grey by the drifting shadows of cumulus clouds, under a cerulean sky.

He turned back to her, to answer her question, 'Before he died your father was concerned that Sandy Leitch might try to kill him.'

Virginia Easterton looked shocked, 'Kill my father, why, what for?'

'Following their Katanga escapade, your father bought this farm and settled down to a law-abiding life. Leitch, on the other hand, embarked on a career of crime, involving the trafficking of drugs into Europe. He apparently made a lot of money, but when he arrived here, prior to your father's death, he had lost most of it. He was attempting to convince your father to fund a drug deal he was putting together.'

'I'm sure Dad would not have had anything to do with drugs.'

'That's right. His refusal to help, angered Leitch. I believe it might have eventually led to his death. Your father let slip to Leitch that he still had his escape fund, which had been transferred into Krugerrands. It was that money that Leitch was attempting to persuade your father to lend him.'

'I cannot believe my father was murdered. What makes you so sure?'

Darke gave her an account of the original accident investigation. He explained the discovery of Leitch's watch, lighter and little finger at the scene of the accident, together with the identification of Leitch in Scotland.

'Add these factors to his criminal activities and your father's concerns about him, together with his disappearance following the accident,' he concluded, 'it is logical for the authorities to assume he was involved in your father's death.'

'Yes, I see,' she said tonelessly.

He felt her sadness, all this was re-opening a chapter of her life, which she had dealt with emotionally and finalised, enabling her to move on. Now it was back with a deeper and more sinister aspect. She would need time to re-assess her feelings, to sort out a new understanding on the loss of her father. A father who now had a past, previously unknown to her.

She stood and crossed to the edge of the veranda, to leant against the wooden pillar, her arms folded as she gazed at the distant scene. Darke felt awkward as he viewed her well-proportioned figure. She was a very attractive woman, who could readily turn a man's thoughts to other things, but this was not an appropriate moment. He looked away and fixed his stare to his left, where a stag beetle lay on its back, at the top of the steps. It was buzzing loudly as it frantically rocked around trying to right itself.

'For many years I have thought of Muzindi as my home. It was a part of me, somewhere to return to. It is hard to learn that in truth that I hadn't the right to feel that way.' She fell silent for a while, then turning to him, with a wide smile, remarked, 'That's a selfish point of view. I might never have had Muzindi at all, so I must be thankful it was here when I needed it most.' She crossed to him holding out her hand, 'You must forgive me, this has all been a shock. I appreciate you carrying out my father's wishes and coming to see me, it must have been somewhat daunting?'

He shook her slim cool hand. 'Not really,' he answered, 'I was under the impression your father's letter would explain everything. It only perturbed me when he had not mentioned the possibility of his own murder.'

She frowned. 'I need time to think and come to terms with all this. It changes so many things.'

Having delivered Tanwick's letter, he took his leave declining the offer of refreshments. He felt Virginia Easterton needed time on her own, to absorb the disturbing news he had brought.

Over the following week, Lucas Darke was involved in assisting Inspector Desabi with the details of the original investigations concerning Bodell's death. Also, the disappearance of John Warren, the company manager of Kalagan 'B' farm.

Initially he had been concerned that Alison would become bored with being restricted to the hotel all day or visiting Fort Albert's main street, with its single department store. However, within a few days the 'bush telegraph' did its work. Each evening old friends and acquaintances, from six years before, called at the hotel to say hello. Realising that

Lucas was involved each day helping with the re-opened cases, Alison was quickly invited to join in the local social scene. A new face was always refreshing. Her only problem was trying to explain she was not romantically involved with Darke.

Her efforts only partially worked at best. Eventually, she allowed them to think she was just being coy about their relationship. She was invited to a farm to ride, water-ski on a local dam and to go game spotting with Charlie Garthright, a game ranger friend of Lucas.

Charlie showed her tracks of a leopard in the dust beside a bush path. Fascination gripped her and she could not help but bend and lightly touch the indentations. Somehow it brought home to her that this was Africa, it was all so raw and fascinating. Charlie quietly led her up to a stony ledge, overlooking a rock formation. Upwind of them, beside a water hole, a leopard was languidly washing itself, in the shade of a mopane tree. she gazed in awed silence. Each lazy movement of the sleepy animal, caused the muscles to ripple beneath its glossy fur. The wild free animal she saw before her bore no comparison to the poor creatures she had seen on display in zoos.

The murder investigation moved to Mount Muzindi farm. It was necessary to reconstruct, as much as possible, the original scenes for the files. Kalagan 'B' had been investigated as a murder and terrorist incident. All the necessary detailed scene-of-crime work had been done at the time. In the absence of evidence to the contrary Bodell's murder had been treated as a road traffic accident, requiring a less intensive scene investigation. Now it had been upgraded to murder, it needed more comprehensive information from the location. If basic details, such as measurements, angles and a detailed map, were not available, it could undermine the prosecution's court case. Fortunately, the scene had not been completely cleared of debris. On the steep hillside, glass and small rusting parts from the wrecked vehicle were still to be found scattered about, enabling an accurate reconstruction of the location to be made. Additional photographs and measurements were taken.

Seven days after arriving in The Kingdom of Kwazania, Alison stood leaning against a pale grey police Peugeot 404 saloon. She was looking across the slope at Superintendent Kufanu, Inspector Desabi and Lucas Darke moving about what was now the possible, eleven-year-old scene of Lew Bodell's murder. Darke had told her of Bodell's death before they left Scotland, to see the exact location brought his account eerily to life. It had become even more poignant, now that it had been confirmed as the site of a double murder. They moved carefully about the scene, reconstructing the final position of the wrecked vehicle, using their memories and enlarged copies of photographs Darke had taken at the time. She had been invited along the previous night, after Superintendent Kufanu and his wife, Samanca, had joined them for dinner at the Leopard Pass Hotel.

Towards the end of the evening the big policeman turned to her and said, 'We are, I'm afraid, monopolising Lucas which is leaving you little time to see our country, Miss Falkener. Why not come along tomorrow, at least you will see Mount Muzindi, our highest mountain?'

She found Elias Kufanu instantly likeable. He gave the impression, on purpose she felt, that he was a simple, happy giant of a man. Very quickly she became aware of the incisive mind that he camouflaged, with his easy-going manner. Samanca Kufanu was also easy company, she was well educated and a naturally considerate person. Her tall slim figure and flawless skin could have earned her a career as a fashion model. They made a striking couple. By the end of the evening, they were all on first name terms and promising a further dinner, before Alison and Luke returned to the U K. In the meantime, Samanca and Alison had arranged a two-day sightseeing and shopping trip, to Umbaka. Hearing this

Lucas and Elias Kufanu glanced at each other, raising their eyebrows in mock surprise.

The crunch of tyres, on the gravelled surface of the escarpment road, drew Alison's attention back to the present. Further up the hill beyond the two pale grey police Landrovers, an olive green open-backed vehicle, of the same make, had stopped partly off the road. Virginia Easterton stepped down from the cab. She moved slowly round to the near side of the vehicle, intent on watching the figures working on the slope below, unaware that she, in turn, was being observed. Alison walked towards her. The other woman was too engrossed in the police activity, to be aware of her approach. Her face looked pale and drawn.

Alison called 'Hello,' twice before there was a response. Virginia Easterton turned in surprise to see Alison approaching.

Relaxing, she gave a slight smile. 'You must be Alison Falkener, I'm Virginia Easterton.' They shook hands.

'It must be a harrowing experience to look at this spot?' Alison suggested.

Virginia Easterton looked back down the hill before replying, 'I've driven past here so many times, over the past eleven years, but I've always been reluctant to stop and look at it close up.' She changed the subject. 'I came to invite everyone up to the house for refreshments, whenever they finish here. I understand they want to look at the house and to question any of the employees who were here eleven years ago.'

The sun was setting before the convoy of police vehicles finally took leave of Mount Muzindi Farm. Six long-term employees had been interviewed. The farmhouse had been comprehensively photographed inside and out. Detective Inspector Desabi, looking less dishevelled than the others, felt confident he understood all the aspects of the case. There would be some details yet, to complete the picture, but he had much more of an understanding of the eleven-year-old events, than he had that morning. Lucas Darke had added as much additional background information as he could, with the assistance of Superintendent Kufanu. A meeting was arranged for two days later, at provincial headquarters, in Fort Albert, before they all said their goodbyes.

Darke and Alison bade farewell to Virginia Easterton, before driving of in the Peugeot, ahead of the police Landrovers.

'What do you think of her?' Alison asked.

'Virginia Easterton?'

'Yes.'

'Why?'

'Just curious.'

He glanced quickly sideways at her, not wanting to take his eyes for too long off the twin beams of light, boring into the fast-fading twilight. 'What do you make of her?'

'Well, under that veneer of finishing school polish, I think she is a very lonely person. Did you know she lost a son in childbirth a year before her husband died?'

He shook his head. 'No. No, I didn't.' He exhaled deeply. 'That means she has suffered the loss of a mother, father, a baby and a husband. That's quite enough to handle for anyone.'

'I think she's a brave woman. She is trying to busy herself with the farm, to use it as a means of coming to terms with her multiple loss. This final business of her father having been murdered, coupled with his brush with crime, has given her a further jolt.'

'It's bound to have done. An attractive woman like that, hopefully she will get over it fairly quickly.'

Alison looked at him scornfully. 'You men. You haven't got a clue. She didn't have a stable life to begin with, having lost her mother. Then her father is killed. When she does manage to put things together, with her marriage, it all comes apart again. Now when she believes nothing else can happen, she is told her father's death was murder, not accidental. Furthermore, if that wasn't enough, he had a criminal past. A lot of what she has painfully put together, in her mind, has come apart. She's in a very fragile state.'

'I must say in two hours of talking to her you seem to have gathered an awful lot of information and made some dramatic deductions.' He did not disagree with her. Alison was astute. On reflection, much of what he had seen of Victoria Easterton supported her theories.

'Oh, it didn't take two hours we talked of other things too.'

He glanced at her, in the semi-darkness, her tone had been too matter-of-fact.

She saw his look and smiled conspiratorially. 'We talked about you.'

'Me! What have I got to do with anything?'

'She told me a story about a tall, dark policeman, covered in dust, who called at Muzindi one day, when she was eighteen, on holiday from finishing school.' She stopped and turned her face to watch his profile in the reflected light, from the main beams.

'And?'

'She said she had been deliberately rude to him and he had taught her a lesson. She believes it was you. So, what did you do to her?'

'As I remember it, she more or less did it to herself.' He explained about the body box and the need to identify Petrol Mugwani, as a farm employee.

'Anyway, she says she's forgiven you.'

He grunted noncommittally.

'What do you think of her?'

'What do you mean by that?'

'Well, do you fancy her?'

'Back off young lady. I'll let you know in my own good time, if and when I "fancy" someone.'

Alison studied her own reflection in the side window and said, 'You could do worse. It's about time you settled down. The whole of Kilpicton thinks so.'

He replied, almost speechless with amazement, 'Well bully for the whole of Kilpicton,' was all he could think to say, in lame reply.

She grinned into the night, 'I just thought you might like to know.'

'Thank you for your consideration, but somehow, here in the middle of the African bush, the opinions of the good people of Kilpicton hardly seem relevant.'

'You must admit she's very attractive?'

He knew her well enough to know she would continue baiting him until he replied. 'She's not ugly,' he temporized.

'I'm not suggesting this is the time to woo her, but maybe in the longer term. Anyway, I like her and think she would be ideal for you.'

He began to laugh. 'Woo her! You really are something, Alison. What gives you the right to meddle with another person's love life? Other than being a woman, of course?'

'It's a suggestion that's all,' she said haughtily. I've said what I think, it's up to you.'

'Well at least we finally agree on something.'

Alison could not let the subject drop without a final gibe, 'I just think you're silly not to at least consider the idea.'

Chapter 13

The following day Darke waved Alison off with Samanca Kufanu, for their two-day shopping trip to Umbaka. He watched as the car disappeared along the hotel drive. On his return to his room the telephone was ringing. The well-modulated voice of Virginia Easterton filled the earpiece. Despite his denials of the previous night, he found the sound of her voice disturbingly attractive.

'I am sorry to trouble you, when you're busy with other matters, but I don't know who else to ask. I was wondering if you would be good enough to help me solve a problem. It's a rather private matter and you are the only one I know I can trust.' She was eager to persuade him, 'It's to do with my father's letter, the one you brought from Mister Tanwick.'

The last sentence caught his attention. 'Of course, I'll do whatever I can.' He sensed her relaxing, at the other end of the telephone.

'Thank you. Would you and Alison care to come for lunch today?'

He explained that Alison had just left for Umbaka, on a shopping trip and that she would be back in two days. He suggested she might care to wait until then.

There was a moment's silence then tentatively she said, 'Could you come today, if you don't mind. It is rather important?' There was a pause. 'I think you will agree, when you hear what I have to say.'

His next meeting with Elias Kufanu and D I Desabi was set for the following afternoon. He had decided to enjoy the benefits of the hotel pool and relax for the day, particularly as the Kwazanian government was now paying for his accommodation, whilst he was assisting with the case.

He had little to do that day, Virginia Easterton's plea for assistance was intriguing him. 'Of course, is twelve-thirty, okay?'

'Perfect,' she said with relief.

Three hours later he parked his hire car in the shade of the eucalyptus trees, before walking to the farmhouse. Virginia Easterton was on the veranda to greet him. Her hand was cool as he shook it.

'Thank you for coming, I'm sorry not to have given you a clearer idea of why I asked for your help. But, as you know, the telephone is not very private.'

She was simply dressed in a pale blue cotton skirt and white blouse, with just a suggestion of a sleeve. Her tan was light and even, indicating she was not an avid sun worshipper. They chatted generally until they were on the veranda and he was sitting with a glass of the local lager, on the table beside him.

'Lucas,' she began, using his name for the first time, 'You knew of my father's 'escape fund'. You mentioned it the other day. May I ask you what else you know of it?'

Darke outlined the events, prior to her father's death, including the conversation concerning the cache of South African gold coins.

'Krugerrands!' She said, then laughed. 'That's typical of my larger-than-life father. A hoard of gold coins, no less!' She seemed more relaxed than he had seen her, the light golden tan of her skin glowed with an inner radiance.

He chose his words carefully, 'The discovery that your father's death was no accident means there must have been a reason he was killed; a motive for his murder. It is quite likely that Leitch killed him to get the money. He was the only other person at that time, who knew your father had a significant hoard of gold coins.'

'You think he took it?'

'It's a strong possibility, as I can think of no other reason why your father was killed.'

Shaking her head she said, 'According to his letter he hid it, up at the knoll.'

'Have you found anything?'

'No. I've been up there, but I can't think where it could be. I was hoping you could help me look for it.'

'Hidden treasure,' Darke mused, raising himself from the comfort of the wicker armchair, 'I'm your man,' he said, rubbing his hands together, 'It was always a childhood dream of mine to hunt for a chest full of Spanish doubloons. Do you have a lantern and spade?'

She laughed. 'I think we can wait; lunch is ready.'

They talked of other things as they ate at a table set at the corner of the veranda, to take advantage of what little breeze there was. Darke found Virginia Easterton easy company, she was the consummate hostess. Maybe, he thought, it was down to her finishing school education. The conversation ran easily along, under her guidance, moving smoothly from subject to subject. She gently sidestepped his attempts to draw her into conversation about herself. She in turn encouraged him to talk of himself, with little success. He parried her questions with brief replies. He did not enjoy talking about himself. If she was going to be reticent, he would follow suit. She quickly moved onto more neutral matters. The subject, of her father's 'fund' was not broached until they had left the table, to move back to the comfort of the wicker chairs for coffee.

'How do you suggest we begin the search? I was reluctant to make it obvious I was searching for something.'

He had been pondering the point himself. The 'bush telegraph' was aptly named. It was a constant source of amazement how events in the bush were seen, interpreted, not always accurately and disseminated over many miles within hours. Yet it was a well-documented fact. It would be necessary to take precautions against prying eyes.

'I suggest we take a picnic basket and walk up there with a pair of binoculars. You must have done something similar, many times?'

She nodded. 'Good idea. I'll take some flowers for the grave.'

The stroll up to the knoll took no more than ten minutes. By the time they arrived he had all but forgotten the purpose of the walk. He had become so engrossed with his companion. Their conversation had continued to flow readily, he found himself chatting in an unusually relaxed fashion. She enjoyed slowly drawing him out. He was a tall, attractive, self-contained man who seemed unaware of his appeal to women, or if he was, he failed to monopolise on it, which she found refreshing. She felt comfortable in his company.

They continued past the outcrop of rocks and on towards the grave. There was no head stone. A slab of the local rock had been set into the ground with a few words chiselled into its surface. At its centre a cavity held a small metal container, in which she carefully arranged the small bunch of flowers she had been carrying. She watered them from the plastic container Darke had carried for her.

He watched the tender way she went about the process and felt awkward with himself, for finding her so desirable, at such a moment. He turned away and to distract himself he walked back towards the rock formation. In the distance, a troop of baboons was idling away the afternoon among some rocks in the shade of acacia trees. They were safe enough, if he kept an eye on them. Moving past the overhang of rock, he came to the tall cave entrance, which allowed light well into the interior. He called out and shone the torch into the gaping darkness: there was no reply. He threw three stones, one after the other, deep into the blackness without evoking a response. He had heard of a local farmer who once entered a cave without taking precautions, only to be faced with an equally surprised leopard. How he managed to escape unscathed was beyond him to explain. He could recall nothing in his panic, until he found himself sitting in his vehicle, shaking like a leaf, with the front of his shorts covered in his own urine.

The bushman paintings started no more than six feet inside and stretched to the rear of the cave, where it widened out, twenty feet further on. In the light from the torch, the dull red, black and ochre colours, looked as fresh as the day they had been painted. Kept in the dark dry atmosphere, away from wind, rain and direct sunlight, there was little to cause deterioration. He had seen them before, there were a number of similar paintings in the area. Most were in relatively inaccessible locations. On patrol, he would visit known sites and detail ones newly discovered. They fascinated him. He kept a file of them, recording them for posterity. The cave contained nothing of significance. Underfoot was mostly dust covered rock. The walls, save for the paintings, were featureless and smooth, hence their appeal to the bushman artist. Using one of the stones he had thrown into the cave, he tapped the sandy floor experimentally here and there, to check for sound. There was no significant difference wherever he tested.

Outside the cave he turned back towards the rock overhang and the shelter Bodell had made to enjoy the full vista beyond the escarpment. It was easy to become engrossed in the panorama. With an effort, he turned to study the structure as a potential hiding place, for a cache of gold coins. He began to calculate the sum involved. Lew Bodell's letter mentioned transferring one hundred thousand US dollars into krugerrands, each coin weighing one troy ounce of fine gold. Assuming a krugerrand was worth thirty-five dollars, in nineteen sixty-seven, that would translate into approximately two thousand eight hundred and sixty coins. He whistled under his breath, wondering what such a hoard would weigh. After a quick calculation, writing in the dust at his feet, he came to the conclusion it would be about one hundred and eighty pounds. Amazed, he obliterated his calculations with a sweep of his boot. After some thought he concluded he was looking for something akin to the size of a medium suitcase.

He moved into the shade and ran his hands along the smooth stone, looking for something different. The stonework construction of the shallow shelter gave way in places to the natural rock, as he moved around the recess. Only where there had been cracks or faults, had the rock been filled with shaped stones cemented in place, to provide a more even surface. Two steel cabinets were fastened to the rear of the overhang, with double steel doors, which housed: folding tables, chairs and barbeque equipment. There was nothing to indicate a secret hiding place. Darke stepped out into the sunlight to meet Virginia Easterton. He stooped and picked up a medium sized stone.

'Any luck?' she asked.

'No,' he said slowly, retracing his steps into the shade. Here, tapping the walls produced a variety of sounds but nothing that sounded hollow. It was difficult to determine whether the exercise was of much value. He explained what size the cache must be and its weight. They looked at each other in puzzlement.

'Did your father mention anything else in his letter, that might be of use here?'

'Not that I recall.' She took the letter out and read the relevant section several times, before handing it to Darke. 'He just says he hid the "pot of gold" at the knoll.'

Darke also read it over several times. 'He says nothing of its whereabouts. It's almost as though he expects you to know.' He looked at her, almost through her, as he concentrated. 'Have you ever hidden anything here in the past, or even found something, which your father would have known about? Something your father might expect you to remember?'

She frowned. 'I don't know. I'm not sure.' She turned to look to the north, her eyes resting on a four feet high single rock, about forty yards from the shelter. 'There was something.' She stood motionless, thinking back over the years. 'I must have been about twelve or thirteen years old, soon after Dad bought the farm. We were standing on the veranda of the house, when I saw the most vivid rainbow. I pointed it out to Dad. He said there was a "pot of gold" at the end of the rainbow. I told him I thought its end was half way between here and the stone outcrop over there.' She pointed to a lone rock. 'He laughed and ruffled my hair saying, "If it was there, you would need a pneumatic drill to dig with, it's solid rock".' For some time after that, when we walked to the knoll, we would often say we were going to look for the pot of gold.'

'Well, it's worth a try.' He paced the distance out from the main formation to the isolated rock, to discover the mid-point fell in the centre of a stone bench. It was one of four set in a semi-circle. 'I suppose it makes sense,' he commented, doubtfully.

'Why do you say that?'

'Well, it's not a site I would choose to hide a hoard of money. Out here in the open, we can easily be observed from some distance away. However, if you use reverse psychology, no one would expect it to be exposed like this and the stone bench marks the spot well. It disguises the fact that there could be a space underneath.'

'Oh,' she said, half convinced, 'It would take at least two people to move the seat and then there's the pedestals.'

'I shouldn't think so. That wouldn't make sense. It was your father's escape fund. He wouldn't want another person to know his hiding place. And he would want to get at it, easily and quickly, without help.'

'That's true. So where does that get us?'

'Looking for an easy solution.'

He knelt down to scrutinise the bench more closely. His logic made some sense, but quite how it could be used to help him in his search, was not immediately obvious. He studied the stone slab below the seat. He was keen to take out his penknife and scrape the dust away from the edges.

However, they were in the open so he did not want to make his actions too obvious, in case they were being observed. Using his fingers, he quickly brushed away the dust at one end to reveal an edge. The slab butted up to the inside of both pedestals and was the width of the seat. Standing up and wiping the dust from his hands, he suggested the two of them stroll around the semi-circle of benches.

They stopped at one of the other seats and sat down. Darke leant forward with his forearms across his knees, casually looking down below the bench. Here the slab at ground level was different; it continued underneath and slightly beyond the outer edges of the pedestals. Shortly they rose and continued their stroll around the semi-circle. Now that he knew what he was looking for, it was easy to see from a standing position, that all the other benches differed from the first. Only on the first bench did the ground level slab finish at the inner side of the supporting pedestals, which were set directly into the ground. For all the others the pedestals stood on top of a longer horizontal slab.

He explained everything to Virginia, she remained outwardly calm, but he could tell she was excited. He smiled at her.

'Do you think this could be it?'

Her excitement was so infectious his previous doubts receded. 'It would be worth trying to lift the slab to see what's underneath. But not now. I suggest we come back just before sunset, with a vehicle. We can park it in such a way that would screen us from the direction of the farm.'

By the time they returned to the house two hours of daylight remained before sundown. Darke found the time passed all too quickly in her company. Soon it was time to return to the knoll. Within five minutes of leaving the house, he had positioned the Landrover to screen the bench, from the direction of the house. They watched the sun set in the west. As it sank below the horizon, he opened the rear door of the Landrover and took out a torch, a hand brush, spade and crowbar. Noise could carry great distances in the still evening air, so it was with caution he set to work clearing the dust and soil from the base slab. He removed enough to reveal the entire length of its lower edge, which would allow the crowbar to be inserted underneath and ensure no soil dropped in under the slab, as it was lifted.

He looked up. Virginia Easterton was keeping watch in case they were observed.

'All clear?' he queried.

'Yes, I can't see any movement.'

'Right, here goes.'

He gently applied his weight to the crowbar. The slab lifted sufficiently to allow him to place a stone under its lip to support it, whilst he withdrew the crowbar and inserted both sets of fingers beneath its edge. He was able to lift it and wedge the blade of the spade, on its side, under the angled slab, leaving a gap of ten inches. Switching on the torch, they both stooped and craned forward to inspect the space beneath. There was nothing to see. The surface beneath the slab was solid rock, chipped away to make it level. It was filled in here and there with, what appeared to be, a dry mixture of sand and cement, compressed by the weight of the slab. There was certainly no space to hide anything.

'Well, there's nothing there,' he said flatly.

They both straightened up.

'Why then was the slab a different size from the other benches?' she asked. He thought for a moment. 'Beneath this bench, unlike the others, the rock is immediately below a thin layer of soil. To have put a long slab down, would have meant cutting much more of the rock away. On this seat the pedestals have been set directly onto the rock. Therefore, unlike the other benches, the slab has been cut to fit between and not under them.'

'So, what do you suggest we do now?'

He grinned wryly. 'There is only one thing we can do. Think the whole thing through again.'

By the time they returned to the house their despondent mood had changed to laughter at how easily they had fooled themselves, into believing the hoard had been hidden under the stone bench.

Fifteen minutes later Darke stood by the fire in the large farmhouse sitting room, holding a heavy crystal glass charged with brandy and ginger ale. As the ice clinked against glass he relaxed, as 'L'appuntamento' by Ornella Vanoni was playing on the music system, in the relaxing ambience of the large comfortable room. The open log fire crackled sporadically in the huge stone fireplace. It took the chill out of the still mountain air. A vague scent of woodsmoke permeated the room. It was the typical scent of Africa: visit any kraal and woodsmoke was the predominant smell. The lighting was low. Here and there, beams of light from the narrow apertures at the top of the lampshades shone up to the timbers of the vaulted ceiling. Along the walls hung paintings, individually lit, by overhanging brass wall lamps. He had viewed them before in daylight, but carefully lit as they were, he could fully appreciate the delicate skill Lewis Bodell had employed, in copying the cave paintings faithfully in watercolours. In his mind he reviewed the events of the afternoon, as he studied each of the seven subtly lit paintings.

'Dinner is ready.' She had entered the room before he knew it. Her perfume, light and delicate, touched his nostrils. She stood elegantly tall, just inside the door, she was wearing a simple black silk dress and high heels. Her hair had been tied back in a ponytail during the day, now it hung loose, falling in a natural style to her shoulders. A combination of the soft lighting, the discreet style of her perfectly fitting dress and her shiny cascading hair, he thought, created a most attractive vision.

His silent appraisal embarrassed her.

'I'm sorry,' he said recognising her discomfort, 'My mind was far away, I didn't hear you, then to see you looking so......'

She relaxed, enjoying the implied compliment. She said quietly, 'So.....?'

'So..,' he searched for the right word. It was his turn to feel awkward. He was here to help her, not to take advantage of the situation. It would be too easy to be boorish and make some trite remark. 'So, different,' he said lamely.

'Different?' she gave a slight smile. 'Would that be different 'good' or different 'bad'?'

'Oh, good,' he said hastily.

'Oh good,' she echoed, and they both laughed. 'I forgot to ask whether you like guinea fowl,' she inquired, as she led the way to the dining room.

Elspeth, Virginia Easterton's housekeeper was used to serving her mistress solitary meals. She was clearly delighted to see her with male company. She kept giggling as she waited on the table. It was when she asked Darke whether he thought Mrs Easterton looked beautiful, that Virginia, in mock anger, order her to stop her nonsense and be off for the night. Elspeth departed, her ample bulk quivering with suppressed laughter. Once alone, they returned to the events of the day. They spent the remainder of the meal attempting to make sense of Lew Bodell's cryptic clue. Try as they would, they could think of nothing to solve the mystery, until Darke froze in the act of sipping his wine. He swivelled his head to meet Virginia's puzzled look.

'What is it?' she asked.

He put down his glass and took her hand. 'Come,' he said.

He rose from the table, she followed, intrigued by his intensity. He still had hold of her hand as they entered the sitting room. He went straight to the final copy of the cave paintings, quickly scanning it.

'There is no rainbow in that painting!'

She glanced at the picture, 'No there isn't. Should there be?'

'I'm sure the last painting in the cave has a crude depiction of a rainbow.'

'If that's the case, why did Dad not show it in this picture?' Her eyes widened and she answered her own question, 'Because it wasn't there when he painted these pictures.'

'Exactly. He must have added it to the painting in the cave, to indicate the hiding place.'

'Clever old Dad and clever you for spotting it.'

'It's a strong possibility anyway,' he said with caution, remembering the way they had misled themselves that afternoon.

'I'll change quickly and we'll see whether your theory is right.'

'Ah,' it was an involuntary remark.

She looked at him questioningly. 'What's wrong?'

He paused before admitting, 'Your dress. It suits you perfectly and fits so well it's a shame to change.'

She gave him a wide smile as she left the room, and called, 'I can always put it on again, later.'

She returned after ten minutes in slacks and a safari jacket, her hair once again in a ponytail.

Chapter 14

Darke repeated the stone throwing precautions before entering the cave. Eagerly, Virginia followed him to the end of the row of paintings. In the light from the torch, they both stared at the crude suggestion of a rainbow, in the style of the rest of the paintings. It was cleverly done, as both of them admitted.

'When you think about it,' said Darke, 'he had faithfully copied the whole tableau, so he'd already mastered the bushmen style. So, it's not so surprising that he was able to quickly add the rainbow.'

'Why do you think he was so secretive about the hiding place? Why not just write down where the gold was hidden?'

'It's my guess he moved the gold here from the house after Leitch arrived. He probably realised that once Leitch knew his fund was still intact and converted into krugerrands, he might try to get his hands on it, by fair means or foul. To commit its whereabouts to paper without encrypting the solution could play straight into Leitch's hands. According to your father, when I last saw him, he implied that Leitch was unstable enough to resort to force, at any time, if given a reason to do so. The rainbow idea was a bit of insurance. Leitch had become suspicious of your father's every move; the simplest thing might have triggered him to violence.'

Dust covered the cave floor below the last painting. Using a trowel and brush Darke cleared the loose powder, to reveal a rock slab, roughly fashioned into a rectangle, two feet by two feet six inches. A knife blade around each edge quickly freed most of the dust, enabling him to insert the blade of the shovel under the slab, to lift it sufficiently, for his fingers to get a grip. He lifted it with relative ease and slid it to one side, to reveal a sheet of yellowing newspaper, covering a number of slats lying across the space. He removed them to reveal six black shallow metal boxes, stacked in two piles of three. The weight made it awkward to lift the first box from the cavity. He placed it beside the hole and lifted the hinged lid. Inside lay neat rows of shiny golden Krugerrands, individually enclosed in clear plastic sleeves. He slid one coin out. It was marked with the distinctive head of Paul Kruger, the first President of the Transvaal Republic. The reverse side displayed a springbok design. As Virginia shone the torch Darke rapidly counted the coins in each row.

They both remained silent staring at the wealth of gold, that partially filled the box, until Virginia audibly exhaled, having held her breath from the moment he had started to lift the slab. 'How many coins do you think are there?'

Darke tested the weight of the other boxes. After a brief pause, he said, 'At a rough count there are four hundred and eighty in this box and there are six boxes weighing roughly the same. Just short of three thousand, I would think.' He took one coin and handed it to her. 'I suggest you leave the rest here whilst you decide what to do with them. Having this treasure in the house is going to be a liability. Besides they're heavy.'

She nodded in agreement.

The cavity contained one other item: beside the boxes, wrapped in oiled cloth, was a loaded .38 calibre, Smith and Wesson revolver. It had been placed beside the boxes, a clear indication that Bodell had been alive to the possibility of trouble. Ten years buried in the cave had done it no harm at all. The dry atmosphere ensured that no rusting of its lightly oiled surfaces had occurred. He checked it over carefully before returning it to its hiding place. He closed and fastened the box, before replacing it in the ground. By the time he had finished there was no indication that the floor of the cave had been disturbed.

The relative contrast between the claustrophobic heat of the cave, compared with the cool night air hit them, as they emerged. It served to loosen their tongues.

In a guarded, conspiratorial tone, Virginia whispered, 'That was amazing, to see all that money lying in a hole in the ground. How much do you think its worth?'

It was as though she had read his mind. He had been estimating the value of the golden stockpile. Assuming Bodell's emergency fund, of one hundred thousand dollars, had all been converted into krugerrands, which is what Bodell had indicated, then it would have increased directly in proportion to the gold price. He knew gold was at an all-time high and must be at least worth four times its value, of ten years previously.

'At least four hundred thousand US dollars. Maybe four-hundred-and-fifty-thousand. You're a very wealthy woman.'

They drove back to the farmhouse. Darke switched off the ignition as she turned to him. 'I can't keep it. It would be wrong. How do I give it back?'

'We've had this conversation before.'

'I know, it's so frustrating. I want so desperately to make amends for my father's....', she paused, frowning, searching for a word, '......transgression,' she looked at him saying diffidently, 'I don't want to call it a crime. I hate to call him a criminal, because I know he was doing it for me.'

'He was never tried for any crime. He's innocent until proved guilty.'

'Good, but that doesn't help me resolve the issue of how to make amends. What would you do in my position?'

He thought for a moment. 'Put it to good use for the benefit of the Africans, either in the Katanga region, or here in Kwazania. Simple water purification plants can make a significant difference to the sickness rate in the villages. Providing tools and equipment, to improve productivity. Things like that. There is no shortage of ideas you could use it for. I imagine it would soon be used up. Alternatively set up a charitable trust, invest the money and use the interest to fund small, basic projects on a regular basis.'

'Yes, that makes sense.' He felt her hand on his arm. 'Thank you for that. Are there no end to your talents, Lucas?' her tone was half-earnest and half jocular.

They walked to the veranda and into the house. He washed off the dust of the evening's work, in the guest bathroom where he had cleaned up, earlier in the day. He returned to the comfortable sitting room, where Ornella Vanoni had given way to Frank Sinatra. Two fresh drinks had been placed on the side table. A log of eucalyptus wood was newly settling in the dying embers. The bark began to smoulder then ignite. Small flames came and went, licking their way upwards, round the bark, gaining in size as they progressed, releasing its distinctive aroma.

'You're far, far away.'

He turned to see her standing, as before, just inside the doorway. She had changed back into the black silk dress. Her hair, released from the pony tail, once again fell in long, dark, natural curves to her shoulders.

'...So..', Darke paused, this time he did not feel the constraint of the previous occasion, she had obviously changed back into the dress because he had liked it. He smiled slowly and said, 'breath-taking!'

'Thank you.' There was a slight smile about her eyes. 'You're very kind.'

Her grey eyes held his as she walked towards him. In her high heels she was barely an inch shorter than him. He caught the faint scent of her perfume again.

'I'm grateful for your help. It's been an interesting and exciting day. I doubt I would have solved the mystery of the 'pot of gold', without your help.'

She came close, without thought, he took her in his arms. He felt her firm body yield to his touch, through the fine material of her dress. It was a slow, gentle kiss, full of unreleased passion. Even through his ardour he realised she had been through so much in recent times. It was crucial to treat her gently, to move at a pace she could control. She gave an all but inaudible sigh as they parted. Her arms slid slowly from round his neck, her eyes holding his. She gave a wry smile, as she leant back in his arms.

'It's been a long time since I kissed a man, I'm out of practice I'm afraid.'

Darke drew her close, his lips touch her forehead, she looked up at him. 'It worked for me,' he murmured as they kissed again.

Eventually she gently disengaged herself from his arms, picked up their drinks and handed him his glass. Also on the side table was the krugerrand showing a springbok. She turned it over to reveal the head of Paul Kruger, President of the South African Republic before and during the Second Boer War.

'I wonder why Dad bought krugerrands?'

'As I recall, South Africa began producing them in nineteen-sixty-seven. It was the first time for many years that an individual could purchase gold there, without a licence. Your father would have known that the krugerrand, being one troy ounce of fine gold, was an easily convertible commodity. Also, it was an investment and likely to appreciate in value, which it has done. In this case by four or five hundred percent. Its only disadvantage is its weight. He could have gone for stamps or diamonds but for those you need to find a ready buyer. It's easy to sell gold, anywhere in the world.'

'Alison said you are not involved with each other. Is that true?'

It always intrigued him how a woman's mind could leap from one subject to another, totally unrelated one, as though it was perfectly normal.

He smiled. 'Yes. We're more like brother and sister than anything else.' She looked at him askance. He laughed, saying, 'Why ask me if you're not going to believe my answer?'

'She's very attractive.'

'So are you.'

'Thank you, but you have just kissed me. Are you saying you have never kissed Alison in that way?'

'That's right, I have never kissed Alison in that way.' He raised an eyebrow at her, 'Why bring Alison into this?'

'Because I like her, I wouldn't like to hurt her.'

'Rest assured, my kissing you, will not hurt Alison. We work well together. We both know getting involved would undermine that arrangement.'

She drew him to the chesterfield and they both sat down, she said, 'I'm tougher than maybe I look, you know.'

'I don't doubt that.'

'You have been treating me like a china doll all day.'

'I don't go around kissing china dolls.'

'That was the first time you dropped your guard.'

'Alright, I admit I have been tiptoeing around. What with all that you have been through, I didn't want to create an awkward situation.'

She rested a hand on his arm. 'I appreciate your consideration, but, as I say, I am not a china doll.' She paused looking at her hands. He waited. She seemed to make up her mind before continuing, 'I have used Muzindi as a hide-away for the past year, to come to terms with everything. The letter you brought with you was a shock, but it is time for the grieving mother, wife, and daughter to take up her life once more. The gold has made me realise that there are things to be done. It offers a way to make a new life for myself, to make amends for my father's misdeed.'

He took both her hands in his. 'You're right. I think you're a whole lot tougher than you look.' He looked at his watch. 'Nearly midnight, I had better be going.'

They both rose and slid into each other's arms; he gave her a long kiss, enjoying the sensation of her responding to his caresses.

'Lucas,' she said breathlessly, the hint of a frown crossing her brow, 'it has been a long time since I was close to a man, other than my husband and more than a year since my husband died.'

He held her at arm length and said quietly, 'Don't worry, I understand.'

'No...,' her eyes could not meet his, 'No,' she said again, 'That's not quite what I meant. The thing I have missed most is being held close.'

He drew her back to him and held her tight, kissing her hair.

Her head was resting on his shoulder when she spoke, 'I know I can trust you Lucas, I don't want you to feel committed in anyway.' She turned her head to look up into his eyes, they were surprisingly expressive eyes in a strong face and now they were gentle. They gave her the desire and confidence to continue, 'I would like you to spend the night with me,' the eyes that boldly held his wavered, momentarily, until he cupped her face in his hands and gently touched her lips with his, 'I will understand if you don't...'

'Shhh,' he breathed touching a forefinger to her lips, 'I have spent the day forcing myself not to desire you, you have just destroyed the last vestige of resistance I have.'

She was flushed. 'I'm amazed at myself for asking you.'

He gave a slight smile as he bent to pick her up and carry her from the room.

Chapter 15

'You slept with her! After all I said to you, you slept with her!' Alison Falkener was standing in the middle of Darke's hotel room, glaring at him in exasperation.

'Hang on a minute, Alison, you're jumping to conclusions.'

'Two and two makes four. Simple addition. The housemaid said your bed had not been slept in the other night. You say you spent the day with Virginia Easterton. With your reputation it doesn't take a genius to fill in the gaps.'

He looked at her quizzically. 'Alison, you are the only one who says I have a reputation, which is grossly unfair. Anyway, I'm not accountable to you. And I'm certainly not going to encourage you to cross-examine me, by confirming or denying anything. What may, or may not, have happened between Virginia Easterton and me is none of your business.'

'But I'm responsible. She's still coming to terms with the loss of her baby, her husband and the revelation of her father's past. I encouraged you to consider her as easy prey. You couldn't stay away from her, could you?'

'Good Heavens woman,' the words burst out of him, at the thought of himself as a sex-crazed predator, 'What do you think I am?'

She was warming to her theme. 'We both know what you are, you don't have to tell me whether you slept with her, I can tell by your face. And I encouraged you.'

'Alison, I'm not going to be provoked into answering any of your questions. If you're now feeling guilty, for some reason, because you believe you acted as some sort of matchmaker, then so be it. It might teach you not to glibly interfere in peoples' lives, in future. My relationship with Virginia Easterton has nothing whatsoever to do with you. Do I make myself clear?' There was no reply from Alison. 'Well?'

She remained silent and in so doing they both knew she had begrudgingly accepted what he said. He knew she was one of those women, who in spite of their emotional judgement, could respond to a reasoned argument.

Instead, she turned on her heels, walked to the door saying, 'Very well, have it your own way.' Every movement of her tall frame revealing the utter contempt she felt, for anyone who could stoop so low, as to introduce logic into an argument. She passed through the door, closing it behind her with the teasing words, 'But you did, didn't you?'

He decided to leave her for a while, as he had an appointment at Police Headquarters, in town.

Sunlight glinted off the silver laurel leaves and crossed spears of Superintendent Kufanu's badges of rank. They were set on stiff dark blue sleeves, threaded onto the epaulettes of his khaki short-sleeved, open-neck tunic.

The big policeman leant forward to speak and the reflected sunlight disappeared, 'Progress to date: an international warrant has been issued this morning for the arrest of Alexander Leitch. A request has been sent to New Scotland Yard for any information of his whereabouts. We have given them his known alias plus information on his Glasgow addresses and Rasguneon Castle. The police in Scotland may find something from their searches of those premises. The French police have been contacted concerning any drug-related murders, by stabbing, in southern France, during the early to mid-sixties. It's a long shot, but as we all know, once in a while, these things can pay off.'

Darke and Inspector Desabi nodded in unison, with no knowledge of Leitch's present whereabouts, every possible line of enquiry had to be checked.

The burly Superintendent continued, 'Rather than using the formal channels, I have just been on the 'phone, to the police liaison inspector in the Congo's Shaba Province, previously Katanga,' he smiled, 'It's sometimes quicker and more effective, if we can use the direct approach. He has checked the old files, many of which were lost or destroyed, at the time of the rebellion. They can find no background details for Leitch, prior to his time as an employee of the Katangan railways,'

He sighed and said, 'That is about all we can do for the present.' He looked at Darke searchingly and asked, 'So, what are your plans, Lucas?'

Darke knew there was little more that could be done. It was just a question of time. All they could do was wait on events. His justification for being in Kwazania had come to an end. A warrant had been issued for Leitch's arrest and relevant countries informed, but his and Allison's future remained dangerously uncertain, until Leitch was apprehended. From Leitch's point of view his problems could be resolved if the two main witnesses against him could be eliminated. This meant the two of them would have to remain in hiding, when they returned to the U K. Not an easy task when he had his businesses to run. Also, Alison had family to consider. Someone like Leitch would have little compunction in kidnapping the odd relative, to achieve his objective of locating the two of them.

Echoing his thoughts, he answered Elias Kufanu's question, 'Not a lot more we can do here, except to wait. Hopefully not for long, but it could be weeks, months or years before we have further news of Leitch. We must return to Scotland and try to keep our whereabouts secret, to avoid a visit from him or his men.'

Promising to have a farewell dinner with Elias and Samanca Kufanu, before departing for the UK, Darke took his leave of the two policemen. Feeling empty of emotion, he left Police Provincial Headquarters and walked down Fort Albert's Main Street, to the travel agent. He booked two tickets for a flight from Umbaka International Airport to London, in four days' time. After the many months of pursuing Leitch and the excitement of the past weeks, a future of waiting on events looked bleakly uncertain. His drive out of town and up the Leopard Pass, to the hotel, did nothing to improve his mood. At the reception desk a message was handed to him saying Virginia Easterton had called. There was no immediate sign of Alison, so he returned to his room and rang the number for Mount Muzindi farm.

Visiting the tobacco farm the following morning, was beginning to feel more like coming home. Alison, contrary to expectations, was her usual self. She chatted easily during the drive north, through the farming district. Virginia Easterton had suggested, over the telephone, that Darke tell Alison of the previous day's discovery they had made. She asked for their assistance in transferring the weighty hoard, to her bank in Fort Albert, for safekeeping. Alison was excited to see the "loot", as she referred to it.

As they climbed the three steps to the veranda, the mistress of Mount Muzindi farm, looking happy and relaxed, came to greet them from the interior of the house. After a while, Darke found the atmosphere between the two women disconcerting, their manner was vaguely conspiratorial, he felt slightly awkward having the two of them there. They sat over coffee planning the movement of the gold. It was not as though the task was complicated; it was more that their activities should not arouse attention.

It was decided that all three would visit the knoll, leaving Virginia's long wheelbase Landrover beside the cave entrance. The two women would then keep watch, whilst viewing the scenery. This would allow Darke to remove the gold from its hiding place and bring the boxes to the entrance of the cave. It would be an easy task to alert the two women, load the gold coins into the rear of the Landrover, climb aboard and drive to the bank in Fort Albert.

He continued to feel slightly uncomfortable as he watched the two of them. Alison was nodding approvingly as Virginia outlined her plans for using the gold, to establish a charity to assist African communities in remote regions. Now and then, both would stop and turn to him with warm smiles. He decided that he was out of his depth. He excused himself saying he was going to check the Landrover, to ensure it did not breakdown on their way to town, for the want of oil, fuel, and water. Alison would be following the Landrover in the hire car, as a backup vehicle.

Ten minutes later he returned to the veranda to find Alison sitting alone.

'You are forgiven,' she said quietly.

'For what?'

'I knew I was right.'

'What about.

'She's less tense.'

'Who, Virginia?'

'Not that that entirely exonerates you.'

'It doesn't?' This is weird, he thought. 'From what?'

'You can be so self-centred at times.'

'I'm not sure I'm enjoying this disjointed conversation.' He looked at her intently. 'What on earth are you talking about?'

'Alison returned his gaze and through closed teeth said, 'you made love to Virginia.'

'You were discussing me?'

'Not in that way. Don't be silly,' she said dismissively. She saw the question in his eyes. 'She said you had been very kind and considerate.'

'So?'

'Under the circumstances that reveals a lot to a woman.'

'Well, I would say Virginia was also kind and considerate to me.'

'That's not the same thing at all. And you know it.'

'It isn't?' he queried, raising an eyebrow and shaking his head.

'Of course not. You wouldn't understand. Only a woman would understand the significance of what she said.' Her fingers circumnavigated the lip of her coffee cup.

'So, I'm forgiven, you say?' he queried, in an attempt to bring the conversation to an end.

'Up to a point.' Her eyes, viewing him askance, gave her words added meaning.

'That's nice,' he said, contritely, as Virginia Easterton reappeared on the veranda.

Fifteen minutes later he entered the cave leaving the two women outside with the Landrover. He uncovered the boxes of Krugerrands, stacked them close by the cave entrance, tucked Bodell's revolver into his waistband, under his shirt, replaced the slabs and swept the dust back over them. To anyone entering the cave there was no indication the hoard had ever been buried there. He exited the cave and savoured the cool, clean, dust-free air allowing his eyes to adjust to the bright sunlight. He became aware of figures standing in a semi-circle around the entrance.

The barrel of a Kalashnikov rifle raked his ribs, none to gently, accompanied by the words, 'Hands up,' shouted in a thick Bantu accent.

He froze as the scene before him became clear. There were three men, uniformly armed and dressed in camouflage tunics, trousers and caps. Cheap cloth badges on their caps and tunics carried the legend "KAPU" in faded yellow letters. Darke realised these were so called 'freedom fighters', from the Kwaza African People's Union. Lack of local support had turned them into marauding bands of thugs, that preyed mostly on the more remote kraals, further to the north, where the Royal Kwazanian Army was systematically searching for, and destroying them. Rumour had it that they had been pushed back across the border, into Nambria, east of the Olulopo river. These were merciless, often drug-crazed killers who would hack off a victim's limb, or kill, just for their own amusement. Darke was frightened for himself, but more so for the two women. His mind raced. At least he was armed. Bodell's revolver was out of sight under his shirt. If he had been alone, he might have tried using it and retreating back inside the cave. He did not rate his chances, but a quick death from a grenade or a burst of gunfire was better than an agonising death at the hands of these butchers, as many of their victims would have agreed. What were they doing so far south? He could not understand it.

'Don't try anything stuppit, Darke, we've got yer women,' Sandy Leitch cautioned as he came into view, dragging Alison behind him. Her hands were tied in front of her. Darke spotted more KAPU uniforms guarding the perimeter of the site. Brogan, Leitch's henchman, followed his boss dragging Virginia by the arm.

Leitch waved his automatic pistol at the 'freedom fighters' and grinned. 'You like my private army?'

'You're playing a dangerous game, associating with these fellows, Leitch.' Darke felt a measure of relief. The future of the three of them could not be describe as anything but grim, but even Leitch, he thought, could be relied upon to kill them relatively quickly, compared with these KAPU thugs. Brogan forced the women to sit down on one of the stone benches.

Leitch replied, 'Not "associate" Darke. I don't "associate" with these men,' he paused for effect, 'I command them,' he said it grandly. Seeing the disparaging look on Darke's face, he went on, 'You don't ken it, do ye, Mister bloody, busybody Darke?' His accent thickening as his temper rose, 'I finance these guys. The Russians give them precious little these days. KAPU has shown themselves to be a poor investment.' He waved his automatic at the uniformed men again. 'I picked up the tab. If it wisnae for me they would have disbanded eighteen months ago. I have plans for them that will change their prospects and mine.'

'I wouldn't have thought that was your style. Why are you getting involved in politics, for heaven's sake?' Darke asked with genuine curiosity.

'Politics,' Leitch spat the word out, 'Am no in'erested in politics laddie. I'm protecting ma operation.'

He ordered two of the KAPU men to guard the women. He and Brogan walked up close to Darke. Both men were unshaven and stank of stale sweat. Leitch's breath was heavy with the smell of whisky.

'You have caused me a lot o' grief.' He spat and pushed his face close to Darke's. 'I should give you to these guys for a wee bit o' sport, but it canny be. I have plans for the three of you. It's a pity, but I need you in reasonable condition.' He walked past Darke to the cave entrance and looked at the metal boxes. He hefted the top box, noting its weight. 'Hello. Is this wha' I think it is?' he said. He placed the box back on the pile and lifted the lid. He gave a tuneless whistle and chuckled to himself. 'Nothing like gold to put a man in a gid mood.' He was grinning as he turned away from the cave, 'Now that is what I call a haul. I would ha' made the trip for you and the girl,' he pronounced the word more like 'gurrell', 'or the gold, but to have both, well, that's a bit o' a bonus.'

'What are you up to Leitch?'

'You wait an' see,' Leitch snapped back.

'Let the women go. Leave the gold, it doesn't belong to you, Do one decent thing in your life.'

The Glaswegian gave a bark of a laugh. 'Don't be stuppit, man. This is payback time and I'm gonna enjoy it. As for the gold that's mine, I worked for it.' He turned to Virginia, 'Your father needna have died if only he'd been reasonable...'

'You killed him in cold blood,' Darke growled in a disgusted voice.

Leitch nodded to Brogan. The big man stepped forward and slammed a punch into Darke's stomach. He tried to turn with the blow, but the force of it doubled him up. He went to his knees whooping for breath. Through the noise of his own gasps and the ringing in his ears, he heard Leitch warn Brogan.

'Tack care Carl, no broken bones, man, remember.' Reluctantly Brogan stepped away, he clearly had a score to settle.

Leitch continued conversationally, 'I didnae want to kill Lew, but he left me no choice. I hit him from behind, he never knew a thing. He'd tricked me into thinking the krugerrands were hidden in the house. The safe was too small, so it had to be hidden elsewhere. After the 'accident' I searched the house from top to bottom, I found nothing. By the time I left I was no' a happy man. I'd organised ma own death, but was short o' funds. And my bloody hand was hurtin' like hell.' He smiled happily, rubbing his hands slowly together in satisfaction. 'It's been a long wait, but here's ma gold at last.'

He seemed to genuinely believe he had a right to it. Darke realised how cold blooded a killer this man was. It meant nothing to him to wipe out a life to serve his purpose.

Leitch gave instructions to the KAPU leader and signalled to Brogan. Within minutes the six metal boxes were loaded into the back of the Landrover. Alison was sandwiched in the front seat, between the KAPU leader and Brogan, who was driving. Behind, squeezed in the middle seat sat Leitch, Virginia Easterton and Darke, with his hands bound. KAPU fighters filled the rear bench seats and three others clung to the top of the vehicle.

Bucking and rocking precariously over rough tracks, the over-laden vehicle ground its way, in low range, four-wheel-drive, north-eastwards behind the farm, climbing back into the mountains.

'Where are we going?' Darke asked, twenty minutes later, as they rounded a shoulder of rocks and came upon the Muzindi cliffs.

No one answered. He gazed up at the imposing, sheer, almost smooth granite face, several hundred feet high and over a half-a-mile in length. Many thousands of years before, the face of the mountain had sheared off, leaving a clean surface, largely unmarked by cracks, ledges or fissures. The cliff top leant outwards as it rose, making it impossible for all, but the most experienced and daring climbers to scale. Each end curved outwards. The foot of the cliff wall at its centre lay above and back, from the little used track, by a distance of three hundred yards. The overgrown trail climbed gently to the north, as it found its way across the front of the rock wall, traversing a series of misshapen hummocks and gullies. The bush sloped up at an angle of thirty degrees from the track. It crossed the same track, higher up, where it doubled back on itself, then flattened out as it approached the foot of the smooth rock face. The cliffs were at the same time impressive and intimidating. In Europe or America, they would have been an awe-inspiring visitor attraction, but here, lost in Africa, they had yet to make it onto the tourist agenda.

Twelve years before, Darke had visited the area on patrol, in part, to check on the site of bushman paintings. He did not understand why Leitch had brought them here. The disused track they were on had been made to access a silver mine at the foot of the sheer face, but it had long since ceased operations, back in the nineteen-fifties. The roof had collapsed. Re-opening was deemed to be uneconomic. Beyond the cliffs an overgrown footpath, continued over a pass, eastward through the mountain range. After that, Darke guessed, it met the Olulopo River, that marked Kwazania's eastern border. It was believed to be part of the ancient Arab slave routes that led beyond the river, through the Republic of Nambria, to the coast.

As they began to traverse the front of the cliffs, the men on the outside of the truck dropped off at intervals, to join other KAPU men who appeared to have been waiting on their arrival. At the north end of the sheer face, Brogan brought the Landrover to a halt, there KAPU men unloaded the bullion boxes. At this point the track doubled back on itself, to climb gradually back across the rock face. Darke realised that Leitch and his men must have come this way from the border, on foot. It explained their lack of transport and must have been quite a feat for a relatively unfit Leitch. Darke reckoned it must have involved a march of a day and a half.

Brogan was left guarding the boxes with a repeating shotgun and an automatic pistol. Two of the KAPU men climbed into the rear of the Landrover to guard the prisoners as they continued along the upper track. Leitch drove the Landrover a few hundred yards before halting at a level area. He switched off the engine.

'The end of the road?' said Darke.

'Payback time,' said Leitch.

'Seems a lot of effort to go to, just to shoot us.'

'I dinna intend to shoot yer. In fact, you're free to get out the truck.' Leitch grinned and waved the barrel of his automatic, to give emphasis to his words.

The three of them climbed out into the heat of the day. The rock face was radiating the rays of the sun. Fortunately, a westerly breeze took away some of its intensity. Darke's heart leapt momentarily, when one of the KAPU guards appeared round the rear of the truck, wielding a wicked looking knife. However, he just indicated to Virginia to put her hands forward, when she did so he cut the rope from around her wrists. He did the same for Alison and finally Darke.

'What are you up to Leitch? Darke asked, rubbing the circulation back into his wrists.

'You'll find out soon enough. Just walk along the track.'

No one moved, until two KAPU men came at them viciously flaying the air with jamboks: whips of rhinoceros hide. Darke, shielding the women, pushed them before him up the track, in the direction the Scotsman indicated.

Leitch yelled after them, 'There are men posted all along the lower track. If you try and get to either end of the cliff, they have orders to shoot the women first.'

'What are you up to Leitch?'

'I told you. You'll find out soon enough.'

Darke thought of using the revolver, tucked into the waistband of his trousers, but that was pointless, they had nowhere to go. There were too many men lower down the slope. That was the only direction in which they could escape. Men and cliffs surrounded them. There was no advantage to be gained by using the revolver: he could not win. Reluctantly, he guided the two women ahead of him along the ascending track. After some fifty paces they stopped and looked back. Leitch had started the Landrover and was reversing it round. When it was at a right angle to the track, he selected forward gear, revved the engine, released the clutch and drove it straight onto a rock. The sound of grinding stone and screeching metal, indicated that serious damaged had been done.

Leitch climbed out and looked at the front wheels, which had been lifted off the ground by the impact. He raised the bonnet, climbed onto the front bumper to reach inside the engine compartment. They watched in fascination. The Scotsman was bending down fiddling with something. He straightened up and jumped backwards. Suddenly flames leapt up from the engine, rapidly engulfing the rest of the vehicle. Leitch ran off down the track, behind the two KAPU figures, yelling as he went. His words were lost in the roar from the flaming truck. It was difficult for them to see the three retreating men, as the air between them was shimmering wildly from the heat generated by the flames.

Whatever Leitch had yelled seemed to galvanise the line of KAPU men, stationed at intervals along the lower track, into action. They began darting back and forth. It was hard to deduce what was happening, until they saw the flickering, orange flames. Horrified the women gasped, and Darke swore. In no time, a blazing fire, leaping and crackling, extended from one end of the Muzindi Cliffs to the other, beneath a curtain of shimmering air.

'He means to burn us alive.' Virginia's eyes were wide with fear.

Alison was obviously upset as she looked towards Darke. 'We must do something, Luke.'

'Yeah, but what.' He thought. He said out loud, with more confidence than he felt, 'Climb straight up to the base of the cliffs.'

It sounded as though he had a plan, but in truth he had none. He needed time to think. His knowledge of the area was meagre, having only visited it once before. The disused mine, he knew, was no use to them: the entrance had been sealed for safety. They kept climbing over the rough bush, until the ground began to level off. The going became easier. Here the cliffs seemed to rear up, high above them, leaning outwards as they rose. The rock face had a polished look. It was obvious, there was no way he could scale it. Let alone with Alison and Virginia. He called a halt to give their aching lungs a chance to recover.

The flames were not visible from where they stood, the slope had levelled out a hundred yards behind them, so they were out of view of the men below. On the breeze came the acrid smell of burning, accompanied by sporadic sounds of popping and crackling, as the moving line of flames consumed the tinder dry growth. Maybe it was his imagination, but, now and then, he felt additional heat being wafted towards them. To their left a slight rise of ground caught his eye. He left the women, telling them to wait. He ran, as best he could, to the outcrop. It was a smooth flat area of rock, almost level, one hundred feet wide by one hundred deep. An island of raised bare rock in a sea of bush. Close to the foot of the cliffs, rocks were piled up, where they had fallen over the years.

He called to the women and waved them over. As they approached, he said, 'The only chance we have is to use this rock as a base. It needs to be enlarged otherwise the flames will come too close and the heat and smoke will overwhelm us. We need to set fire to the area around here, before the main fire comes up, to create a bigger firebreak.'

'Will it work?' Alison asked, doubtfully.

'It might,' Virginia Easterton said. She looked back towards the unseen line of flames. 'It depends,' she had helped to fight bush fires when they had threatened Mount Muzindi, or neighbouring farms. 'Usually, you backburn to create a firebreak. It's important to control it carefully, otherwise it gets out of hand and becomes another bush fire, parallel to, and ahead of the first. Here we can let it run its course, until it reaches the foot of the cliffs. The problem is whether we have the time to burn this area before the main fire is upon us.'

Darke nodded, 'Yes, but we only have to run a short line of fire, fifty feet in front of the rock platform, extending it for fifty yards in each direction, beyond the width of the rocks. When we have completed the line, we retreat onto the rock platform. We then move to the base of the cliffs behind the rocks. Thereafter, all we can do is wait.'

It was a plan. They knew that only time would tell whether it would succeed. None of them had matches or a lighter. Darke instructed the two women to pull up handfuls of dry grass to twist into thick strands, to use as torches. He fashioned four for himself and left them to their task, to jog across the flat area towards the fire. On reaching the edge of the slope, he gauged the fire was almost up to the track they had recently left. It was difficult to judge how much time they had to implement their plan. Here and there smaller fires had sprung up, ahead of the main line of flames. Sparks, drawn up by the intense heat, had been thrown forward by the breeze. The track was not wide enough to hamper its advance for long.

The flames of the main fire were leaping fifteen feet into the air and advancing at a slow walking pace, aided by the slight breeze and the angle of the slope. It was all but impossible, to see beyond the roaring flames. If the KAPU men had not already left, they would be still on the lower track. Shielding his face as best he could, he moved down the hill, to a small advanced patch of burning bush. Darke lit his torch before being driven back by the heat and airborne embers. Sweat covered his entire body as he ran back to the comparative cool, of the higher slope. Looking back, he knew it was a race against time. The line of fire was already establishing itself across the upper track. Halfway back to the plateau of rock, he transferred the flames to the second torch, before continuing as best he could over the rough ground, towards the cliffs.

Virginia realised he was exhausted, as he came up to the two women. She signalled to him, to throw the torch to the ground, amid the newly pulled grass, which immediately flared up. Gasping for air and holding his side, Darke watched as the two women, carrying lit torches, touched them to the tufts of coarse grass until they ignited. They set off together, starting a line of small fires, from a point, fifty feet forward of their rock sanctuary. Still panting for air, Darke turned to look out from the cliffs. To his dismay he could see the tops of flames showing above the edge of the plateau. The fire had progressed more rapidly up the slope than he had anticipated. He set off in the opposite direction to the two women, extending the new fire line with a series of small conflagrations, that would soon grow and join together.

Alison and Virginia had finished their series of fires, which rapidly expanded into a single line. The flames grew fiercer, forcing them to back away. Darke finished his line and re-joined them. They were driven back by their line of fire. Darke looked anxiously at the main fire, which was now entirely visible, as it edged onto the plateau. He judged, from the rate at which it had climbed the slope, the flames would be upon them in minutes. The heat from the new fire line was building, sucking the oxygen from the air. The three of them were coughing. The smoke and embers from the two lines of flames was combining above them and bending towards the cliff face, high above their heads. Sunlight was almost filtered out, leaving a gloom lit by the flames alone. Glowing cinders were falling about them as they retreated before the new blaze onto the granite platform. When the fire line met the front of the rock platform, it died. The divided blaze began to spread round each side of their hoped-for sanctuary. Alison was using her scarf to cover her mouth. Darke helped Virginia to tear the sleeve from her shirt and he used his handkerchief to breathe through.

'Time to take cover,' Darke croaked, as he slapped at a smouldering patch on his shirt, where a glowing cinder had alighted. His throat was parched from smoke and lack of saliva. Rising heat and black dust, were taking a heavy toll on the three of them. He began coughing uncontrollably as smoke caught in his dry throat. His lungs felt raw from his recent exertions. The women were similarly suffering. With a great effort he quelled the retching spasms, which sapped his strength. Moving quickly, he led the way to the rear of the outcrop. The heat was intense. He turned as he reached the granite wall to check on the women.

Alison was behind him. 'Look,' she yelled, pointing downwards.

Darke did not need her to tell him. He felt the pain. The bottom of his right trouser leg had been smouldering and had now ignited. He beat at it with his hands until the flame went out. Both women stood looking at him, arms hanging limply at their sides, completely exhausted. The overhanging cliffs masked what little sunlight filtered through the rising pall of smoke. Orange light from the dancing flames, gave the scene an ominously theatrical glow.

At the base of the cliff, they took shelter behind fallen boulders. Their heads were pounding, hot, fire-dried air did nothing to relieve tormented lungs, as they lay back gasping. The sound of the hungry flames changed as the main line of fire came to the edge of their newly burnt firebreak. It was dying out, well to the front of their stone haven, but continued to rage down each side of the newly burnt areas. It sounded as though they were in a vast tunnel. The incessant roar echoed off the smooth rock face, punctuated with the continuous crackling and popping, as the curtain of flames moved around their refuge. They could feel the radiated heat coming at them from the flames, reflected back off the cliff face. Darke had no idea how much hotter it might get, or how unbearable. He used his penknife to cut three buttons from his shirt. He sucked on one and handed the other two to the women, indicating that they should do the same. It helped produce some saliva, but he knew they could not last much longer.

Darke checked the revolver in his waistband. He had put the thought to the back of his mind, but he knew soon, he may have to use it on the two women, rather than see them die in agony. When would he do it? Who would he shoot first? He decided he would know when the time came. They would become distressed, so when he could bear it no longer, he would have to use the gun. At close range he should be able to execute two rapid head shots, for the women. Check they were dead, then finally a bullet for himself. It was a grim thought. He forced his mind to remain detached, devoid of emotion, it was the last thing he would be able to do for them. It would need to be done efficiently.

Time passed and the searing heat reached a peak, but failed to lessen. Sometime later, Darke realised he had briefly half fainted. He came round with a ringing in his ears and a pounding headache. The two women were faring no better, they were also in a state of semi-collapse. All they could do was endure. He kept dreaming of water, as his tongue grew uncomfortably large in his mouth.

After some time, he pulled himself upright; forcing himself to concentrate. The flames were no longer as high as they had been, they were losing their vigour, the continuous roar that had assailed their ears was lessening. In various levels of consciousness, they lay behind the fallen rocks, waiting as the heat about them gradually moderated. The light was changing. Numbly, Darke became aware of the decreasing temperature. He summoned the strength, once more, to raise himself above the level of the rocks.

The wall of flames, having reached the area they had burnt as a fire break, had died for want of fuel. The fire line had divided into two wings, north and south. Each had worked its way round the edges of their recently back-burnt area. The daylight was returning rapidly. The two sets of flames had reached the foot of the cliffs, leaving nothing to consume. Only patches of flickering flames were left, to devour the remaining denser tufts of bush. He watched in wonder as the flames quickly died, leaving wisps of smoke. Somehow, they had survived.

Shakily, cautiously, he pushed out from behind the protection of their hiding place. It was doubtful that Leitch or his men had waited to check they were dead. Anyone viewing the fire, from the track below, must believe nothing could have survived the flames. He hardly believed it himself. They had done so by the narrowest margin, aided by luck and their own ingenuity. The two women were fit and healthy. Both had done their equal share of work. If either of them had been less fit, none of them would have survived.

He checked for movement across the charred surface of the plateau. Only fronds of smoke rose from smouldering clumps of growth, close to the foot of the rock wall, otherwise all was still. Forcing his tired muscles to respond, he made his way out from the forward edge of the rock outcrop. He knelt to feel the ground through the black ash. It was still warm, but not sufficient to stop them leaving the protection of their rock platform. Bush fires, he knew, moved through the vegetation relatively quickly, doing a lot of superficial damage, but not raising the ground temperature long enough, to damage seeds or roots just below the surface. Within a day or two of the next rainfall, the devastated area would be alive with fresh growth.

He aroused Alison and Virginia from their semi-conscious state. They were suffering with dry mouths, as he was. Without complaint they rose, to stare in disbelief, as they surveyed the desolation, caused by the near-fatal fire. None of them could believe they had survived such an inferno. Fatigued as they were, they could not stop smiling.

Fifteen minutes later they had reached the rough track, at the cost of being covered in even more fine black dust, raised by their movements. They could taste it. It tormented their parched throats and had sort out every part of their anatomy. In the distance the remains of Virginia's burnt out Landrover lay wrecked and on its side, from the explosion of its fuel tank. There was no one to be seen. Leitch and his men had long since left, assuming, with some justification, that the three of them were consumed by the flames. He and his men would not have wanted to hang around for too long, for, even in such a remote area, the fire could have attracted attention from the sky. A light aircraft or helicopter reporting the whereabouts of an armed group, was the last thing they would want.

The three survivors dropped down to the lower track and trudged southward, along the unburnt trail. They were surrounded by a sea of black dust to their left. Eventually they reached the end of the cliffs, leaving the area of torched bush behind. Darke calculated, in their present condition, it would take them one-and-a-half hours, walking downhill, to bring them to Virginia's farm. But their priority was water. He led his two uncomplaining companions onto a barely discernible animal path, up a slight incline. The women were bone weary and moved like zombies. For ten minutes more they continued to make their way to the south until they heard the trickle of water. At the sound they looked up in disbelief. Moments later, over a slight rise, they spied a crystal-clear pool, forty feet across, fed by a silver shard of water, tumbling from a cavity in the rock face: a man's height above its surface.

A short while later Virginia asked, 'How did you know this was here.'

She was standing beneath the natural shower. They had removed their footwear, but otherwise were fully clothed luxuriating at the water's edge. The black dust had gone, washed away in the cool torrent. Alison and Darke sat on a convenient rock, allowing the heat to dry them and the clothes they were wearing. They had slaked their thirst in the crystal-clear, life-giving water. After their initial fill, they continued to sip from cupped hands, savouring it like vintage wine. The effects of the dehydrating heat were dissipating.

Darke pointed to a vertical slab of stone, in the shadow of a large overhang of rock, on the far side of the pool.

'There are bushmen paintings over there. I visited them once on patrol. Also, I knew it was used as the water supply by the silver mine, when it was operating. As it had existed for hundreds of years or more. I assumed it would still be here.'

Chapter 16

From altitude, familiar territory looks disturbingly different. It takes time to orientate oneself, to readjust from ground scale to air scale. Things look surprisingly close together from above. Hills merge into the landscape, and lose their significance. Only when the eye becomes accustomed to viewing terrain, from above, is it possible to accurately interpret the topography.

Sitting beside the pilot, as the Allouette helicopter rhythmically beat its way skyward from Mount Muzindi farm, Darke had no problem making out the area to the east. As a glider pilot he had been trained to constantly read the ground beneath his wings, always looking for potential landing sites, should he fail to find lift. In this case, when they rose two thousand feet above the farm, the Muzindi cliffs, with the blackened terrain before it, stood out immediately. As they flew nearer, the tracks were no longer overgrown. They stood out as sand-coloured scars through the blackened earth. The wrecked shell of Virginia Easterton's Landrover was clear to see, across the upper track, cremated by the flames.

It had taken the three of them, little more than ninety minutes to trudge back to the farm from the pool. They had bathed their aching limbs, slaked their thirst and rested for half-an-hour. It did much to rejuvenate them physically from the effect of the fire. It reinforced their determination to turn the tables on Leitch and his men. Virginia was the worst affected by the journey, with blisters on both her feet. Her fortitude to keep going had not held them up. Indeed, they had not known of her suffering until she finally removed her shoes at the farm, to reveal her bloodied heels.

An ice-cold orange juice, his third, sat on the side table as Darke telephoned Police District Headquarters in Fort Albert, to speak with Elias Kufanu. The Superintendent listened carefully to Darke's report of the kidnap and attempted triple murder.

Once, he heard that Leitch was based across the border and was funding the operations of KAPU, he interrupted Darke.

'That'll do nicely, just hold the line, Luke.' He was gone for five minutes before returning, to say, 'Luke, there's an army border patrol helicopter being diverted to you. You know what he'll need. He should be with you inside thirty minutes. The pilot will pick you up and follow your instructions. We don't want to frighten Leitch, so keep your distance, but if you can locate him before sunset, it will give us a better chance tomorrow. I'll be with you in a couple of hours.'

Darke had hardly finished lighting a fire and organising a makeshift "H", of stones, to mark the temporary landing zone, when he heard the distinctive beat of a helicopter approaching. He gave the signal to the two farm hands to feed the fire with green vegetation, to produce smoke. The pilot would use the plume to indicate wind speed and direction, to aid his landing approach. Standing back, he watched the Allouette helicopter, a French built machine, circle and drop onto the zone. He waved to the women on the veranda, before stooping and moving to the empty passenger's seat. The pilot grinned, shook hands, yelled something, rendered unintelligible by the noise of the rotors, and handed him a set of earphones with microphone attached.

An hour later, in the rapidly fading light, they landed back at Muzindi Farm. It had not been a difficult task to spot the twenty men, from the air. There was only one route through the mountains, it barely deserved its description as a path. The experienced pilot used his skill to fly behind the hills, careful to avoid alerting Leitch's men. It was simple enough to penetrate deep in the mountains, land in a neighbouring valley, which allowed Darke to climb his way to a vantage point. From there he could survey the old Arab slaver's route that led to the border.

The army binoculars showed minute figures toiling their way towards him, from the western end of the valley. Their progress was slow, hampered by the terrain and the burden of the six heavy boxes of gold coins. It was evident they would have to stop soon, to make camp before nightfall. It would not be safe to travel over such a precarious path after dark. He watched them struggle on as he marked their position on the pilot's map.

'I don't see why he didn't just shoot us at the knoll, why take us up to the cliffs and go through all the elaborate business with the fire?' Alison looked at Darke and Elias Kufanu in turn.

The Police Superintendent was standing before the fire in the farm's large sitting room. He looked across at Darke, who gave a slight nod to indicate that Kufanu should answer the question. He explained, 'Leitch wanted your deaths to appear accidental. If you'd been murdered, or disappeared, we'd have suspected he was behind it. The last thing he wanted, was to give a reason for the authorities to think he was likely to be somewhere in the area. That would have stirred up a hornet's nest for him, as indeed it has done. He's obviously hiding across the border and the last thing he wants, is for anyone to suspect he's there.'

Alison shivered. 'It's a sobering thought to realise someone has planned your death.'

'I have enough men guarding this house for you to be able to sleep safely tonight,' he said reassuringly, 'hopefully by tomorrow our Mister Leitch will have other things to think about. Anyway, he thinks you're dead.'

'What about tomorrow?' Darke asked.

Kufanu turned to him. 'As soon as you told me Leitch was operating from across the Olulopo River in Nambria and financing KAPU, I knew we'd have all the help we needed. For months the army has been probing across the border, further to the north of here, looking for the KAPU base without success. They've obviously been looking too far north. The problem is its wild dense bush on the other side of the river. Whilst the Nambrians tolerate low level incursions, into their uninhabited north western region, they are likely to take exception to a full-scale invasion, or even unauthorised aircraft overflying their territory.'

'Will they give permission now, do you think?'

'Haven't done so in the past. The problem is, we are a democratic monarchy, they're a one-party Republic. In effect a dictatorship. We're ideologically miles apart. We get on well enough: they need our cheap coal; we need their rail access to the sea. However, they cannot afford to be seen actively aiding a monarchical system, against so called "freedom fighters". It would be a betrayal of their political ideology. In reality there hasn't been much love lost between Nambria and KAPU, even in the pre-independence days.'

'We mustn't let Leitch escape. If he slips through our fingers, God knows when we'll find him again.' Darke's mood had been changing as they spoke, from optimism to bleak pessimism at the thought of letting the Scotsman escape, yet again.

'Everything that can be done is being done, Luke. There is every chance we'll get him tomorrow.' Kufanu stooped and picked up a grey holdall and handed it to Darke. 'To make things official, you are now a Chief Inspector in the Police Reserve. With your background it's the simplest solution. As you will appreciate, we can't have armed civilians wandering around in an operational area. The uniform should fit.'

The army arrived at three in the morning. First, four ten-ton trucks ground their way up the escarpment to the farm, making heavy going of the bends. They were shortly followed by a Westland Whirlwind helicopter, as a replacement for the smaller Allouette. Darke was dragged out of a deep slumber by Kufanu, who had not slept. He had spent the night checking on the armed police and army personnel, guarding the house.

Kufanu just said, 'They've arrived.'

Darke grunted and shook the sleep from his brain. His throat felt raw, his body was stiff from the previous day's ordeal. By the time he had dressed in his new khaki uniform, with the three silver pips on each shoulder, the dining room had been turned into a temporary operations room.

The Allouette pilot, standing in front of a map of the area, was briefing a Major and Captain of the Royal Kwazanian Rifles. The two officers had flown in with the larger helicopter, to take charge of the operation. The Major was medium height, thickset with an aura of boundless energy. The Captain was an inch or two taller, slimmer, and more reserved. They obviously knew each other well. Both were dressed in camouflage uniforms. Their characteristic dull red berets, the colour of the soil covering large swathes of Kwazania, were folded and tucked under their left epaulettes. When the pilot had finished his briefing, the Major turned and introduced himself and Captain Paradzai.

He smiled readily, saying, 'You've had a lucky escape Chief Inspector, mostly of your own making, I hear. Congratulations.'

Major Jubal Abumi's clipped accent and manner, stamped him as Sandhurst trained, Darke decided, as they firmly shook hands. He was able to pinpoint, on the map, the position where he had last seen Leitch and the KAPU fighters.

Superintendent Kufanu, having handed over responsibility to Abumi, remained to liaise with the army.

The Rifle Regiment Major tapped the map, with his pencil, before speaking, 'Twenty men moving along the steep-sided valley in difficult terrain. We have two choices: one, ambush and destroy this unit somewhere between their present position and the river; two, track their progress and locate their base over the border, with the object of destroying KAPU in its entirety, once and for all.'

Abumi had reduced the problem to its simplest terms. Put that way, Darke thought that Leitch's prospects looked bleak.

'What are the chances of taking them alive?' Kufanu knew the answer. As a police officer, trained to apprehend suspects with minimum force, he felt obliged to explore the possibility.

Major Abumi considered for a moment, before replying, 'If we were operating in open terrain with plenty of time to set up the ambush, I would say the chances were good. The majority could be persuaded to lay down their weapons and surrender, with a minimum loss of life. But here,' he looked at the map, 'we are operating in mountainous terrain with little time to prepare. To attempt to capture them all alive, is not a practical proposition. It would put the lives of my men at greater risk. Also, it is still likely to result in an all-out firefight, with much of our advantage thrown away. Frankly it's not an option.'

Kufanu nodded his understanding.

Abumi continued, 'It's very tempting to try to locate the base camp, but the risk is too great that they would spot us and escape. From the information you have given, in this target group we have the top man, the leader and banker as it were. To eliminate him will seriously undermine KAPU's ability to function, so we must take the opportunity to neutralise him whilst we can.' He issued orders to Captain Paradzai, before turning back to the two policemen, 'My orders are to take prisoners for interrogation, if possible. If not, then "take them out".'

It transpired that an eighteen-man detachment was being formed, from army and police anti-terrorist units, based further north in the Hundi Valley. They were instructed to cross to the Olulopo, move down stream, using inflatable craft, powered by outboard motors, to where the river meets the eastern end of the old slave trail. They were ordered to attack and destroy any KAPU units, guarding the boats. They would then proceed westward up the trail to set up an ambush, for the returning KAPU unit, at the eastern end of the valley. They were designated “River Force”. A detachment from the farm, known as “Alpha Force” was to leave immediately, under Captain Paradzai, to follow the trail from the western end, to complete the trap.

The Major, with a radio signaller and two Rifles, was designated “Control”. He planned to follow Darke’s example, of the previous evening, and fly to a neighbouring valley to the North of the slave trail and climb to an observation point overlooking the trail. From this position he would co-ordinate the other units and monitor the progress of Leitch and his men.

Major Abumi invited Kufanu and Darke to join him. The two men readily agreed. Outside the farmhouse the army logistics unit had come and gone. They had left a detachment to guard the aviation fuel, ammunition, petrol and supplies, not immediately needed for the current task. It was strange, Darke noted, for the smell of the eucalyptus trees to be overwhelmed by diesel fumes and to see the tranquil surroundings of Mount Muzindi farm, transformed into a makeshift army camp. The big Sikorsky helicopter was warmed up and waiting for them on the lawn.

Chapter 17

Careful not to let sunlight reflect of the lens of his binoculars, Darke scoured the length of the valley below him. The others lay beside him on the ridge to the north of the old slave trail, with the bright morning rays already warm on their backs. The early morning sun had yet to penetrate deep into the valley. The shadows were slipping steadily down the flank of the valley opposite. Within minutes the primitive trail, running lengthwise along the gorge and halfway down its southern slope, was revealed in the clear morning light. Searching its route from the west, he spotted movement.

'There,' Darke whispered huskily, pointing at the torturous path, almost directly opposite their position. Leitch and his men had covered far more ground than he would have thought possible.

Major Abumi, at his side, swung his heavy glasses in the direction Darke had indicated. 'Blast,' he said, 'they've moved quicker than we expected.'

'Yes, they're not carrying the boxes of gold, so they've made better progress,' Darke muttered, 'They must have hidden them, with the object of returning for them later. Where does that put your two units Major?'

Unexpectedly Abumi grinned. 'That's the first thing you learn in the army, nothing goes according to plan.'

He slid down the slope before standing and conferring with his signaller. In a quiet tone he radioed River Force, to discover their position was two miles upstream from their objective. They expected to be at the landing point within fifteen minutes. Kufanu and Darke were carefully searching the rocky trail, from west to east, through their binoculars. The only movement came from Leitch's party. Alpha Force was not expected to cross over the pass into the valley for another ten minutes.

The KAPU men were making much better progress than the night before, unencumbered by the gold, however the path was rough and little used. Its meandering route mainly descended from the pass they had crossed the previous night. Occasionally the route climbed briefly to negotiate the topography it met along its way. On their left was a two-hundred-foot drop, down to the narrow river that tumbled along its floor. It kept their attention on the path, allowing little time to scour the ridge tops, for any unlikely opposition. They were giving no indication they were aware of being observed.

Abumi estimated it would take twenty minutes for Leitch's party to reach the east end of the valley. It would bring them to a position less than a quarter of a mile from the Olulopo. River Force would have to move quickly to climb from the river to set up an ambush. It was going to be a race.

The Major slid into position between Kufanu and Darke to survey the progress of Leitch's men. 'It all depends on how many men he has guarding the boats by the river,' he said, 'Any gunfire will warn this lot and it'll become messy.' He studied the progress of the fourteen men, then continued, 'I've ordered River Force to report when they're in place. If we don't hear from them, it'll mean they're not ready. In that case we'll fire on these chaps, before they reach the end of the valley. That'll warn River Force they're coming and distract Leitch and his men as they head for the river. I doubt they'll want to stop to find out who's shooting at them from behind. They will be too busy making for their boats. That should make things a little easier for the ambush team.' He checked the progress of Leitch's men on the footpath, before continuing, 'We will move along behind this ridge, to a position above the east end of the valley.'

Abumi briefly spoke with his three men, then led off, keeping below the ridge, out of sight of the KAPU band. The going was slow over the scree that littered the eroding ridge. There was little soil and minimal vegetation. Over millions of years wind and weather had slowly ground down these mountains, from sharp peaks to rounded ridges. Much of the resultant dust and debris had blown away, or washed to the valley floor by rain to be swept into the Olulopo River and eventually out to the Indian Ocean.

After ten minutes the Major called a halt, to climb to the ridge top to check their progress, against that of their quarry. Satisfied, he descended and led them further east. When they had marched for fifteen minutes, he stopped and checked again. 'This'll do fine. We have a good view and field of fire.'

Darke and Kufanu followed Abumi as he climbed back to the top of the ridge. Below, Leitch and Brogan were sandwiched between the KAPU fighters. The KAPU leader and five men were in front, with the remainder bringing up the rear. The path had descended to a height of fifty feet above the tumbling river. Here the terrain was becoming more level, with large loose rocks strewn about, as though ancient glacial movements had pushed a giant pile of debris into the lowest, narrowest, part of the valley. Scrub and the occasional gnarled tree patterned the rockscape below. Leitch and his men were coming close to the end of the valley. The path, at this point, wound its way between the collection of huge stones, before dropping down, out of sight, on its way to the river.

Major Abumi was instructing the two riflemen, 'Wait for the order, aim for the leading men, but keep an eye on Leitch and Brogan, the two Europeans, in the centre, they must not escape back up the valley.' He turned to the signaller positioned fifteen feet below. 'Anything from River Force?' He inquired.

'Just static, sir.' To emphasise the point, he took the earphone from his ears: in the still air the static hiss could be heard by all.

Time was running out. Abumi grunted irritably, 'Call River Force, tell them the KAPU unit is about to leave the valley and head for the river. We will open fire in one minute.'

Before the signaller could transmit, distant bursts of gunfire came from the direction of the river. The Major breathed a sigh of relief. In the valley Leitch's men had stopped at the sound. Leitch moved first, pushing past the men ahead, with Brogan at his heels, making for the front of the line.

'Open fire,' Abumi ordered, as he dropped to a prone position, sighting his SLR down at the path.

The two Riflemen triggered two shots each to test the range and angle. The leading KAPU man went down with the first volley. One of the riflemen at least had judged the distance and angle perfectly. The entire party instinctively turned as one, to look across the valley from where the new threat came. They were momentarily frozen in their actions, until Leitch yelled at them to follow him. Darke shouldered his police SLR. Unlike the army rifles the police models were regulated to fire single shots only. He fired two quick rounds at Leitch. The Scotsman was too quick for him, or Darke had not aimed low enough, to make the correct allowance for a downhill shot. Leitch disappeared behind a large rock. He could only be glimpsed waving at the KAPU men, instructing them to run the gauntlet and make for the river. The two riflemen and the Major sprayed the line with automatic fire. In spite of Leitch's instructions most of his men wisely sought the nearest cover and stayed where they were. The leading KAPU man and two others lay unmoving, where they had fallen.

'Single shot,' called Abumi, above the sharp crackle of volleys, 'make your ammunition count.'

They kept up a steady rate of accurate fire. Darke and Kufanu were not strangers to the Self-Loading Rifle. They had both used them frequently on their annual visits to the police rifle range. Darke was only interested in one target. Whenever he spied any part of Leitch he fired, but his quarry was careful to use his cover well, whilst yelling orders to his men, who were beginning to recover their wits. One by one they began to return fire, causing the riflemen, Kufanu and Darke to use more cover. It slowed their rate of fire. This in turn gave the KAPU unit more opportunity to dart from cover to cover, to make their way towards the final bend in the path, which would take them out of sight. One more KAPU man went down just as he came up to the rock shielding Leitch. The camouflage clad figure sprawled headlong at his feet. Leitch stooped and took up the fallen man's Kalashnikov. He could be seen dragging the man halfway behind his rock cover. From time to time the wounded man's leg moved feebly. Unconcerned Leitch stripped him of his ammunition pouches, before using the man's weapon to return fire.

Abumi rolled over and slid down from the top of the ridge as he yelled to his signaller, 'Where's River Force, Corporal?'

'They're engaging six of the enemy at the river. Two enemy down. One minor casualty. A squad has landed to outflank the remainder. Lieutenant Kufa expects to advance within ten minutes.'

'Warn him a force of up to fifteen men are heading down the path, towards the river from the end of the valley. Radio the helicopter to find and ferry as many men as he can carry, from Alpha force. Tell him to bring them to this end of the valley, opposite our position and above the KAPU force. Tell him, when he's done that, to come and collect us. Got it?'

The signaller yelled his confirmation and turned back to his radio set. The Major returned to his firing position for a further five minutes, to continue firing whenever a target presented itself. By the time the last KAPU man ran the gauntlet and disappeared out of the valley, another of their number was down and lying motionless. In the still air their ears rang with the after effects of the firefight. Even so they were aware that the sounds of battle from the river had stopped, signifying that the opposition there had been overcome. Leitch and Brogan had sent their men on ahead, whilst they gave covering fire. Finally, they both managed to slip away.

'Now they're out of the valley they're in less of a trap,' the Major announced, 'Unless we can get Alpha force forward, they could escape to the north or south, as River Force advances towards us.'

It seemed longer, but it was only five minutes, before the rhythmic beat of its rotors announced the arrival of the Westland helicopter. It flew below hill height along the length of the valley, before it climbed, slowed and hovered above the ridge opposite them. It disgorged eight men before rotating a quarter turn and heading straight for them.

As they climbed aboard the Major donned a headset and microphone, to give his instructions to the pilot. The Helicopter sped back, over the detached Alpha force men, who were rapidly clambering down to the path, to follow in the tracks of their quarry. The Major waved to Captain Paradzai, as they headed for the river, which was clearly visible and close by, from the air. The machine banked and began to circle above the sun-baked terrain. Here eroded rock particles, blown down over millennia, from the mountains above, had migrated into every nook and cranny, to foster life in the form of sparse grass and gnarled shrubs. Aloes with colourful flowers clung to sheltered rock crevasses.

It took time to spot the enemy. Only if they moved or turned their faces skyward did they stand out. Lying prone, as most of them were, their camouflage uniforms were very effective, in allowing them to blend with their surroundings. A section of River Force was exchanging fire, in the area of the ancient track, pinning down some of the KAPU unit. The remaining men of River Force were fanning out, into a pincer movement round each flank. Here and there a grenade exploded. Time was running out for the KAPU fighters. They were clearly uncertain of the size of opposition they were up against. They had no idea they were about to be surrounded, let alone what to do. They were leaderless.

Darke yelled to Kufanu, who was sitting next to him, 'Where's Leitch?'

The big man pursed his lips and shook his head, his eyes never wavered from scanning the terrain beneath. Major Abumi randomly sprayed the bush with bursts from his SLR. Suddenly five faces turned skywards revealing their positions. Simultaneously the six men from Alpha Force, led by Captain Paradzai, opened fire from behind. The trapped men quickly understood they were surrounded. They realised that to continue the fight would mean certain injury or death. Within a moment the first man surrendered. He was called forward, without his weapon, with hands raised. The rest soon followed, in a similar fashion. Only one man retained his weapon and that he used as a crutch. He limped along the path dragging an injured leg, that left a blackening trail of blood in the dust. There was no sign of Leitch or Brogan.

The helicopter spent half-an-hour carefully searching an ever-widening area of bush, rock clusters, cliffs and gullies, without results. The area was peppered with caves and hiding places. The two men had vanished.

Major Abumi yelled over the engine noise, 'We could spend days searching this terrain and still not do a thorough job.'

The others grimly nodded in agreement.

The Major added, 'We're getting low on fuel. I'm afraid we must return to base.'

Fifteen minutes later the helicopter touched down at Mount Muzindi. The farm was rapidly taking on the air of an established army camp. Virginia was packing to take up residence, at the Leopard Pass Hotel, for a few days. There was little she could do whilst the army was occupying the farmhouse.

'Only get in the way,' as she put it to Alison.

It was clear the army was not going to be leaving for some days, the two women were deciding whether to make a trip to the capital, Umbaka, with Samanca Kufanu.

Major Abumi considered his task to be incomplete without making an effort to capture Leitch. After fruitless airborne searches through the day, orders were given to River Force to camp by the Olulopo, with those men of Alpha Force who had been flown forward in support. They were instructed to make a sweep on the west bank of the river, to the north and south of the ancient track, at first light. It was hoped they might pick up the trail of Leitch and Brogan. The balance of Alpha force was to return the following day, bringing their prisoners for interrogation. They would recover the gold along the way.

In the distance, towards the knoll, the helicopter pilot and mechanic were checking their machine, preparing it for operations the following day. Darke, Kufanu and Major Abumi walked up the veranda steps, to be greeted with cool beers, served by Alison and Virginia. The Major took a long pull at the chilled contents of the glass, with obvious delight. He excused himself, to make his way to the dining room, where all the maps were set up, to plan the next day's tasks. Darke and Kufanu gave the women a subdued account of the day's operations. The good news that the gold would be recovered, with the aid of the KAPU prisoners, was overshadowed by the disappointment felt at the escape of Leitch and Brogan.

Alison had been sitting on the edge of her seat becoming more agitated as their account unfolded, eventually she could contain her excitement no longer.

'We may have something that might help.' She looked at Virginia who was obviously in agreement and said, 'You'd better tell it.'

Virginia Easterton nodded. 'One of the women, who lives on the farm, came to see me this morning. Some years ago, her husband was forced to help Sandy Leitch build up drug contacts, along the border. Leitch had picked on her husband because he had caught him selling dagga, to the farm workers. He threatened to tell my father and have him dismissed. Also, through the local witch doctor, he threatened him with dire consequences if he didn't cooperate. Her husband believed the threats. He was terrified of the witch doctor. The plan was for Leitch to develop marijuana plantations, hidden in the mountains, apparently close by the Olulopo River. Her husband, fearful of Leitch, became depressed at being forced to help, which she believes was a major reason for his suicide.'

'What's her name,' asked Darke.

'Hanna Mugwani.'

'Petrol Mugwani's wife?' asked Elias Kufanu, with interest.

'That's right,' Virginia said, 'she hates and fears Leitch, blaming him for the death of her husband. She has been too frightened to come forward before, for fear of what he would do to her. She heard he had tried to kill us.' She smiled. 'Through the "bush telegraph," I suppose. When she saw the army was after him, she resolved to come and tell us her story.'

Superintendent Kufanu stood up, 'We need to talk to this woman.' He called for a constable and issued an order to bring her to the house.

It proved to be a timely instruction, for Hanna Mugwani, having packed her belongings, was about to leave the farm when the policeman found her. She had heard that the army had failed to capture Leitch. She was afraid he would find out she had talked and take revenge. Cross examined by the two policemen, she began to relax and tell what she knew.

Darke had not understood, when he first met Leitch, that he had been staying at Muzindi on and off for a month. In that time, through Petrol Mugwani, he had established contact with various growers of marijuana. When

Lew Bodell had believed Leitch was away, visiting other parts of the country, he was in fact just a few miles to the east, building the basis of his illegal drug business. Hanna Mugwani said her husband had explained to her where Leitch's base was located, but she had never visited it herself. All she knew was that it was in a remote area, on the Olulopo side of the Muzindi mountains, to the south of the old slave route. She described it as a high valley. Within a year or two Leitch joined with KAPU and had located its base across the Olulopo further south, to its present position, so that they might better avoid the army units searching for them in the north. She was unsure whether the marihuana plantations, were still operating.

The Superintendent turned to Darke and said, 'What do you think?'

'He's a man who likes his bolt holes. Where else is he likely to go? He could have reserves hidden there, in case of an emergency. In his line of work, it makes sense. It's worth a try.'

Major Abumi listened carefully to their account of Hanna Mugwani's story, before turning to the large map spread out on the dining table.

Kufanu leant over the map to circle an area with his finger. He said, 'If it's suitable for growing quantities of cannabis. It must be at a lower altitude and facing north. That means it must be here, north and east of Muzindi Mountain.'

They all nodded in agreement.

He continued, 'It will need a good supply of water, but then there's lots of water coming of these hills in all directions.'

Major Abumi spoke, 'At first light we'll use the "chopper", to search the area thoroughly. Searching for a hidden valley should be a lot easier than searching for two men.'

Chapter 18

Above the beat of the rotor blades and the roar of the engine, Abumi's voice could be heard through the headphones. He instructed the pilot to stay high, once they had crossed to the far side of the Muzindi mountain range. The acute angle of the sun picked out the prominent geographical features, leaving the rest in shadow. Many valleys were defined in sharp relief, but most of those that could be seen, supported little vegetation. In the distance, much further to the south of Muzindi Mountain, great rolling swathes of fir trees, shaded the lower slopes; they were planted in wide sections by Kwazania's Forestry Development Authority.

Major Abumi had ordered the helicopter to execute a search pattern of the most likely area, to the east of the mountains, due north of Mount Muzindi. Several possible valleys were identified from height. As the higher altitude reduced the performance of the helicopter, they had taken off with one pilot and the Major in the co-pilot's seat. The other five RKR men with Kufanu and Darke, occupied the main cabin.

The major, having briefed them beforehand, said, 'If we identify a potential valley we will drop down and enter it low and fast, in case of ground fire. We won't have much time to check each one out, keep your eyes open as we make our pass. If you see something get a fix on it, so that you can quickly locate the position again.'

By accident, twenty-five minutes into the flight, they found what they were looking for: it was less of a valley, more of a bowl. It was not one of the locations previously identified on the map. They had exited a possible location to move to another, when Elias Kufanu spotted movement. It was at the end of a low ridge, overlooking the Olulopo, beside a small lake cradled in a deep bowl-shaped depression. It was a sun trap, about a quarter of a mile in diameter, where stunted trees and shrubs grew in profusion. A narrow portion of the eastern lip of the bowl had worn away, allowing the lake, by the way of a waterfall, an access to the river below. What could be marijuana plants were scattered about randomly, as natural growth, to avoid drawing attention to the plantation.

The Superintendent called over the intercom to the Major to report movement. The Major gave instructions to the pilot, who banked the Whirlwind steeply, turning towards the lake.

They could see a group of people, gathered at the edge of the water, close to some rocks. The group, at the sound of the helicopter, had thrown themselves to the ground. As the helicopter drew closer, the camouflage uniforms could be made out, only because they knew where to look. They passed overhead and turned to their right, back onto a reciprocal course and directly into the line of tracer bullets, curving slowly out from the rocks over which they had flown. The Whirlwind's nose came up when the tracers hit, it spun round at an awkward angle, dropping sideways towards the ground, its movements powerfully erratic. Darke realised the machine lacked the height necessary to switch to autorotation; its only means of a soft landing.

'Tighten your harnesses,' he yelled to the others. His stomach lurched as the adrenalin burst into his system. He braced for the impact. Through the open side door, the ground was sliding up towards them, with deadly speed. Just in time the pilot gained a measure of control. The nose swung round in the direction of flight, allowing the helicopter to flare out from its dive, presenting its rotor blades, at a ninety-degree angle to their line of descent. The manoeuvre briefly trapped a cushion of air beneath the whirring blades. The speed of the descent decelerated with a jolt. Darke felt the effect as his spine compressed. Both arms had been raised to protect him from the impact. They became instantly four times their normal weight, slamming down into his lap, with the force of a heavyweight blow, his head sagged violently into his shoulders.

The discomfort was momentary as the downward momentum fell away. The helicopter seemed to hang briefly, fifteen feet above the uneven ground, before falling vertically, towards the ground, once more out of control. A rotor blade scythed into a tree jolting the airframe, swinging it wildly off to starboard. It struck the ground at a shallow angle, reducing the shock of the impact. The fuselage jolted over to one side, but the rotor blades continued to hack through the trees, buckling as they did so, but keeping the cabin more or less upright.

A series of shudders ran through the machine, like the death throes of a mechanical beast. Darke's straps held, but others were thrown about in the cabin, or out through the open doorway. The kaleidoscopic scene, accompanied by the screech of buckling metal, appeared before him, as though he were an observer, detached from reality. The slewing and wrenching of his body, jerked him out of his mesmerised state. The dying, flying machine swirled to a halt amidst the chaos of bodies, twisted metal, broken trees and undergrowth. His overloaded mind fought to think coherently, through the confusion and panic that was overwhelming him.

He felt the surge of adrenaline as he tried to throw himself out through the opening. He wanted desperately to get clear of the stricken helicopter, but he had forgotten to undo his straps. The jolt from the restraining harness, forced a measure of sense into his confused brain. He paused briefly and took a deep breath to force his mind to think. Fire was the greatest threat. Clear everyone from the wreck. Also, they would be useless and in almost as much danger, if they were unarmed. Beside him Elias was shaking his head obviously similarly affected.

'Rifles,' yelled Darke, unclipping his harness and taking his self-loading rifle from the rack on the twisted bulkhead.

Kufanu, still dazed, nodded and signalled Darke to lead out through the door. He was aware that a rifleman had been thrown out of the opening as they hit the ground and noticed the forward bulkhead, behind the pilot, was seriously damaged as he threw himself through the opening.

He rolled as he hit the ground, picked himself up and headed, groggily, for a line of long grass. He stopped and faced back towards the wreckage of the Whirlwind. Kufanu, who was close behind him, did the same. There was a loud 'whumph', heard above the ringing in their ears, as the fuel tank burst into flames. Darke shielded his face from the searing heat and turned away. He ran along the line of the tall grass. At a safe distance he turned to look back. There was no sign of life. He nudged Kufanu's arm. Both turned away from the burning wreck, to see a line of KAPU men, emerging from the tall grass with weapons aimed directly at them.

The best time to escape is immediately following capture, before the guards are into an effective routine. Darke had read this in a book. It made sense, but in this instance, it was not so easily done. The KAPU unit was six men strong. They collected their rifles, tied their hands behind their backs, searched their pockets, before leading them away through the bush. "It is depressing to be captured," the book had said. He certainly felt depressed and demoralised. Looking at Elias Kufanu he could see, by his expression, he felt the same way. He supposed he should be encouraged that these KAPU men had not killed them out of hand. He was also sure that once they met up with Leitch, they would not live long. The time for subterfuge and the need for their deaths to appear accidental, was past. They would just be an encumbrance. Leitch had made it clear what little regard he had for the lives of others.

The entrance to the cave came as a surprise. It was hidden from view, until they were forced, at gunpoint, to push between the foliage at the base of a rock face. Bare light bulbs hanging from flex, draped along the side of the tunnel, lit their way downwards. The still air was thick with dust and heat. A short distance brought them to the head of a series of slopes and steps, meandering deep into the mountain. They veered sometimes left, sometimes to the right, as they kept descending ever deeper. Mostly the tunnel was natural, caused by fissures and faults in the rock. Occasionally, as necessary, the walls had been roughly widened by human hands. Steps had been crudely hewn on the steeper sections, along the route. Darke noticed the soot-stained rock above. The residue, he surmised of countless flaming torches, from centuries past; probably in the days of the Arab slavers.

Darke's theory was justified, as their descent flattened out, they entered a sizeable cavern. It was like a wide hall. The lighting was poor, but the air was cooler and they could feel the difference. They passed darkened doorways of cells hewn into the sides of the cave. They caught the scent of dank air as they passed by. There was daylight ahead. Their captors prodded them to move faster. They passed a lit chamber where uniformed figures were working amid wooden storage boxes. Around the walls were iron rings set into the rock about waist height, confirming his opinion that these were old slave cells. Another was lit, but unoccupied and equipped as a workshop. A heavy-duty cable ran from its doorway, in the direction they were moving; towards the daylight.

Their journey through the mountain had brought them down several hundred feet, almost to river level. As they stepped into the blinding daylight, Darke tripped and nearly fell down a narrow path. The cable from the empty workshop ended at a generator running noisily in the shadow of the cave's entrance. They continued their descent. Lush undergrowth grew to the edge of the path and in many places overhung it. The river was close by, for they heard the splashing of water, coming from a short distance below. They descended a combination of stone and wooden steps.

Abandoned tools here and there, of different types, indicated that some steps were still being repaired or re-enforced. The path brought them down, under overlapping camouflage nets, onto a crude wooden jetty. Involuntarily, in spite of the vicious prods from their guards, both Kufanu and Darke stopped. They gasped in amazement, for moored in front of them lay the familiar shape of the "Olulopo Princess", her white hull and superstructure stained and rusted from years of neglect. She looked enormous under the camouflage covers, draped around her funnel, from bow to stern. A mottled relic, sitting in dappled sunlight, filtering through olive drab cloth and netting.

The history of the hundred-and-twenty-foot Olulopo Princess, Darke knew, was in large part the history of Kwazaland. The river steamer had been constructed in sections, on the river Clyde, in eighteen-ninety-three. She was then disassembled and shipped from Glasgow to the mouth of the Olulopo River, on the East Coast of Africa. From there the sections were transported upriver on barges, to the Agani Falls in Kwazaland. Each piece was then transported overland, to a point above the Falls. There it was re-assembled at a temporary-built encampment. From the moment the Olulopo Trading Company took delivery of her, in eighteen-ninety-four and sailed her upriver to the growing settlement of Fort Albert, she played an integral part in the development and expansion of the colony.

Most of the imported freight to develop the colony was brought to a point above the Agani Falls, loaded onto the Princess and ferried to Fort Albert, either in her hold, or on her decks. Even after the railway line was completed from the coast to Fort Albert and further westward to Umbaka, she was needed to open up the northern region of the colony. Expeditions were mounted, from her wide deck, to the lower lying territories, beyond the northern escarpment, thereby circumventing the barrier of the Eastern Highlands. She was able to sail one hundred and eighty miles north of

Fort Albert, in two to four days depending on the load she carried, time of year and water level in the river. An overland journey would have taken several weeks, by wagon.

As time passed the need for the Princess's services increased, to serve the north's growing demands. Each year, following the end of the rainy season, the river level would drop, the current would slacken; no longer fed by the seasonal rainfall. Her powerful wood burning twin steam engines, housed in her ample twenty-three-foot beam, would be used to full effect, towing barges upstream. She carried heavy machinery and building materials, to serve the needs of the burgeoning northern population. Her heyday lasted until the nineteen-fifties, when metalled roads were constructed down into the extensive northern valley, to accelerate the final development of the region.

After that the Princess still plied her trade, relying increasingly on locals and visitors to the area, to replace the reduction in freight. Darke, like many in the colony, had sailed on her, in the sixties. He remembered his trips with fondness, but her time had passed and her days were numbered. The Princess's final owners could only offer competitive freight rates by not spending money on her maintenance. In nineteen seventy-two, fifty miles north of Fort Albert, having struck an underwater obstacle, she sprang a leak. Her poorly maintained pumps broke down and she began to sink. Her Captain, Rory Blacker, relatively sober at the time, had the sense to beach her, at the entrance to a creek, on the Kwazaland side of the river. He sent the crew, except the cook, down river to Fort Albert, in her tender, to report the incident, whilst he attended to his remaining stock of whisky. It was decided she was uneconomical to repair and re-float. The Olulopo Princess was left abandoned and forgotten, in an inhospitable and remote stretch of the river. Like many others, Darke had heard of her fate with sadness.

A vicious jab from a gun butt brought Darke back to the present. It took him all his attention, to stop himself from pitching forward, over the side of the jetty, as he staggered under the blow. They were directed past stacked boxes of ammunition and mortar shells, onto the gangplank, to be halted on the deck, below the companionway to the wheelhouse. All around them men in sweat-stained KAPU uniforms were too busy carrying sandbags on board to take much notice of their presence. Through their feet they could feel the vibration of machinery. The Olulopo Princess was pulsating with life again. They waited whilst the corporal in charge climbed up to the wheelhouse and disappeared from view.

Darke exchanged glances with Kufanu. Both men were fascinated with the activity and the appearance of the rejuvenated river steamer. Aft of the superstructure containing the living quarters, there was approximately thirty feet of open uncluttered deck, except for the hatch cover for the aft hold. The steel rails upon which Darke had, some years before, leant to watch the riverside scene slide by, were being reinforced with sand bags, to waist height. Gaps were left at intervals. A similar arrangement, but more advanced, had been constructed on the twenty-five feet of the deck, forward of the wheelhouse. Within this area two heavy machine guns had been positioned to fire to port. On the starboard side sat the belts of ammunition in boxes stacked, two high.

Raised voices from above drew their attention back to the head of the wheelhouse steps. As they looked up the corporal was unceremoniously thrown through the door and ended up hanging over the bridge guardrail. As he hung there, a massive Sergeant, his skin blue black in hue, far darker than that of the local Kwazanians, strode into view. He took the frightened Corporal by the throat and drew him close. Specks of saliva, caught in the dappled sunlight, issued from his mouth, as he yelled a string of epithets into the face of his junior. The feet of the unfortunate man were almost off the deck. He was swung round and half thrown down the companionway. The corporal tumbled to the deck below. He quickly jumped to his feet limping slightly, muttering to himself. He signalled his men to return the prisoners ashore. They rapidly retraced their route, onto the jetty, up the steps and back to the cave. Once inside the entrance, the Corporal limped his way to a darkened, unoccupied, cell to the left of the central chamber. Darke and Kufanu were ordered inside, the door was slammed shut and locked behind them. Dank air filled their nostrils. The only light available came through the barred, one-foot square, opening in the upper part of the door. They could see a guard had been set to watch over them.

'What was that all about on the Princess?' Darke asked. His knowledge of the local dialect, was rusty after ten years. The big foreign sergeant had spoken with a strong accent, which had rendered his speech, all but unintelligible to him.

'He was furious that the corporal had brought us to the boat. Asked him if he wanted the whole world to know what they were about. Told him if he did anything like that again he would be "dead meat". It certainly looked like he meant it.'

Darke asked, 'Did you see the boxes of mortar shells on the jetty?'

'Yes, they must be planning an attack. The target has to be Fort Albert down the river. It's the only thing I can think of. They couldn't do it via a land route without being spotted well in advance and intercepted. But a raid on Fort Albert would need a few hundred men or more.'

'They've been forced to stop their activities up north. Maybe Leitch needs something spectacular to revitalise KAPU's standing with their Russian paymasters. He will not want to keep subsidising them any longer than he needs too. This could gain him a lot of credit with the Russians, not to mention other supporters around the world. The more money KAPU gets from other sources, the more he can siphon off for himself. Also, if they did succeed and were able to destabilise the country. it would offer him an ideal opportunity to expand his drugs operation. It could also give him a degree of legitimacy and power. He obviously thinks it's worth a try, but he's taking a hell of a risk.'

Elias Kufanu sucked in his breath. 'They haven't gone to the length of using the Princess for nothing. They're not going to gain anything by going up river. It can only be a large attack on Fort Albert. They usually use guerilla tactics in small units. Attacking a town will require a few hundred at least, That's why they're using the Princess. How did they manage to re-float her?'

Before answering Darke suggested they turn back-to-back, to try and undo their bonds. He managed, albeit slowly, to loosen the rope around Kufanu's wrists. As he did so, he reminded the big Policeman of Leitch's steam locomotive background in Katanga. The Princess's twin engines had not failed; only her pumps. To a man with Leitch's knowledge, the repairs to, or replacement of, her steam pumps would have presented little difficulty. How they sealed the damage to her hull he did not know. As far as Darke knew she had been abandoned further north. Therefore, she had been secretly sailed, probably by night, to her present location in the creek, below the old slave cave.

He recalled the vibration beneath their feet when they were on board. That was not her main engines, he decided. More likely to be auxiliary diesel power, but more than that, her pumps had been working. He reminded Kufanu of the sound of water being expelled into the creek. She had been patched, but was still leaking, only the pumps were keeping her afloat. It made sense, they decided. If it was that easy to re-float her, the owners would have done so soon after she was originally damaged. The hull damage was most likely significant, but Leitch had made some temporary repairs, sufficient to keep her afloat, long enough to lead an attack on Fort Albert.

Kufanu rubbed his wrists as the rope fell away. He turned his attention to freeing Darke and said, 'I think we can assume that Leitch is not here at present, otherwise we would have seen him by now. I don't know what you think of our chances, but knowing Leitch's history of violence, once he appears, I think our chances of survival will be slim.'

He heard a grunt of agreement from the darkness, Darke replied, 'He has no need to stage an accident anymore. He can get rid of us straight away. And having tried to kill me three times, he will make certain the next time. So, the sooner we get out of here the better.' He thought for a moment. 'How about chatting to the guard. Ask for food and water, to see if he knows where Leitch is, or what they intend to do with us.'

'Worth a try,' Kufanu agreed. He crossed to the door. Speaking through the bars he engaged the bored guard in conversation for some minutes, before falling silent and returning to Darke.

'That was useful,' he whispered his report, 'Leitch arrived last night and left almost immediately, to join his main force, further to the south on the Nambrian side of the river. Once the Princess is ready everyone will be sailing on board, to meet up with him. As we thought, he doesn't think much of our chances once we meet with Leitch.'

'Did he say when they would be leaving?'

'He didn't know, but the rumour is either of the next two nights. They are waiting on instructions from the man himself.'

'Well, that gives us a bit of time. What did he say about food and water?'

'"Wait and see", was his only suggestion.'

They were interrupted by noise from outside. The door opened and three uniformed men entered the darkened room. The door was firmly closed behind them. Darke tensed, thinking momentarily that they were about to be assaulted, before realising that it was Major Abumi, with a bandaged arm. He was accompanied by two of his men; a sergeant and a rifleman. After their excited greetings they exchanged information. Abumi had been thrown clear, during the helicopter crash, after a bullet grazed his left arm. He had been knocked unconscious and by the time he came round, KAPU men had surrounded him. The other two men, Sergeant Cheruwa and Rifleman Aaron, had also been taken prisoner before they could take defensive action. three riflemen, as well as the helicopter pilot and winch-man, had apparently died in the crash.

It was generally agreed that their chances of being rescued were nil. The helicopter flight plan had covered a wide area of the Eastern Highlands. Finding the wreckage of the Westland might take days, even weeks. That was assuming the KAPU men had not removed, or covered up, the remains of the machine. It was hours later, after the daylight from the cave entrance had faded, that food and water were brought to them. They asked for a light. Surprisingly an extension lead was fed through the grill with a car inspection lamp attached. It took its power from a socket from the main cable that ran the length of the main cave. It gave sufficient light, with which to inspect the cell. They occupied a room some thirty feet deep, by fifteen feet wide. As expected, it had solid rock walls, ceiling and floor. It was empty of anything except two buckets, which they assumed were to be used as toilets.

Their request for further creature comforts, such as blankets and mattresses fell on deaf ears. Their gaolers were not trained to the task and showed no interest in the welfare of the prisoners. They spent their duty carelessly idling their time away, rather than monitoring the activities of their charges. Occasionally they could be drawn into conversation, giving away more information of what was happening on board the riverboat. Adding snippets of conversation, between the guard and passing KAPU soldiers, soon enabled the prisoners to build a picture of what was afoot.

The Olulopo Princess was soon to sail south, with all on board, to meet with additional forces further downstream, on the opposite shore. As they had guessed she was to be an artillery platform, to support the night attack on Fort Albert. The Princess would tow attacking units, in rigid hull, inflatable barges, and release them close to the town. The men aboard would make their way to the shore. The Princess's role was to provide machine gun and mortar fire from her decks, as the attack was launched. The plan included taking the road bridge, across the Olulopo River. This would allow additional forces, hidden on the Nambrian side, to cross into Kwazania to maximise the destruction of the town.

KAPU attacks rarely involved more than one, or two, of their seven-man operational units. They are guerrilla fighters. Hit and run units, unused to conventional warfare. This was something beyond their experience. The prisoners sensed a tense air of excitement, amongst the guerrilla soldiers, at the forthcoming massed battle. The chance for looting would be particularly attractive to them.

Darke discussed the situation with the others. It was agreed that this was a significant change of tactics, therefore Leitch would be taking a big gamble. For the first time the KAPU forces would be united in one large scale attack. It was felt that, with the element of surprise, Leitch's plan stood every chance of success. However, to avoid annihilation, all the KAPU forces would need to disperse rapidly, back across the river, before the better trained and equipped Kwazanian forces moved against them. As a propaganda exercise, it would hit the front pages of newspapers around the world and be worth the risks involved. No doubt KAPU's new found leader was aiming to attract more funding, from their erstwhile Russian sponsors.

The prisoners agreed that they must expect to be moved down river within the next day or so, to an almost certain death sentence once they met up with Leitch. They were in no doubt, that with the imminent attack, he would have them slaughtered without ceremony. They made their plans and settled down to await their fate.

Chapter 19

Their prison aboard the Princess was pungent with the stench of damp wood and diesel fuel. As it was a steam vessel, that runs on timber logs. they assumed the diesel must be for the auxiliary motors, to provide power, when the steam engines were not in use. The five prisoners were below deck, forward of the wheelhouse, on the port side. The accommodation was spartan compared with that experienced by Darke, on his last pleasure trip aboard the Princess. Their prison had originally been the quarters for the crew. The cabin consisted of four bunks on each side, in two tiers, with lockers under the lower bunks. Opposite the entrance door was the inwardly curved shape of the hull, wherein was set a porthole, which allowed a meagre amount of daylight to penetrate the gloomy interior. Their only view was of the side of the rough wooden jetty, below the level of the walkway.

A narrow steel table was bolted to the floor in the centre of the cabin. Two dim bulkhead lights supplemented the faint daylight from the porthole. The five prisoners stood tensely round the table, whilst Darke put his ear to the door. He could hear nothing from the outside, above the regular throb of the ship's pumps. Before he gave the "all clear" to his expectant audience he pointed to the hole in the ceiling, covered by a mesh grill.

He whispered, 'That's an air vent, it leads directly to the deck above. Anyone listening will hear everything we say, unless we keep our voices down.' They all raised their eyes to the ceiling grill before looking back at Darke and nodding.

'What have we got?' he asked, keeping his voice low.

Just before sunset they were marched down from the caves, to the river, by four guards, two in front, the other two bringing up the rear. Their guns cocked and ready for immediate use. After their two-day sojourn in the cell, it had taken a brief time for their eyes to become accustomed to the early evening sunlight. There were ominous storm clouds forming to the north. As they started down the path toward the steps, leading to the jetty, Elias Kufanu slipped, dragging Sergeant Cheruwa down with him as he tumbled into the undergrowth. Both men had yelled with pain, as they landed. Darke went to their aid. Major Abumi, who had been in the lead, put his hands in the air, as the leading guards swung round, levelling their guns, as they did so. He called to the man, saying that the others had tripped, and that there was nothing to worry about. Rifleman Aaron at the rear also had raised his hands, to show no resistance. The rear guards, on seeing the event, were more inclined to grin, as they watched Darke's attempt to help the fallen comrades.

The two men had grunted with pain from their fall. They had tried to right themselves on the banking, and began to laugh and gasp for breath. The guards shouted and pointed their weapons at the floundering threesome, for, by this time, Lucas Darke, in his attempts to help, had also fallen. They had all quietened down and disentangled themselves and with Darke's assistance had climbed back onto the steps. Sergeant Cheruwa, holding his chest, was slightly bent with pain as he took shallow breaths of air. He had signalled that he was not too bad, just winded. Elias Kufanu had twisted his knee and was only able to negotiate the steps one at a time, whilst keeping his right leg as straight as possible.

As the jetty came into view, it was evident to the captives, that much work had been done on the vessel, since they had previously been onboard. Sandbags now surrounded all the deck to waist height. Mortars and heavy machine guns were positioned forward of the wheelhouse and also on the open rear deck area. They had been draped with camouflage covers, but at that short distance, were easily identifiable through the broad squares of netting. The derrick on the rear deck had been removed. Sizeable aluminium Skiffs were stacked inside each other. They measured approximately fifteen feet long, by six feet wide. Three were lashed lengthwise, along each side of the steamer. Their matt black painted hulls faced outwards.

Twenty men were taking it in turns to carry logs of wood up the gangway. The passage of the prisoners onto the Princess had halted work temporarily, allowing the KAPU men to wipe the sweat from their brows, regain their breath and rest their glistening bodies. They took little or no interest as the prisoners filed past.

In answer to Darke's question Elias Kufanu winked and with a wide grin withdrew a pickaxe handle from down his trouser leg. Cheruwa, the RKR Sergeant straightened up, with an equally broad grin, proffered the crowbar he had been clutching to his chest.

'Hopefully we can do something with those,' Darke said approvingly.

They had laid their plans and rehearsed the mishap on the steps. It was hoped that the lack of thorough military training and discipline, displayed by the KAPU soldiers, would mean it was likely they had not tidied away the abandoned tools that had been spotted, near to the steps, on their earlier visit to the jetty. Clothing had been loosened to allow equipment to be secreted away as quickly as possible. The task of tool gathering went to the two biggest men: Kufanu and Sergeant Cheruwa. Darke's roll was to act as cover and prolong the confusion, to improve their chances of success. Their time in the cell had not been wasted, they had discussed a variety of options. Finally, they settled on a simple, flexible plan of action. It had depended on them being able to affect an escape from their next prison aboard the Princess, which would require tools.

Major Abumi suggested, in a low voice, that they thoroughly examine the cabin. The wooden bunks had no mattresses. Everything was bolted to the floor. The lockers beneath the bunks were empty. The room was dank, with mould on the walls. Using the crowbar, Elias Kufanu opened the stiff porthole for fresh air, more in hope than expectation. There was no breeze and the aperture was too small for the passage of a man's head. The forward wall behind the bunks was varnished plywood.

They could not tell whether a guard had been left outside the door. It was arranged that Rifleman Aaron would sit on the floor, with his back to the door, to delay entry, should any one attempt to enter the cabin unexpectedly. Kufanu took up the crowbar. He began working on the edge of the decaying wood panel, on the forward bulkhead, between the two tiers of bunks. The throbbing of the pumps and the rumble of boxes and drums, from the deck above, covered any noise he made. As he scored the damp wood just below the upper bunk, the panel unexpectedly split, with a dull crack. They all froze and listened. Nothing happened and no one came. They relaxed and Kufanu continued once more. He used the forked end of the crowbar as a crude cutting tool to tear a slot in the wood. He marked out a panel three feet long by two-feet-six-inches deep. When he tired, the others took it in turns, until the wood had been scored through on all four sides. The panel could then be prised away, to reveal a narrow cavity with more, but rougher panelling beyond.

Before they could progress further, a warning came from the seated rifleman, followed by a commotion outside their cabin door. The panel was pushed back in position. A key was inserted in the lock, the rifleman, on a signal from the Major, stood up and moved away. The door swung inwards revealing two armed KAPU men: one wearing sergeant's stripes. The Major lolled against the bunk they had been working on, Elias Kufanu lay stretched along its length and Darke crowded close to the opened door. The guards waved their levelled Kalashnikov automatic rifles in the direction of Darke. The meaning was clear, so Darke retreated back towards Kufanu's bunk. The KAPU sergeant silently counted them. Nothing was said. They withdrew and the door was pulled to and locked behind them.

'Checking on us,' Abumi said, 'we have been in here about half an hour. If we intend to break out, we'll have to time it, for just after a visit from the guards.'

'Or we do it now, if we can get through this second panel,' Kufanu whispered, rising from the bunk.

'Better have a plan worked out first,' Darke added. 'I suggest we wait until the Princess sails and it's dark. We don't know what lies on the other side of that bulkhead, yet.'

Half-an-hour later they had created a large hole and forced a passage into the adjacent disused store room. Major Abumi clambered through and eventually returned to say the door was not locked and there was an armed guard dozing outside the door of their cell. They replaced the panel of wood beside the bunk as best they could, to disguise their handiwork from prying eyes. They settled down to await their next visit from the guards. An hour had passed since the previous visit when a clatter of feet was heard coming down the companionway, from the deck above. The key turned in the lock and the same two men stood outside. One was their guard, bleary eyed from having his sleep interrupted. The sergeant counted their number, without entering the room, then stepped aside whilst the guard pulled the door closed. They heard the key turn in the lock.

Their plan was simple. Abumi worked his way back through the hole. Once there, Kufanu passed him the pickaxe handle and crow bar, before also wriggling through into the forward cabin. The transition from one cabin to the other, took several minutes, as the hole was small and the needed to avoid undue noise. It became easier halfway through the exercise. With the onset of night, there came an increase in the sounds from the deck above. Gone was the thud and tumble of wooden logs being thrown into the ship's bunker, to be replaced by loud rumbling noises, as though, the fore and aft gang planks were being hauled aboard. The throbbing of the engines increased.

Elias Kufanu passed through the hole to the adjacent cabin. At the same time, they all felt the movement of the vessel as it swung away from the jetty. With all the additional weight brought aboard, her movements were sluggish. She wallowed ponderously, taking a long time to right herself before rolling back in the opposite direction. Darke could feel, by her delayed responses, that she was dangerously top heavy. The Princess was built to carry heavy cargo in her hold or tow barges. It was a different matter with the walls of sandbags and weaponry they had installed upon her decks. The balance of her weight had shifted uncomfortably high above the waterline.

A signal from Sergeant Cheruwa alerted Darke who began banging on the cabin door until a muffled demand came from the other side.

'On the floor,' Darke yelled and pushed a slip of paper beneath the door.

In the next cabin Major Abumi watched through the slightly open door. When Darke called and banged on the cell door, the dozing guard had come instantly to his feet and moved to the door. The noise Darke created made it easy for Abumi to open his door further. The guard glanced at the floor as a sliver of paper appeared below, pushed from the other side by Darke. The guard, leaning on his semi-automatic rifle, stooped to pick up the piece of paper. He never completed the move. Abumi slipped out of the stockroom with the pick axe handle. There was no room to swing it. Instead, he jabbed it, with as much force as he could muster, into the side of the guard's head, behind his ear.

The KAPU man went down, ending in a heap on the floor. Superintendent Kufanu had come, armed with the crowbar, to assist the major and was slightly aggrieved at having nothing to do. Between them they raised the man, sat him in his chair, relieved him of his two spare magazines of ammunition, before searching him for the keys to the locked cabin, without success. They arranged him to look as though he was sleeping. Kufanu returned the way he had come and called through the hole for the other three to exit their prison, via the stockroom.

It was a temptation to climb the steps to the cooler air on deck, but first they explored the remaining forward accommodation, leaving Sergeant Cheruwa and Rifleman Aaron to cover the steps from the deck above. Forward of the cabins a hatch led into the large unlit chain locker, full of greasy anchor chains and old coils of heavy ropes. A musty, all-pervading smell of tar mixed with grease, hung heavy in the air. Darke had an idea. He ran his hands over the sticky chains, testing the glutinous accumulation of dirt, grease and rust over the backs of his hands, to obliterate the paleness of his skin. Satisfied with the result he smeared his face in the same way. The others helped by telling him of any areas he had missed.

Kufanu handed him the guard's bush hat, and advised, 'Stay out of strong light, keep that on and no one will tell the difference.'

They were in the compartment that formed the bow of the vessel: the walls narrowed, and sloped inwards to the floor, forming the prows. This could be felt rather than seen, as very little light penetrated from the corridor. At its opposite end, the short passage leading aft, finished with a door, which lead under the bridge to the boiler room beyond. On the opposite side to their prison was another larger cabin, equal to two of the cabins on the port side. Its door refused to open more than halfway. Just inside, large timbers could be detected, angled and jammed in position. It was difficult to see in the gloom, but they decided that this was where the original damage to the hull, had been done. The timbers were shoring up the hole. Clearly a temporary measure. Water could be detected sloshing in the bilges, beneath the broken decking.

Before leaving the confines of their prison they had agreed they could not leave the Princess. By doing so they would have no chance of contacting the Kwazanian authorities, to warn them of the impending attack, or to find some way of preventing it. They would have to hide. By doing so they hoped their captors would conclude they had immediately left the vessel, soon after freeing themselves from their prison. They decided to hide in the chain locker. However, it was clear that the ropes and chains were only sufficient to cover the Major and his two men.

Kufanu and Darke left the guard's Kalashnikov in the charge of Major Abumi and went to look elsewhere. The cabin with the shoring had nothing in it, except the jammed timbers. Anyone with a torch, would soon have spotted them hiding there. They were becoming desperate when Darke suggested they make their way back, into their recent prison, to hide in the lockers beneath the lower bunks. Kufanu was dubious.

Darke said, 'Look, as soon as they unlock the door and find that five men are missing, they're going to be in a panic. Five men can't hide under the bunks, there's a big hole in the wall. We've obviously escaped. They'll rush out, in the hope that we haven't left the boat yet, and search for us on deck.'

Kufanu reluctantly nodded. 'We don't have much choice,' he said, leading the way.

Once back in the cabin they slid the locker doors open. There was a damp three-ply vertical partition, dividing the space into two, which soon gave way with pressure from a heavy boot. Darke was able to wriggle into the space quite easily.

The Superintendent on the opposite side had more difficulty, he was eventually able to slide the door shut, with a disgruntled, 'Good job I'm not claustrophobic!'

They settled down to wait. It was perhaps an hour later that Darke, almost asleep, was jolted from his semi-slumber. The motion of the steamer had ceased. It took him a moment to realise they had run aground on one of the Olulopo's many sandbanks. There was much shouting and movement on the deck above. Soon order was restored. Following a series of shouted instructions, many feet began to tramp in unison and the boat started to rock from side to side. The engines were put in reverse and under maximum steam. The whole craft rolled and vibrated with the effort until finally she came unstuck. The commotion overhead subsided as the Princess, once again, continued on her journey downstream.

Another half-an-hour passed before boots were heard on the companionway, followed by a shout and a dull clatter, as the body of the guard hit the floor. A key scraped in the lock and the cabin door thudded open. A moment of silence, followed by expletives. There was a shout from the corridor, followed by the clatter of more men descending the steps. The sound of boots moved close to Darke's head. His heart was pounding, but they were just examining the hole in the wall.

Whoever was in charge shouted something indecipherable. The footsteps retreated to the neighbouring storeroom, then to the other compartments. There were muffled curses and a brief pause, followed by the treading of boots along the short passageway and up to the deck above. Over the following ten minutes an increased level of activity was noticeable on the main deck, overhead. It was apparent that a search of the boat was in progress. Eventually a party of searchers descended to their level and ran through the cabins. One of their leaders came to their prison and stood close by Darke's hiding place. The KAPU man was obviously examining the hole above where he lay. Darke held his breath as a beam of torchlight penetrated through the cracks of his hiding place. The search continued with more haste than care. He waited, listening intently, expecting at any moment to hear that one of the others had been discovered, but nothing happened.

The search party's efforts, below the main deck, were cursory. These men were not used to such work. Their limited training concentrated on hit and run tactics of the terrorist, or freedom fighters, depending on which side you were on. They were looking for a group of five escapers, so failed to consider spaces that could contain less than that number. They knew that in the prisoners' position, they would have been long gone. Probably thinking they had slipped over the side onto one of the sandbanks, that had interrupted their progress.

In time the hubbub settled down to the previous level. In addition, came the steady drum of heavy rain on the canopies and wooden decking above. Darke could only guess what the KAPU leader was saying. Someone's head would roll for allowing the prisoners to escape. Another thirty minutes passed. Darke heard a scuffling in the cabin, followed by a gentle knock on his locker door. 'Lucas, are you awake?' whispered Elias Kufanu.

Darke struggled to extricate himself from his hiding space.

Kufanu was exercising his limbs, 'Couldn't take any more of that: it felt like a coffin,' he said, waving at the opposite locker. 'What do we do now?'

Darke had been thinking and said, 'It's raining and dark. They won't have any lights showing, for fear of attracting attention, so we should be okay to move around on deck. Let's find the others and get out of here.'

It was simple to slip onto the deck. At the Major's suggestion, they removed all their badges of rank, to make them less conspicuous. He suggested they did not move around in a group of five. That would be too obvious. The three Rifle Regiment men left together. Kufanu and Darke followed a few minutes later.

The rain was heavy, all the KAPU fighters were huddled in groups, many were dozing and a few were talking. The sound of the rain, assailing the taught canvas canopies, was loud enough to require anyone to shout, to be heard above the constant drubbing. As Darke had surmised there were no lights showing. The two of them unhurriedly made their way to the wide stern, as pre-arranged, guided by the walls of sandbags. The KAPU men had moved inboard, away from the sides of the steamboat, when the rain had started. The water was cascading from the awnings, onto the top of the sandbags, some of which bounced inboard. The KAPU men were huddled in the centre of the deck, leaving a damp, wide walkway between them and the sodden sand-filled bags. They were used to fighting in seven-man sections, rarely operating with other groups. Most did not know anyone beyond their own unit. Consequently, the likelihood of being identified in the dark was small.

Darke noticed, that whilst the canopies kept the men on deck dry, the sandbags lining the rail were steadily absorbing more and more rain. It was adding additional weight to the already overloaded vessel, reducing her freeboard. The upper deck above the passenger cabins, he knew, was also screened with sandbags. This additional weight, high up above the waterline, was having a marked effect on her handling. He also noticed that the Princess was hardly moving above the speed of the current. The vibration of her engines had reduced to a barely perceptible level. Darke wondered if they were reaching the meeting point with Leitch. Then he realised that the torrential rain had reduced visibility to a few yards.

It became apparent the captain had reduced speed, for fear of running aground once more. The steamer was drifting with the current, but still in danger of grounding on unseen sandbanks. Instructions were yelled from the port side of the bridge, as a spotlight beam pierced the darkness, followed by a second from the opposite side of the superstructure. The beams swung erratically, then, following further instructions from the bridge, steadied down to slowly sweep the river ahead, on each side. There was no need for a black out. As long as the heavy rain fell, no light would be seen, for any distance, horizontally or vertically. No aircraft would be flying in these conditions. Darke turned to look over the stern as a means of hiding his face. The weak glow from the lights, reflecting off the myriad shards of rain, falling and bouncing off the river's surface, created an eerie confusion of shadows across the deck. The spotlights did little to improve the steamer's progress. They showed a few yards of river on either side. the water was so disturbed by the downpour, that it was impossible to detect sandbanks just below the surface. Several times, the tell-tale jolt, of the flat-bottomed hull against an unseen sand bar, rocked them on their feet. It evoked a murmur of concern, from the drowsing soldiers.

Elias Kufanu leant close to him and said, reassuringly, in a low voice, 'You look fine, no one's taking any notice of you.'

It eased his mind somewhat, but he still felt exposed. Darke asked, 'Did you notice the bundles of paddles in the skiffs, as we passed?'

'I noticed bundles, but didn't realise they were paddles.'

'They must intend to use them to ferry the men to the western bank, before the attack, to cover the Princess when she disembarks the rest of the force.'

The Superintendent grunted his agreement.

Darke continued, 'If we can dump the paddles overboard it'll make life more difficult for them.'

A brief discussion followed. It was agreed that Abumi, Darke and Kufanu would work along the deck checking that the lashings of the skiffs were holding securely. Whilst the other two men were around him Darke would remove the paddles and drop them over the side. As they stopped beside the skiffs a voice called out to them. Abumi answered the man and backed away, pulling Darke with him, followed by the Superintendent. The man followed. They nearly fell as the boat grounded to a halt on a sandbank. They all staggered, their interrogator lost interest in them, he immediately turned and moved rapidly in the direction of the bridge.

'Thought we were for it that time,' Abumi whispered with obvious relief, 'That was a stroke of luck.'

They abandoned the idea of dumping the paddles. Instead, they retired to the stern and sat down to make themselves as inconspicuous as possible. The engines were reversed. As the power was increased the steamer juddered, violently, under their feet. The men on deck were not used to life aboard the Princess, anything untoward added to their fears. An air of despondency hung over them, brought on by the rain, the groundings and their apparent slow progress. Most could not swim. Others, with more imagination could easily visualise the boat sinking: they could picture their own watery demise. They were lost in their own dispirited thoughts. Eventually the vessel churned herself free to continue down river, to the relief of everyone on board.

Several times the Princess grounded again and could not be re-floated by reversing her engines. Once again, they had to resort to using some of the reluctant passengers to rock the boat. The makeshift crew used long poles over the side, to push the ageing Princess off the sandbank. Judging by the shouts from the bridge, the KAPU leader was feeling frustrated with the unexpected conditions. He was quick to take his anger out on his men.

The five of them, in two groups, were ignored as they slowly worked their way back to the companionway, leading to the deck above the passenger cabins. It was darker here and they were surprised to find the small upper deck deserted. Two heavy machine guns, surrounded by sandbags, were protected from the weather by covers. Being narrower than the deck below, splashes from the rain on both sides left only a narrow strip of dry deck, down the centre. When the rain had started, those men on the upper deck, had sought a drier refuge, under the bigger awning of the main deck, below.

The forward end of the upper deck was occupied only by the narrow funnel situated immediately behind the wheelhouse. In days gone by this upper deck was where the passengers would sit to take afternoon tea and watch the passing flora and fauna. Three of the group hung around at the top of the steps, to hinder anyone coming up from below. It enabled Elias Kufanu the opportunity to explore, and Major Abumi time to immobilise the heavy machine guns. Both men returned together.

The Major grunted, ‘Okay,’ which they took to mean he had been successful. The Superintendent reported that he could squeeze under the forward edge of the awning and climb onto the roof of the wheel house. If the rain ceased or the Princess reached her rendezvous point, they could quietly climb onto the roof of the bridge, if they needed to hide or await events.

Chapter 20

It was after one o'clock in the morning when the riverboat nosed awkwardly into the east bank of the river. Her unskilled crew threw the bow lines ashore, which were hurriedly tied to a tree, allowing the current to swing the stern downstream, until the steamer could be moored parallel to the recently constructed jetty, facing upstream. On the roof of the wheelhouse Darke stretched stiffly. They had climbed onto their hiding place when the rain had suddenly ceased, giving way to a quarter moon, frequently obscured by heavy cumulus clouds. The spotlights had been extinguished and the vibration of the engines increased, as visibility improved.

Almost before the mooring lines had been secured, the gangways were lowered. Darke heard voices and footsteps climbing the companionway to the bridge. He recognised the voice of Sandy Leitch. His anger at the delayed arrival of the Princess was apparent. Once inside the wheelhouse his voice was muffled and incomprehensible, but still clearly angry. The odd word was discernible, when the commotion from elsewhere on the boat momentarily quietened.

More men were filing on board carrying additional equipment and stores. Darke's concern at the uncomfortable way the vessel moved had not diminished. He wondered, in her condition, how overloaded the Princess could get before becoming dangerously unmanageable. She was a flat-bottomed vessel and therefore unlikely to capsize, but her handling was seriously impaired. He had a whispered conversation with the others. They agreed their main priorities were firstly, to warn Fort Albert of the impending attack and secondly, to stop the Princess, if possible, from reaching her objective. They were severely restrained in their conversation, by having to whisper for fear of being overheard.

Darke suggested they go ashore to see what might be found. There was little they could do to stop the riverboat at this time. The longer they stayed aboard the greater the risk of being discovered. All agreed it was time to make their move. Leaving their hiding place was awkward as once the rain had ceased a few men had moved back onto the upper deck, so the five of them lifted the awning and climbed down, making sure they stood on no one in the process. The men below made way for them with only the odd grunt. When they reached the steps down to the lower deck, Darke looked back through the gloom. Only one man seemed to be curious, as to where they had come from. He stood up, lifted the awning and looked out onto the roof of the bridge. His silhouette gave a shrug before the awning fell back into place. The man resumed his seat in the deep shadow cast by the wheelhouse.

The five of them made their way along the main deck. A second gangway had been lowered to the temporary jetty, to hasten the loading of additional supplies of ammunition. The men loading, were using the more substantial forward gangway. Once they had stacked their burden, they quickly made their way ashore, by the narrower white painted gang plank at the stern.

The five of them moved to the rear of the steamer. Darke led the way and chose his moment. A gap occurred in the flow of men filing ashore. Imitating the man in front, he stepped onto and half ran down the planking, ducking, as he went, under the camouflage netting hanging over the jetty. Once ashore they were in an area of almost total darkness. The others were on his heels. Above the sounds of men coming and going, came the inevitable chorus of cicadas. It was almost deafening after the relative quiet aboard the Princess. Darke noticed, with interest, that the edges of the pathways had been marked in white and were just discernible. About two hundred yards from the river, a red glow indicated a centre of activity. He stepped aside from the path and caught the others, as they came by, to guide them to his side. They needed no hiding place. Just by standing still, away from the path, they could not be seen by anyone passing.

It was beginning to rain heavily again. There was activity astern of the steamer. By keeping away from any of the marked routes and cautiously feeling their way along, at the same distance from the river's edge, they were eventually able to discern the nature of the activity. After five minutes of watching all became clear. Four large collapsible boats, with rigid hulls, were moored behind the Princess: two side by side with two more behind. The first boat was filling with fully armed men. Darke estimated each craft would take thirty men in total. They were boarding in fours. As soon as they were seated another four followed, to avoid upsetting the craft.

On the river side of these four barges, they could just discern an inflatable dinghy, with two men aboard, acting as a safety boat. Its outboard motor was ticking over to keep position against the current. They roughly estimated that the Princess would land two hundred and fifty men and equipment, as a substantial advance guard. That number would easily take the bridge, allowing a force, of possibly battalion strength, to cross from the Nambrian side of the river. Together the combined force would move on to attack Fort Albert.

The Major's voice came from the gloom, 'We need a plan.'

Darke nodded in agreement, for all the good it did in the pitch black, rain-soaked night. He said, 'But until we have a clear plan of action, we need to keep together, otherwise we'll never find one another again.'

Elias Kufanu suggested in his deep whisper, 'Why don't we head for the light and see what's there?'

They agreed. The Major gave brief instructions to his men and led off with Darke and Kufanu bringing up the rear. They were able to use the marked path that gently rose in the direction of the light. Only one person came towards them and he was silhouetted against the dim light, giving them ample time to step aside from the path. The unsuspecting man splashed by without noticing them. Soon they could make out the structure of a crude hut, from which the red glow radiated. The tell-tale hum of a generator could also be heard merging with the sound of the cicadas.

A sentry suddenly confronted Abumi. He was waving a torch and an automatic rifle tipped with a glinting bayonet, He demanded the password. Abumi scolded the man for being less than diligent. He asked why he had not been challenged sooner and exactly what instructions, he had been given. The sentry, who had been half-asleep, sheepishly began to answer. Then his eyes opened wide, having recognised the major's uniform in the light of his torch. Abumi, seeing the danger moved towards the man, attempting to parry the rifle as he advanced. The sentry jabbed twice with the bayonet. The first thrust caught the major in his injured left arm, Above the elbow. Before the next jab reached its target, the sentry was felled by Sergeant Cheruwa, who had circled around behind the man. The blow with a stone was struck to the head with such a force, that Darke, hearing the thud, was convinced the sentry had breathed his last. The body was dragged clear of the path and hidden in the undergrowth. The Sergeant brought the sentry's Kalashnikov and spare magazines, to the Major.

Abumi, holding his left arm, told the Sergeant to keep them, emphasising that stealth was the order of the day and only to use the weapon when no other option was available. The last thing they wanted was to advertise their presence with gunfire. Darke asked the Sergeant for the bayonet. Using it he cut the blood-stained sleeve off Abumi's shirt, to use it to bind the arm. The major grunted in appreciation when Darke had finished.

'Best I can do, I'm afraid, until we find something better,' Darke replied.

The rain was still falling as they approached the hut. Major Abumi ordered the Sergeant to check the path beyond the structure for any other sentries. Inside the hut two men sat bathed in the faint red glow of a single bare light bulb. It was suspended from a wire, stretched across the centre of the single room. Their soiled tunics were undone to the waist as they lolled lethargically, in canvas chairs. They giggled, occasionally talking quietly, sometimes together, sometimes to themselves. On a rough wooden desk beside them sat a radio transmitter, quietly hissing with static. The sickly smell of sweat and marijuana filled the air.

A movement beside Abumi signalled the return of the Sergeant. A second sentry had been located and dealt with on the farther side of the shack. He had brought with him a second weapon and ammunition. Abumi posted the Sergeant to cover the path to the river. He armed rifleman Aaron and sent him to guard the path, on the opposite side of the hut.

They withdrew from the window to form a plan. It was decided to rush the two occupants. Superintendent Kufanu would take one and Darke the other man, nearest the radio. The Major would follow and assist where necessary, as his arm had stiffened from the effects of his two wounds.

The door was ajar. Kufanu burst through with the fury of a stampeding bull elephant. His target just had time to gape, open-mouthed, before he was felled with a right-handed punch to his head. Darke followed Kufanu into the room and dived at the other man, who was instinctively reaching for his pistol beside the radio. He fumbled the move. Long before he could wrap his fingers around the butt, he and his chair were knocked over sideways, by the impetus of Darke's tackle. He landed heavily with Darke on top of him. Before he could move, Darke brought the butt of his hand up hard beneath the man's jaw, his head snapped back hitting the floor. Darke rolled to one side rising up on his knees. The man groaned and tried to raise himself, only to be struck down by the Superintendent.

The pistol lay on the desk, Darke took it and offered it, butt-first, to Major Abumi as he entered the hut. 'Easier for you to use, with that arm,' he commented.

'Thanks. Won't say no,' Abumi answered lightly.

In spite of his injury, he managed to check the magazine of the weapon, before tucking it, casually, into the waistband of his uniform trousers. The two of them searched their victims and the room, whilst Abumi righted the fallen chair. He settled down at the desk, to work the radio. Darke presented the Major with additional clips of ammunition for the pistol. He slipped them into the side pockets of his uniform, as he worked the dials. Darke and Kufanu helped themselves to a Kalashnikov each from where they were stored in a vertical rack against the wall. They each took three loaded magazines and a bayonet belt. They ignored the tools: pickaxes, spades, ropes and all variety of equipment, stacked against the same wall.

Further exploration yielded a box of standard Russian hand grenades. Darke slid it towards the door, to be taken with them when they left. Other wooden boxes were filled with rations, including corned beef. Kufanu grunted and held up a first aid box. He left Darke to continue the exploration and crossed the room to dress Abumi's wounded arm.

Abumi, noted down radio frequencies from memory, on a pad. He picked up the hand microphone and repeated the same call on different channels. He made the same call again and again: identifying himself and naming Superintendent Kufanu. He warned of an imminent KAPU attack on Fort Albert, giving approximation of strength and warning of the approach from the direction of the river and across the Fort Albert Bridge from the Nambria. Once in a while the static increased, but there was no reply.

'I've used all the frequencies I know and a few besides, without success. The mountains across the river are likely to be masking the radio signal, to and from the army.' Wearily, he relaxed back in the chair before switching to short wave. He began sending urgent warnings again. Bursts of increased static, raised their hopes, but the radio always settled back into the usual background noise.

Every moment they remained in the hut increased the chance of being discovered. Having armed themselves and pocketed tins of corned beef and grenades, they withdrew. The two KAPU soldiers, now semi-conscious, were dragged outside to the rear of the hut, tied back-to-back and gagged. Two haversacks from the hut were used as improvised hoods. Major Abumi gave them a clear warning, any noise and they would be 'silenced'. The hoods hurriedly nodded their understanding.

There was a general sense of disappointment among the group, that no positive contact had been made with the army or Fort Albert. It meant the matter remained in their hands. It was still up to them to find a way to thwart the attack.

The Major, nursing his injured left arm, grunted and said, 'Just thought of something. I've one more broadcast to make.' He turned, unfolding a piece of paper as he went, retracing his steps to the hut.

Immediately, without instructions, Sergeant Cheruwa and Rifleman Aaron separated and melted into the night, to take up their previous positions, beside the path, on either side of the shack. Darke and the Superintendent followed Abumi to the hut. He re-tuned the radio to the frequency he had previously noted down.

He pressed the send button saying, 'We're under attack,' he repeated it three times in an excited tone, finishing with, 'signing off.' He stood back from the table and said to Kufanu with a grin, 'Wreck that if you'd be so kind.' It was delivered in his best Sandhurst accent.

Kufanu nodded, 'My pleasure.' He lifted the radio up and away to the extent of the wires, then gave it a great pull. The radio came free of the batteries with a clatter. He carried it to the door and threw it as far as he could. It landed with a satisfying crunch on the sodden ground.

Major Abumi nodded in approval. 'That was on the KAPU frequency. Maybe that'll give the other units something to think about. With luck they'll decide not to head for the rendezvous.'

Once the five of them were re-united they retraced their route down the path. They had no satisfactory plan of action, except to find some way of neutralising the forthcoming attack. They moved cautiously along the muddy track as it descended to the jetty. Halfway to the river they became aware of cries of distress ringing out from ahead, followed by sounds of branches breaking and other confusing noises. The familiar background sound of the cicadas had ceased. More alarmed voices were raised closer to hand. Something was clearly amiss. They stopped and stepped to the side of the path, uncertain of what to do; unable to interpret what the sounds meant.

As they stood listening, water washed over their feet and began steadily to rise. Through the darkness, a vague shimmering light was penetrating the foliage from the direction of the river. Darke and Abumi were first to realise what was happening. There was little need for stealth anymore,

'A flash flood,' Darke yelled, 'Quick, back up the track.'

As they turned to retrace their steps the water rose rapidly. A few KAPU men, in panic, were splashing their way up the path from the river, their energetic movements discernible through the trees. Kufanu led their small group back onto the path, retracing their steps up the shallow slope, moving as fast as they could through the rising waters. It was up to their knees when a three feet high wave swept round them, bringing a clutter of flotsam in its wake. A floating mass of vegetation that pushed round them, clutching at their legs, threatening to push them over and drag them under. Instinctively Darke, the rear-most member of the party, raised his Kalashnikov above his head, then quickly began to use the butt as a paddle to force his way through the matted clutter of rising debris.

The others disappeared from sight in the darkness. The path was gone, lost beneath the rising tide of detritus that held him in its grip. The soil beneath his feet had turned to greasy mud. He threw his arms wide clutching for anything to keep him upright. He grasped a handful of brittle twigs, but could do nothing to stop himself from sinking beneath the chest high water. His shoulder hit a tree trunk, he grasped for it, but it was gone. Undergrowth pulled him in all directions, as he rolled over the ground, beneath the surface. He pushed an arm upwards, breaking through the mat of flotsam, to feel air above. With tortured lungs, he twisted his body to push upwards against the flow of water. He stood, momentarily, in water above the waist, drawing air into his lungs, before tripping and slipping beneath the surface once more.

Panic subsided: he forced himself to think. He swung arms wide as he bumped into obstacles. His shoulder hit the roots of a tree; he caught its trunk in the crook of his arm. Pushing the tangle of flotsam aside, he swung his legs to the base of the tree, forcing his body upwards to the surface. Once again, he felt the blessed, cool air on his face. He took deep breaths waiting for his thumping heart to steady. He found it easier to swing to the downstream side of the tree, to avoid most of the vegetation swirling past. It would have been better to climb above the water level, but the tree was not strong enough to bear his weight. His rifle was gone, he began to shiver, in part from his soaking but also through shock, he supposed.

'What to do?' he wondered. He decided to call out for the others, raising his voice above the sounds of swirling water and snapping twigs. There was no reply. Occasional shouts could be discerned from the direction of the river. It was obvious his voice was not penetrating far into the night, for he dared not call out at the top of his voice. Occupied, as everyone was, there was no point in advertising his presence. The others might come looking for him, once the immediate danger was over. He had a choice: to stay where he was, or move towards the river. There was little point in moving up or down stream. Away from the river everything was lost in pitch darkness. He could make out the trees along the river bank, silhouetted against the reflections from the open water. He headed in that direction, moving from tree to tree. It was important to find out if the Princess had survived the flood.

After much effort, with one treacherous foothold after another, he reached a position from where he could see the outline of the Olulopo Princess, further upstream. She was anchored by her much-shortened bow line, completely surrounded by eddying water. Her other mooring ropes were gone. Otherwise, she seemed to have successfully survived the flood. There was no sign of the jetty. Darke assumed it would be under several feet of water, if it had survived intact. The inflatable barges were still astern of the riverboat, with men aboard. A few men had been swept away by the current: their heads bobbed along, drifting rapidly, in the fast-flowing stream, bracketed by waving arms. Their unheard pleas for help hopelessly lost, amid the noise of the swirling flood waters.

The inflatable dinghy, he had observed earlier that night, was doing its best to rescue the drowning men. Its powerful outboard engine was no match for the river's main current. Anyone unfortunate enough to be swept out into the centre of the river was being left to cope alone or drown. It's two-man crew were switching its spotlight on briefly, sweeping the river in a wide arc. They were picking up survivors, closer to the tree line, which marked where the river bank had been. Here the current was not so strong. Once hauled safely into the dinghy, the rescued survivors were ferried up alongside the Princess, to be transferred aboard.

Forcing his way through the sodden tangle of floating matter, Darke reached the edge of the tree line. A man was leaning exhausted and spluttering against a tree trunk, half under the water. It was only at the last moment that both men saw each other. The face of the KAPU fighter, seeing Darke for the first time, took on an instant look of horror. He tried desperately to swing his rifle from his shoulder. Darke realised his face was obviously not so disguised any more. Clearly the other man had identified him as a European. As the muzzle of the Kalashnikov swung round in his direction, he grabbed the weapon and forced it hard against the other man's chest, pushing him down beneath the tangle of floating vegetation. His opponent struggled to rise above the surface. Kicking out with his legs, but without success. Finally, he released his grip on the rifle and attempted to roll away. Darke could not hold him and the man burst to the surface, side on to him, his lungs desperate for air. Before he could orientate himself Darke swung the rifle, driving the edge of the butt into his right temple. Off balance, the KAPU man sagged and sank back, to float away face down, amid the debris.

Darke was conscious his priority was still to warn Fort Albert of the impending attack. Finding the others was a secondary consideration. In the distance, the dinghy appeared around the stern of the Princess, moving rapidly toward him. The crew were looking for stray survivors along the tree line. The appearance of the dinghy made his mind up. He would attempt to lure it towards him and overpower the two-man crew. To avoid his pale features giving him away, he moved a short distance downstream, to a half-submerged bush overhanging the water. He used a branch as cover and waited for the dinghy to approach. When it was twenty yards off, he shouted incoherently, at the same time swinging the branches back and forth. The craft accelerated briefly downstream past him, before arcing away from the bank in preparation to circle back, into the current, to come up alongside the bush. As it did so Darke slipped the automatic rifle from his shoulder and attached the bayonet from his belt. He was unsure whether the weapon would fire after being submerged for a time; if it did not, it would be safer to rely on the bayonet.

Since shooting the man in the chair, at Rasguneon Castle, he had pondered the sense of quiet detachment that had overcome him, when he had entered the library. Almost as though he was drained of emotion. He had come to the conclusion that having settled on a course of action, there should be no room for doubt or apprehension. It had surprised him, as it was alien to all his police training. It obviously tapped into a more primitive instinct than mere conditioning. He felt the same stillness steeling over him again. He drew the branch backwards, as far as he could, curving it like a bow towards the bank. He hung his head and hid his face behind the leaves, as the boat came round. He grunted and groaned loudly as they came closer, to encourage them to think he was injured and in need of help.

The outboard motor was cut before it cautiously nudged its way in amongst the branches. One crewman stood precariously balanced, using a paddle to part the leaves. The man called to him and at the last moment Darke released the bough. It struck the standing crewman in the chest. He had no chance, it flung him over the opposite side of the craft, before he could react. The second man ducked the leaf-laden branches that swamped the boat; briefly lost to sight before emerging through the foliage. With as secure a footing under water, as he could manage, Darke launched himself forward with bent arms. As he closed on the boatman, he straightened his arms, adding more power to the forward thrust of the rifle. He felt the bayonet blade jar against bone as it penetrated, twisting the rifle in his grasp, before sliding deeper. The man looked directly at Darke, exhaled in a low moan and slumped into the bottom of the boat. The angle was awkward making it difficult to extract the blade from the body. He let go and threw himself up and over the side, into the boat, pushing the branches partially clear of the dinghy.

The man was dead with the rifle projecting from his chest. It was leaning at an angle and swaying precariously with the movement of the craft. Darke had to put his foot on the body to pull the bayonet free with a twisting motion. The sense of calm detachment had left him now, the adrenaline in his system was subsiding. Withdrawing the bayonet made him shudder with revulsion. He stole himself to continue, as he still had to complete his task.

Darke glanced at the river. The second crewman was clearly not a swimmer and it was an even match between him drowning or reaching the stern of the safety boat. He had been swept along close to the trees, by the sluggish current. The wooden paddle was the only thing giving him a little buoyancy. His desperate flailing hands found the end of a hanging branch. Spluttering and gasping he pulled himself up to the boat, against the current. He looked up to see Darke with rifle in hand above him. He was too desperate to let go of the dinghy. It was simple for Darke to lean down, beside the outboard and hit him between the eyes, with the gun butt. He slipped soundlessly back through the leaves and under the water.

Darke retrieved the paddle before it could float away. His heart was pumping fast. He was sure that no one on the Princess could have heard any noise he had made, as it was too far away, however he was not so sure about anyone else who might be close by. He needed to clear away from his present position quickly, to review his situation. It took seconds to remove the bayonet from the rifle, give it a cursory wash over the side, and safely return it to the sheath on his belt. The body of the boatman was heavy, he pushed and pulled at it, until it rolled over the side of the inflatable, into the river.

The current was holding the boat against the branches, locking it in position. It took a great deal of effort to overcome the pressure of the water, to move the craft a few feet. It would be unwise, he knew, to start the outboard. The propeller might become fouled or damaged by branches under water, which would make the capture of the dinghy a hollow victory. The branches filled the boat. Darke used the bayonet once more, to hack away at the foliage. It was hard going and he began to wonder whether he would be able to free the craft. He swore half under his breath.

'Lucas?' came a whispered question.

He stopped in mid swing at the sound of his name. 'Elias?' he called.

From the foliage rose the bulk of the Superintendent, automatic rifle in hand. The big policeman was alone. He too had been overwhelmed by the tidal wave. Once it had partially subsided, he had made his way to the river. He had seen nothing of the other three. Like Darke he had observed the manoeuvrings of the rescue boat, as it closed with the trees and had the idea of capturing it. It had taken him time to make his way to where he had last seen the boat swallowed up by the bush. He was about to attack, when he recognised Darke's silhouette. Between them they were able to free the craft from the clutches of the branches. The outboard was started, once clear of the bush.

Darke said, 'We'll cruise slowly upstream close to the bank and see whether we can find the others.'

Kufanu nodded, anxiously scouring the dark line of trees. It was a disheartening task as there was absolutely nothing to see in the gloom. Eventually they decided to call out the Major's name, as it would not signify anything to the odd KAPU man in the vicinity. At one point there was activity near the trees, made apparent by the thrashing of water. Darke nudged the craft towards the turmoil, keeping his head low to ensure his pale features were not seen. It turned out to be one of Leitch's men. Darke heard the thud of the Superintendent's fist and saw the man being tossed back towards the shore. Kufanu held up the man's rifle as a trophy and waved Darke away from the waterlogged trees.

They continued their search upstream until they could see the Princess clearly. Darke throttled back the engine and allowed the boat to drift back downstream with the current. At regular intervals Kufanu called out the Major's name. Another commotion along the shoreline drew their attention. Again, Darke guided the boat in. Kufanu was in his line of view and it was only when the grinning face of the Major, was hauled unceremoniously into the boat, that he knew they had been lucky. Sergeant Cheruwa followed. Both had retained their weapons. Rifleman Aaron was missing. All agreed they could wait no longer. It was decided they must head downstream to warn Fort Albert of the impending attack.

Chapter 21

It took the four of them more than two and a half hours to reach the locality of Fort Albert. It had not been plain sailing. The strength of the current aided their journey, but all too often swept them into danger on the bends. Sending them, bouncing on turbulent, eddying waters. They came perilously close to the flooded banks, where the inflatable was in danger of being ripped open, on any submerged obstacle. Without the outboard and spotlight, they could never have avoided some of the dangers. As it was, luck played a large part in their survival.

Darke and the Major were the only ones who had experience of boats, so it was left to them to handle the craft and navigate the swollen river. There were occasions when the turbulence nearly swamped the craft. It was only by sitting Kufanu and Sergeant Cheruwa in the bottom of the dinghy that they were able to avoid capsizing. On the sharper bends Darke swung the bows round to point up stream. By playing with the throttle and tiller, he was able to control the rate at which the craft navigated the bends, to avoid dangerous whirlpools that could easily have engulf them. They had no way of knowing how far ahead of the Princess they might be, or how the riverboat was managing on the flooded river. That was assuming she had set sail.

The four of them only realised they had reached their goal when the road bridge across the Olulopo swept into view, half a mile ahead. The two border posts at each end were brightly lit with high slung spotlights. Fort Albert itself lay off to the right, out of sight, some half mile back from the river. The early settlers had established it on higher ground, to avoid potential flooding and the mosquito ridden marshes, that used to flank the river. The distant loom of the town's lights tinted the scudding clouds with their warm glow. The marshes had been long-since drained, but were still liable to flooding, as was all too apparent. The immediate problem was finding a safe place to land, as the river was far wider than normal. There was the ever-present threat of underwater obstacles. Darke guided the craft into slacker water towards the west bank. The road leading to the bridge was built on a causeway above the level of the flood. Close to the bridge seemed the safest place to land.

The Major splashed ashore and called out, 'We'll go for the road and make for the border post. We can use their 'phone and radio to alert the authorities.'

They nodded in agreement, their faces tense, as their eyes scanned the opposite shore for signs of the KAPU forces supposedly lying in wait for the arrival of the Olulopo Princess. There was nothing to indicate their presence. All was quiet except for the rush of the turbulent river racing by. How long before the Princess would come into view, only time would reveal.

The Superintendent followed Major Abumi to the bridge, leaving Darke and Sergeant Cheruwa to secure the boat. The two men splashed ashore, up to the road and ran for the border post at the western end of the bridge. Darke and the Sergeant followed at a more leisurely pace carrying the Russian-made rifles. By the time the two of them came up to the customs post, Major Abumi was on the telephone, talking to Army Eastern Command unit in Fort Albert. Superintendent Kufanu was on the direct link, talking to the Nambrian customs post at the far end of the bridge.

Major Abumi finished his call and said, 'There's only units of territorials at the Fort Albert camp. I've impressed upon the captain in charge to form a defensive line covering the approach from the river, with an advance party to assist us here. I have requested more ammunition. In the meantime, it's up to us. There is an army column heading for the town. They don't know what it consists of or when it will arrive.' He looked around before continuing, 'There are three men here and four of us. The weapons we have, together with the contents of the Customs gun cabinet, will have to do. We have the Kalashnikovs. All they have here is four SLR's, two point three-eight revolvers, with ammunition and some out-of-date tear gas grenades.' He paused as a Chevrolet pickup truck drove up to the red and white barrier. Turning to the Customs men, he said, 'Get the people out of that vehicle and put it sideways across the road, over there. Do the same with your own Landrover.' He indicated a point approximately thirty yards along the bridge from the Customs post. 'Explain to the occupants that we are commandeering it, that we're expecting a major terrorist attack, imminently. Tell them to get back to town as quickly as possible.'

The two men, who looked like father and son, were both irritated, confused and prone to argue. It was only when they saw Sergeant Cheruwa checking all the weapons, that they realised it would be prudent to do as was suggested.

Elias Kufanu finished his telephone call. 'I suggested to those fellows guarding the Nambrian side of the bridge to get onto their headquarters and explain the situations as soon as possible. I suggested they come and join us here and bring any weapons. They seemed sceptical. There's no way they'll survive an attack on their own. He turned to Darke and Abumi saying, 'It's up to them now.' The Major nodded his agreement.

Darke asked the question, 'Molotov cocktails?' pointing to a crate of Coca-Cola bottles, inside the door of the Customs Office. Some were full, others were empty.

The Major agreed, 'Good idea, can you get onto it?' He eyed the full bottles, saying, 'Might as well make use of the contents rather than waste them.'

Following the instructions given by the Major, the Customs Officers drove their Landrover, together with the Chevrolet, to position them sideways across the bridge east of the Customs post.

Darke asked one customs officer to find strips of cloth, 'Anything will do, rags, dusters, anything that will absorb petrol.'

The man nodded and left. Darke opened a bottle of Coca Cola, using the metal edge of a window sill, and passed it to Abumi. He realised they must all be parched, not having drunk for several hours. He passed the rest of the full bottles around.

'Quick as you can,' Darke said, 'I need the empty bottles for bombs. What you can't drink throw away. When you have finished, put the empty bottles back in the crate.' He took several mouthfuls himself. Almost gagging as the gaseous contents expanded in his dry throat. It was good, very good, he was surprised how much he needed the liquid.

Two Customs men carried the crate of empty bottles and followed him to where the Landrover was parked. He instructed them to open the bonnet. It took them a while, in the semi-darkness of the engine compartment, to undo the fuel pipe. They filled a dozen bottles with petrol. The wicks made from the assortment of rags, used for cleaning the Customs vehicles, were twisted into the top of the bottle. They carefully carried the crate of petrol bombs to the side of the bridge and stowed them there, near the two vehicles.

Darke led the men back to the Customs building, to hear the Major say, '....... and remember the vehicles and building will not give you much protection. Best to use the bridge uprights: they're solid steel.'

Two small slashes of lights up river caught Darke's eye, he pointed and shouted, 'Look! The Princess!'

They had been watching for the arrival of the riverboat, but in the darkness their eyes could distinguish little. The Princess was well clear of the bend before announcing her presence by switching on her bridge-wing spotlights. A flare arced from her bridge. It burst in the night sky, partially obscured in the low clouds that blotted out the crescent moon. In the pale green glow of the flare, they could make out the dark bulk of the steamer. Briefly, like giant arms, the two beams tracked out across the tumbling surface of the swollen river. A red answering flare came from behind the dense foliage on the east bank.

The Princess steered toward the Nambrian bank, in preparation for a turn to starboard. The machine guns on her deck were sighted to port and over her stern. To support the landing the Princess must turn across the current and head back upstream close to the west bank. She was well down in the water and not riding the turbulence easily. Some of the rolling waves were crashing into her hull, throwing spray over the huddled souls on her deck. She swung awkwardly across the river but failed to complete the turn upstream. She was floundering, held by the current and in danger of drifting sideways towards the bridge. The turn across the river revealed to the watchers on the road bridge, the four large rubber barges being towed behind. There were two side-by-side with another two behind. Their full complement of guerillas was huddled down against the spray and cool of the night. Darke could see each barge contained about thirty men.

The overladen steamer was still struggling to manoeuvre. The intention was clear: once facing into the current she would drop anchor, release the barges and offload the men onboard, into the aluminium skiffs being unlashed from her sides. She would need to use all her power, to maintain position in relation to the riverbank in order to drop anchor. But her overloaded engines could not cope. She was drifting. The craft she was towing swung past her at the end of their tow ropes. Their weight came to her rescue, dragging her stern round to complete the turn. She was rocking dangerously and having difficulty keeping position. Darke noted the turbulence under her stern, showing her engines were running at full power. The crew were working to release the tow ropes, to allow the KAPU men to paddle the barges the thirty yards to the shore. Once relieved of the four barges the Princess had just sufficient power to combat the current. She clawed her way upstream, closing with the west bank.

The spotlights swung wildly as they tried to compensate for the rocking of the vessel. Eventually they locked on to each end of the road bridge, highlighting the two customs buildings. As they came to rest, tiny streaks of light could be seen arcing from the stern of the steamer, heading for the bridge, followed by the delayed rattle of heavy machine guns.

The Major gave a yell, 'Incoming fire, get down, take cover. They'll aim to take out the buildings, to stop any communications with Fort Albert.'

Almost in unison the seven men flattened themselves on the bitumen surface of the bridge. Darke felt exposed as the beams swept over the bridge structure. Tracers whirred overhead like angry bees. The Princess's top deck was lower than their position. The steel box sections forming the sides of the bridge gave them cover from the steamer's direct line of fire: not so the buildings. The tracers wavered, wandered lower, until the flimsy wood and metal structures began to shred and disintegrate in the hail of bullets. The occasional hollow thump of mortars could be heard, followed shortly by a distant crump, as each shell landed. Darke knew they had more to fear from this plunging fire, than anything else, but so far nothing had landed in their direction. All the mortars seemed to be aimed toward the town.

Major Abumi apparently oblivious to his injured arm, grinned across at Darke and Kufanu and commented, 'Time to get stuck in. I hope we get support soon.'

He wriggled across to the edge of the bridge and looked over, then ducked down. He rolled onto his back, to look at the rest of them, as they took up their firing positions.

'We have here a choice of targets,' he said conversationally,' I suggest the rest of you concentrate on the men in the boats nearest the shore, whilst the Superintendent and Chief Inspector help me shoot out the spotlights on the bridge wings.' He looked at Kufanu and Darke and they nodded their agreement in unison.

They checked and cocked their rifles. The Major asked, 'You ready?' They nodded again, 'Let's go,' he said.

There came the hollow thumps and distant explosions of mortars once more. Unless the vessel stabilised, in quieter waters, the mortar crews did not have a steady platform to aim and fire their weapons with any degree of accuracy. Almost as one, the men rose up to aim their weapons at the steamer. The starboard wing light was hit within seconds. The port light went soon after. Having extinguished the spotlights, they turned their attention to the men huddled in the barges now making for the river bank.

As soon as the crew of the Princess had dropped the tow ropes, the men in the barges rapidly paddled for the shore thirty yards away. At three hundred yards they presented an easy target. Soon men were being hit and one barge was sinking. Men on board, waiting their turn to land, were attempting to return fire but the rocking of the boats disturbed their aim. Some men in the remaining barges, not wishing to wait, were jumping into the water. Others made it to the river bank, a few were swept away by the current. The men aboard the Princess were queueing to board the aluminium skiffs, which had been untied and lowered alongside.

Under the withering fire, panic ensued among the KAPU men. Whatever rehearsed routine had been practised, was falling apart under the hail of bullets from the road bridge. One of the newly launched aluminium skiffs began to sink, its hull riddled by gunfire. The KAPU men, in danger of sinking, were discarding equipment as fast as they could, knowing they would soon be in the water. Darke wonder how many could swim. He closed his mind to the problem to concentrate on changing the magazine on his rifle. He aimed at the Princess herself. Here their fire was largely ineffective, the KAPU men were well protected by all the sandbags around her deck. The machine gunners, having identified the location of their assailants, turned their heavier firepower towards them.

The Major ducked back behind cover, calling to the others to do the same, ordering them to change their positions before firing again. He spotted four men running from the far end of the bridge. He yelled and waved to them to get down, but the noise of battle was too loud for them to hear. A chain of phosphorescent tracer bullets climbed lazily up from the deck of the Princess. It wavered and wandered towards the running men. As they watched, the leader turned into a limp rag doll, in mid stride, as he met the luminous fusillade. He collapsed onto the bridge surface in an untidy heap and lay without moving. The others, horrified, instantly recognised the danger. They threw themselves flat and wriggled their way towards and past their fallen comrade.

Movement beyond them caught Darke's eye. Looming slowly into view at the far end of the bridge was a cumbersome mechanical contraption. It took him seconds to realise it was some kind of home-made ironclad truck, surmounted by a heavy machine gun. The barrel was poking through a vertical aperture of a steel shield. At a second glance he realised it was a lorry protected with steel plating. Tapping the Major's shoulder, to draw his attention, Darke pointed towards the vehicle.

'Hit the tyres' Abumi instructed. He rolled over and slid round in the prone position to aim at the vehicle. Elias Kufanu joined them and the three men aimed at the vulnerable areas of rubber below the welded steel plates. The armoured leviathan trundled forward and began to spray tracers along the bridge, at the two vehicles blocking its path.

'It's no good,' Darke shouted, 'the steel plates guarding the wheels come too close to the ground.' He indicated the Superintendent and himself to the Major, 'Elias and I'll wait with the petrol bombs, until it comes closer. Give us the tear gas grenades. You take the rest of the men back to the end of the bridge and do what you can to stop the units from the Princess.'

Major Abumi paused briefly, obviously weighing up the options and realising his choices were limited. Unless the vehicle could be stopped it would overwhelm them, but his priority was to stop or delay the attack on the town, that was the growing threat from the Princess. There was no real alternative.

He nodded his agreement, wished them, 'Good luck', before turning and waving to the others to keep low and set off to the west end of the bridge.

The three Nambrian customs men were darting from stanchion to stanchion, to give them cover. They were nearing the two vehicles forming the road block. The armoured truck ignored them and concentrated its fire on the Chevrolet pick-up and Landrover, blocking its path. As the three men edged past the roadblock Elias Kufanu told them to keep going, to join Major Abumi at the end of the bridge. They were in shock. The loss of their leader and the ordeal of crossing the bridge stopped them from answering; they just nodded in response. They hurried on, barely pausing before continuing, careful to move between the stanchions and mindful of the proximity of fire from the crawling scratch-built tank.

Keeping low on the upriver side of the bridge, Darke yelled into Kufanu's ear, 'The wind is in our favour. Its blowing towards the far end of the bridge. If we use the tear gas first, as a smokescreen, that thing will have to move through it. Some of the gas is bound to filter inside. As it emerges from the smoke, we'll be ready to throw the petrol bombs. Hopefully either the gas or the bombs, or both, will be enough to stop it.'

The Superintendent agreed, saying, 'Let's give it a try. I'll take the other side of the bridge. I'll throw my tear gas first, when she comes into range.'

Darke nodded. It made sense. He had no doubt the big policeman could outthrow him by some distance. Between them they divided the stock of gas canisters and petrol bombs. Kufanu's half was left in the crate. Keeping low, judging his moment, between burst of fire from the armoured truck, he ducked and ran, dragging the crate with him. He made it safely to the opposite side of the bridge. Once safely in the lee of a steel stanchion he turned and gave a wide grin and 'thumbs up' to Darke.

The steel-clad monster, advancing towards them, was now half way across the bridge. There were men on foot following behind. Darke held up a teargas canister and signalled the Superintendent. Darke waited for Kufanu to throw two of his canisters, over the roadblock, into the path of the oncoming juggernaut. Clouds of dense smoke hissed and spewed from the canisters as they hit the bridge surface and rolled forward. After a third canister Kufanu stopped. Dense billows of gas were climbing eastward in the steady breeze, towards the advancing vehicle. It was now masked from view. Some of the men following were skirting the dense smoke cloud. Judging it was time, Darke let fly. He threw one canister to the left of the vehicle, another to the right, to stop the men on foot from avoiding the gas. His third canister he threw towards the centre, where the armoured truck was now obscured by swathes of grey smoke.

Both Darke and Kufanu had been deliberately exposed to teargas, as part of their police training to understand and appreciate its effects. It was unpleasant stuff. He knew the fumes would infiltrate the home-made vehicle. It would attack the eyes of the occupants and any damp areas of the body, causing them to itch excessively. The more these areas are rubbed or scratched, the worse the symptoms become. Washing with water or, if nothing else, exposing the affected areas to a fresh breeze would help to alleviate the symptoms. Unless the KAPU attackers had gas masks or were supermen, they must rapidly lose interest in the attack.

The grey gas cloud rolled eastward, slowly revealing the, now, stationary armoured lorry. Men could be seen tumbling from its rear, gasping for breath and rubbing their eyes. Some had even left their weapons behind. Darke and the Superintendent fired at the standing men as more disgorged from the rear. They appeared not to realise their danger, until a few began to fall, calling out in pain. Panic ensued. Some of their number threw themselves to the ground, others tried to slip beneath the vehicle, but the steel skirts came too close to the road surface. One man was having none of it: he obviously lost all reason. He leapt over the parapet of the bridge, into the water twenty feet below, to be swept away by the fast-flowing current. The few still standing had the initiative, in spite of their discomfort, to return poorly aimed shots. They retreated behind the vehicle, using it for cover as they following the teargas cloud. They carried their wounded with them. Three bodies were left motionless, beside the abandoned vehicle.

Darke fired in their direction, to hasten their departure. As he changed the magazine on his rifle for a full one, relative calm returned to the bridge. Close by, came the crackle of a small fire in the Landrover, as a result of the heavy machine gun rounds from the KAPU truck.

Off in the direction of Fort Albert, small arms fire could be heard. Also, the distant thump of mortar rounds landing in the town, fired from the decks of the Olulopo Princess. He looked across the bridge at Elias Kufanu. They grinned at each other with relief at their little victory. Adrenaline was coursing through Darke's veins. He understood the battle madness that affected some men. He experienced a primal urge to leap up and rush forward, to slay his enemies where they stood, but common sense prevailed.

Superintendent Kufanu pointed to the petrol bombs and indicated with a throwing action of his arm, that it was time to use the Molotov cocktails. Darke took a deep breath to calm his nerves and gave him the "thumbs up" sign.

He diverted his adrenaline-fuelled urge to action, by gathering four homemade bombs and stacking them at his feet. Kufanu joined him with his stock of petrol filled bottles. They lit a fuse each from the fire taking hold in the Landrover. Both men threw them as far as they could at the stalled, steel-covered lorry. Darke's bomb landed in front of the vehicle, with a satisfying 'whoomph,' spraying the front steel plates with burning fuel. Kufanu's bomb hit the shield, guarding the silenced heavy machine gun, engulfing it in orange flames. By the time they had thrown four bombs each the machine was the centre of a brilliant fireball, completely covered in flames; effectively barring any further assault from the east side of the bridge, for the time being. The conflagration drew erratic machine gun fire from the Princess. The bullets made bee-like sounds as they zipped passed overhead or smacked, with a ring, into the bridge girders. One after the other the tyres, of the burning armoured truck, exploded. The vehicle sagged down onto its steel wheel rims, in a shower of sparks.

Shouting above the noise, Darke called, 'Time to pull back, before the petrol tanks blow on these trucks.'

Together, in a low crouching run, they retired to a position to the west of the shattered remains, of the Kwazanian border post. Both men sank down in their new positions, breathing hard from the exertion and excitement. Darke looked over the bridge, to see the final skiffs leaving the side of the Princess. Major Abumi's men were engaging the units that had reached the shore. An abandoned craft, was drifting rapidly downstream, away from the shore. It was sinking fast. All of the few men left aboard were injured or dead. The others had taken their chances by diving overboard, some had made it to the shore, others were struggling in the strong current.

Another skiff had gained the bank, but was also foundering. A quarter of the occupants were casualties. Men had leapt overboard into the shallows, they pulled the aluminium skiff half out of the water, before throwing themselves flat onto the sodden ground, to take stock of their situation. The senior KAPU soldier had abandoned his wounded and dead comrades in the half-grounded skiff. He swung his men towards the Kwazanian end of the road bridge. Despite the concentrated fire from Major Abumi's squad, the remaining skiffs, were closing with the shore in a ragged line. One boat was sinking, its hull riddled with bullets. Two wounded men were hanging over the side. Most of the other occupants had taken to the water, clinging to the side of their craft to gain as much cover from the fire coming from the west end of the bridge.

It was apparent that more support was needed to halt the advancing KAPU force. Major Abumi's small team had disrupted the attack, but as more men came ashore the odds were moving in the favour of the attackers. Units were moving toward the town, but an increasing number had turned their attention toward the defenders on the bridge. Darke swung round to take in the view of the Princess. With the last of the skiffs away the crew of the riverboat were making efforts to anchor her bows upstream, to give the mortars and heavy machine guns a more stable firing platform. Already the steady explosion of mortars could be seen, in the distance, falling within the town boundary of Fort Albert. Yellow flashes were reflecting off the low, fast-moving clouds.

Looking back at the Olulopo Princess, Darke spotted the wiry frame of Sandy Leitch. He was silhouetted on the port wing of the bridge, surveying the scene on the left bank through night glasses. He obviously did not believe in leading his men from the front. Darke swung his rifle up to his shoulder, taking careful aim along the sights. He aimed fractionally high, gradually expelling the air from his lungs, causing the barrel to gently drop, bringing the front sight to a point slightly below Leitch's head. He held his breath and gently applied an even pressure to the trigger. He was anticipating the rocking motion of the steamer. As the crew pulled her tight to her bow anchor, the rifle kicked, just as the stern of the Princess swung across the current. Leitch fell against the bridge rail clutching his neck. Before Darke could line the rifle up, for a second shot, the Scotsman had yelled at the fighters in the stern of the vessel, gesturing towards the bridge. Still clutching his neck, he leapt back into the wheelhouse, out of sight.

Inwardly Darke cursed. He felt no remorse in attempting to kill the man. It was a difficult shot to hit Leitch, on a moving boat in semi-darkness, but if he had succeeded, his and Alison's problems would have been over. A machine gun in the steamer's stern instantly targeted Darke's section of the bridge. He ducked behind a steel girder, yelling at the Superintendent to take cover. The urgent clatter of bullets, against the iron girders and others whirring overhead, was loud and intimidating. He took a deep breath to calm his nerves. Changing position, he glanced briefly at the riverboat. Those men aboard, waiting for boats to ferry them to the west bank, were huddling behind the sandbags.

The anchor was not holding the overloaded vessel, nor were the engines powerful enough to fight the strengthening current. The anchor was dragging. It was clear to all aboard she was losing the battle with the river. The Princess swung to port closing with the shore. The port side rose sluggishly, as the she slid onto the muddy bank. The men aboard, including those manning the heavy machine guns, rose up, without orders and ran to the port bow, to eagerly leap ashore. It was a general exodus, but Leitch was not among them.

There came an increase in activity from the east end of the road bridge. The units there had been reorganised into firing parties, now the flames of the wrecked armoured truck were subsiding. They poured a fusillade of bullets at the two wrecked vehicles blocking the bridge. Mortars were also ranging onto the structure. Being based on land they would soon be falling accurately on the defenders.

Darke detected movement from the burning armoured vehicle. 'It's moving,' he shouted above the noise of battle.

The Superintendent peered along the bridge and called out, 'They've managed to hook a line to it, and are dragging it to one side.'

It was obvious they must leave the bridge. A mortar bomb landed twenty feet in front of the smouldering remains of the armoured truck. Once the bridge was clear the KAPU men would be streaming across.

'Time to go,' Darke murmured to himself. He squirmed his way across to Elias Kufanu who was ruefully checking the magazine of his automatic rifle. 'We'd better get out of here Elias,' he yelled, 'Once that mortar finds the range, we'll be for it.'

Kufanu nodded. 'I've only a few rounds left anyway. We should get rid of these gas canisters whilst we can.'

Darke agreed. They pulled the pins on the remaining tear gas grenades and toss them as far along the bridge as possible. The teargas would obscure the view from the far end and hopefully delay the attack for a while longer.

Darke called out, 'Time to go. Let's get back to the Major.'

As they retired the burning Landrover erupted in flames, as its petrol tank exploded. It instantly triggered the eruption of the Chevrolet's fuel tank. The flames were useful in covering their retreat. Even so, they were spurred on their way by the zip of bullets passing close by. The rebels were firing blind, from the far end of the bridge. Moving from stanchion to stanchion, Darke became aware the sounds of battle had changed. Off toward Fort Albert, there was an increase in automatic fire, and the occasional flash of orange lights. He fervently hoped it indicated a counterattack was imminent.

Chapter 21

The major's little force, was located beyond the West End of the bridge, behind a stone wall, on the north side of the road. He looked concerned as they crawled up and dropped down alongside him.

He spoke first, 'The KAPU units are getting their act together and starting to advance. If they have any sense, they will soon outflank us to our left: then we'll be in trouble. What's happening at the other end of the bridge?'

'They've managed to get a line on their burnt-out truck and are pulling it back to one side,' Kufanu explained. 'We have just used the last of the tear gas. It will hold them off for a while. Once the truck fires calm down and the tear gas dissipates, they'll be swarming across, unless we do something." He added, 'We're low on ammunition.'

'Sorry, can't help, we're low as well,' Abumi explained.

To Darke the situation was becoming desperate, unless help arrived shortly, they would be overrun. Once they had the upper hand, the KAPU forces would make short work of them. There would be no mercy, no making them captive, to be taken before Leitch. A quick end is all they could hope for. He allowed himself the brief luxury of wondering how the hell he had got himself into this mess. Grimly they joined the Major's men, firing at the units advancing in their direction. They used their remaining ammunition sparingly, making each round count.

Sergeant Cheruwa called to the Major and pointed towards the town. There was movement at the far end of the road that curved around from Fort Albert. Two, armoured cars were racing along it, towards them, firing their machine guns at the KAPU attackers as they came.

'Cutting it a bit fine, but here comes the cavalry. They'll be useful,' the Major observed with relief.

They watched the two Ferret armoured cars as they approached, firing bursts at the attackers as they came on. The turreted vehicles pulled up before the bridge, behind their position, and immediately opened fire over their heads. They fired in short, controlled bursts, which were having a marked affect in forcing the attackers to take cover.

The Major recognised the young subaltern in command, who jumped down, 'Took your time Silas,' he said smiling, as he returned the young officer's salute.

'Better late than never, sir. We were on the move shortly after receiving your radio messages, earlier this evening.' He grinned. 'Colonel's compliments. He thought you might like some ammunition and grenades. The counter attack is due to start any time now.'

As he finished talking the sky was lit by six parachute flares, launched from the direction of the town, accompanied by increased small arms and heavy machine gun fire. The flares arced high into the low cloud, which created a white diffused glow, creating an eery sensation of daylight.

Darke turned towards the Olulopo Princess, the bright light allowed him to see the riverboat clearly. He stopped, grabbed Kufanu's arm saying, 'Look, she's beginning to drift downstream, away from the bank.'

Kufanu studied the riverboat out on the fast-flowing water. He agreed, 'There's an anchor rope stretched over the bows, and the screws are hardly turning. She's definitely slipping backwards.'

As they watched the taut anchor cable parted. What was left of it snaked back towards the Princess in a series of loops before falling into the water. The current swung her away from the bank and down towards the bridge.

'Her engines have stopped. She's drifting. She'll be under the bridge soon.' Darke paused before saying, 'I'm going to try and get on board.'

Kufanu shook his head. 'Not a good idea.'

'There's no one on deck and Leitch is still on board. We can arrest him.' It was a long shot, but the possibility of finally settling with the Scotsman spurred him on. He could not forego the opportunity. He needed to bring this whole business to an end. Not to try would haunt him. All that had happened since arriving in Kwazania would have been wasted if Leitch escaped. 'It's worth a try.'

Kufanu nodded his head. 'Okay, let's see what happens. I'll let Major Abumi know what we have in mind.'

The bridge was still under sporadic fire from the eastern side. Several bursts from one of the armoured cars had subdued most of the activity from that direction. Fire from the Princess had ceased altogether. The last of the crew had left. She had failed to act as the support platform as intended. It was clear that the KAPU assault on the town was faltering. Leitch was still on board. He was obviously abandoning his men to the mercy of the Kwazanian forces.

Darke led the way back, along the road bridge, using the stanchions for cover. The two men made their way towards the remains of the still burning vehicles. The riverboat was slowly slipping towards the bridge. There was no one visible on the rear deck.

Elias Kufanu tapped Darke on the shoulder and yelled, 'She's swinging towards the first stone pillar, it looks as though she'll straddle it, right side on.'

It was true, Darke realised. If the Princess collided with the supporting masonry of the bridge, it would hold her up sufficiently, to give them a chance to climb down to her deck. The riverboat was drifting sideways to the current, apparently devoid of sufficient power to prevent her being swept away from the battle. She was helpless in the fast-flowing current. A large KAPU figure appeared on the starboard bridge wing to stare at the approaching stone pillar. One shot from Elias Kufanu caused him to hastily withdraw.

The stricken Princess seemed to accelerate over the last twenty yards. She slammed, almost amidships, into the stone column, starboard side on. The screech of tortured steel and the crunch of splintering wood could be heard above the sound of gun and mortar fire. She shuddered to a halt. Darke and Kufanu seized the moment to swing over the chest high rail, to drop onto the awning of the upper deck, whilst all the attention of those few left on board was concentrated on the collision. They were not too soon. The Olulopo Princess sawed up and down, against the masonry pillar, to the motion of the river, before swinging clockwise round the rough stone support. She gave another tooth jarring squeal of torn metal, before ripping herself free, to drift off downstream.

Even with all the KAPU men and their equipment offloaded, the ageing, flat bottom vessel, was still top heavy, her deck was heaving sluggishly in the turbulent wash below the road bridge. Darke was convinced the she was showing less freeboard than previously. The Princess was seriously wounded and was surely taking on water. He told Kufanu of his thoughts. They would need to achieve their objective and get off the crippled craft as quickly as possible.

Both men swung down from the awning onto the rear of the upper deck. Darke covered the port wing of the bridge from the upper deck at the top of the steps leading down to the main deck. Superintendent Kufanu bent down to pick up an ammunition belt of heavy machine gun rounds. He extracted four bullets. With a nod to Darke, he threw them at the bridge structure, to draw a response. A moment later Leitch appeared, on the starboard wing, with a bandage round his neck. He spied Darke and fired a snap shot, but missed. Darke and the Superintendent fired simultaneously, but Leitch had ducked back inside the wheelhouse. Another KAPU man appeared on the port wing. This time Darke fired two well aimed shots, the man buckled forward, staggered to the railing and disappeared overboard, into the swirling torrent. The two men retreated down the steps to the main deck.

An arm appeared on the port side of the bridge. An object was tossed onto the upper deck. The grenade landed, rolled and struck a machine gun mount. The two men threw themselves flat on the lower deck. The grenade exploded harmlessly above them. Flames danced on the underside of the upper deck awning, as something flammable caught fire. Having lost the element of surprise, they both realised it would be foolish to continue.

'It's a stand-off,' Darke yelled, feeling exposed in the flickering light from the fire above.

Kufanu nodded. 'Can't stay here any longer, the Agani falls are not far down river. We need to get off.' He paused, then added, 'We should come close to the right bank soon. We'll have to swim for it.'

There was a movement on the left wing of the bridge, Darke fired and the man disappeared.

'A decoy, I think. Just checking if we're still here,' Darke guessed.

As they retreated towards the stern, keeping watch on the bridge for any further action, Darke almost fell as his foot caught the edge of the engine room hatch. He looked down to see the cover slowly lifting. He bent and roughly pulled it fully open, to reveal a man in overalls on the ladder. There was a look of shock and fear on his face. In his hand he held a live grenade. Darke aimed and pulled the trigger on his rifle. There was a click but nothing happened. The hand with the grenade came up. Darke instinctively rammed the barrel of the rifle at the man. It struck him hard on his breastbone. He slipped of the ladder, dropping down the hatch, taking the grenade with him. Darke kicked the hatch shut. Both men dived onto the deck. They felt the shock of the explosion through the decking. It blew the hatch lid off, followed by a rush of smoke and flames that were quickly dispersed in the strong, damp breeze.

Picking himself up, Kufanu said, 'This is unhealthy, let's get the hell out of this mess.'

Darke realised any chance they had to capture or kill Leitch, had gone. The first grenade had started a fire on the upper deck and the second had started another below. The Princess was dying. She was crippled, powerless and drifting. He nodded his agreement. Kufanu fired two more shots as they made their way to the stern. The main deck awning obscured their view of the bridge wings as they retreated. Once out of sight they turned and ran for the stern.

The big policeman pointed and said, 'That's the bend coming up.'

Darke called out, 'There are some overhanging trees. It could be our best chance.'

As he watched, Kufanu aimed his rifle in the approximate direction of the bridge and fired three rapid shots, to discourage any further action. With a nod both men discarded their weapons and swung over the sandbags by the guardrails. Judging the moment, they leapt into the water. Kufanu, slightly ahead, disappeared below the rushing waves, as Darke was still in the air. Both men surfaced quickly and struck out for the shore. Darke was shocked by the speed of the current. The bigger man was the stronger swimmer. The overhanging trees were coming up fast. Kufanu grabbed hold of Darke with his left hand and swung his right arm up and round a branch. The bough dipped dangerously with their weight, but held. The Superintendent used his enormous strength to haul Darke alongside, enabling him to take hold of the branch. They rested briefly before pulling themselves through slacker water to the bank. They looked down river, but the Olulopo Princess had disappeared into the night.

Chapter 23

Four days later, following the departure of the last of the army units, Virginia Easterton held an evening gathering at Mount Muzindi Farm. Following the failure of the attempted KAPU attack on Fort Albert, there had been much to be done: a search for the Olulopo Princess, debriefings, statements to be given and much needed sleep. Superintendent Elias Kufanu was standing by the open fire, dressed in civilian clothes. On the other side of the sitting room Darke was refreshing their drinks from a decanter.

'We had no idea what had happened to you both,' Alison spoke, her voice betraying the concern she had felt. 'We had to assume the helicopter had crashed, but we had no idea where it might be. I don't think they have found the crash site yet.'

Samanca Kufanu, sitting beside the fire, raised her hand to touch her husband's arm, almost to reassure herself that he was really there. He looked down and smiled affectionately.

'What do you think happened to Leitch?' Virginia Easterton looked at the two men in turn and asked, 'Do you think he's still alive?' She voiced the thoughts of them all.

Kufanu turned to face her, 'We just don't know what happened to him. We could find no trace below the Falls. That's not surprising. Not to put too fine a point on it, any bodies are likely to have been swept miles further downriver or taken by crocodiles. The Princess definitely went over. There is enough of her wreckage spread around, below the falls and down river to prove that. Of Leitch there was no sign. It will not be healthy for him east or west of the river, if he has survived. The Nambrian army is scouring their side for any KAPU forces and so are we on our side.'

Alison Falkener looked at Darke, 'So what do we do now, we're still no safer than we were before? We'll spend the rest of our days wondering whether he'll suddenly appear, wanting revenge. He's just a vicious animal.'

'I agree,' said Virginia.

Kufanu addressed the two women, 'We have a warrant out for his arrest. He has been listed as 'dangerous' and high on our "Most Wanted" List. All relevant information has been passed to neighbouring countries, the UK police, and Interpol. We're still searching the hills for the helicopter crash site. After our debriefing, they have a clearer idea of where to look. We need to recover the bodies of our chaps and close down the marijuana plantations. It is quite possible Leitch, if alive, will attempt to return there.' He gave a slight apologetic shrug of his broad shoulders. 'At the moment, that is all we can do. His entire operation has been destroyed and he's on the run. That should make him easier to trace.'

As he finished speaking, there was a commotion outside. The French windows onto the veranda exploded inwards, with the shattering of glass and rending of wood. A thunderous burst of gunfire and flames from an AK47 rifle, aimed at the rafters, marked the entrance of a dishevelled, wild eyed Leitch. He stepped in amid the debris. The rifle was held in his left hand. His right arm held behind his back. The women screamed.

'Yer F-----G BASTARDS,' he yelled, then in a quieter, sing-song voice, 'It's payback time!'

It was a hopeless task, Lucas Darke realised, even before he threw himself forward. Out of the corner of his eye he caught a similar movement from the opposite side of the room, as Elias Kufanu moved in unison. Leitch swung the weapon from side to side with a weird, twisted grin on his face: watching, judging. Darke felt the weight of the decanter still in his hand. He swung it underarm at Leitch, it was a good throw; accurate enough to get the Scotsman's full attention. He used the butt of his Kalashnikov to easily deflect the crystal flask. it slammed to the floor. It was not sufficient to gain the time they needed. With a confident smile Leitch swung the rifle back toward Kufanu and with a flourish he brought his right arm from behind his back. He held a hand grenade in his hand. The pin had been removed. Both men stopped.

'Get down on the floor,' Darke and Kufanu yelled to the women.

It was clear that the pin had been pulled and only Leitch's grip on the sprung lever stood between them and oblivion.

Darke put both palms forward, 'Easy, Leitch. What do you want?'

'Want? What I want Laddie is retribution. That's wha' I want and I'm gonna get it!'

It was clear to everyone in the room that he was crazed beyond reason. Darke took a step forward.

Leitch's eyes widened with excitement. 'Ah, naughty,' he said, raising the hand holding the grenade higher, in an obvious warning.

Darke felt despair. He was facing a deranged man bent on vengeance, even if it meant destroying himself in the process. He had the attention of the room and was revelling in the moment.

Suddenly there was a transformation. A demonic screech came from the veranda, followed by a dull thud. Leitch's eyes grew wide and his body went rigid. He rose on tiptoe, froze for a moment, teetered, before collapsing, full length, on the wooden floor. His body twitched twice, amid the debris from the shattered French doors, before becoming still. A long-handled African axe was protruding from the back of his skull. Its narrow triangular iron blade was buried deep in the back of his head. Silhouetted in the doorway, behind, stood an African woman, her hands to her mouth, quivering with fury, her eyes fixated on the prostrated form before her.

The grenade, released from nerveless fingers, rolled gently along the wooden floor. Darke leapt forward, in one motion, scooped it up and tossed it out through the broken doorway, past the frozen form of the woman and over the veranda, onto the lawn below. He tackled the women to the floor as the grenade exploded. The raised veranda shielded them from the effect of the blast, deflecting the force upwards.

Elias Kufanu slowly picked himself up, the explosion was still ringing in his ears. He kicked the rifle away from the limp grasp of the fallen man, before stooping to check for life. He straightened up slowly and nodded to Darke, who was helping the African woman to her feet.

'He's dead alright,' he said.

Darke, his hearing similarly affected, just made out the words.

'Can't say I'm sorry,' he said flatly, deliberately not displaying the rush of relief he felt. He turned back to Leitch's assailant. Her eyes were locked on the lifeless form of the man she had just slain. Darke touch her shoulder. The muscles were taught, her entire body rigid, as though in a cataleptic state. He lifted her to her feet, put his arms around her shoulders and talked quietly to her, but he could get no response.

At the sound of gunfire and explosion, two of the constables, the Superintendent had organised to patrol the property, came running onto the veranda. Darke nodded to them, telling them to take the women to the nearby table, to hold her there, but to treat her gently. They seemed uncertain as they surveyed the scene inside the room. Both men looked at their Superintendent for assurance. He gave a single nod to confirm Darke's instructions.

A short while later, after Elias Kufanu had made the necessary telephone calls from Virginia's study. They were gathered there to keep the crime scene undisturbed. He had ordered one of his men to protect the scene, the other stood guard over the woman. He had cautioned and questioned her on the veranda, after she had recovered her senses. She slowly opened up and gave her story. He had taken written notes of her account, before returning to the study.

The three women were calmer now. Darke had given them a stiff drink each. They were obviously still in a state of shock.

'Who is she?' asked Samanca, sipping her brandy.

Kufanu answered, 'Her name is Hanna. Her husband, Petrol Mugwani, was coerced into working for Leitch against his will. He was made to sell drugs and recruit workers for the illegal dagga plantations in the hills. Lucas and I investigated his suicide, more than ten years ago. She has continued to work here on the farm since that time. Ever since she has been resentful for the part, she believed Leitch played in her husband's suicide. She has been constantly in fear of what he might do to her, if she spoke out.' He turned to Virginia, saying, 'You talked with her a few days ago. You know how fearful she was of Leitch. How she held him responsible for the death of her husband. Apparently, this evening one of the farm workers was returning from a 'beer drink', on a neighbouring farm, when he saw a man, with a rifle, acting suspiciously. He recognised him as Leitch. When Hanna heard of this, she became furious. She had had enough. She went in search of Leitch, with her husband's axe. It appears she just wanted an end to her years of fear and anxiety.'

'Lucky for us,' remarked Samanca.

Virginia nodded, 'I didn't recognise her. Her face was so distorted with rage. What will happen to her?'

'It will be a matter of going through the formalities of course,' Kufanu said. 'However, with our statements, it will be a case of justifiable homicide. It is clear she saved our lives, whether that was her intention or not. She will need a solicitor. Can you arrange that?'

She looked strained but instantly responded, 'Of course. It's the least I can do.'

By the time the scenes of crime team arrived it was well past midnight. While they waited Darke and Kufanu encouraged the three women to talk about Leitch's attack amongst themselves. They both realised the need for the women to process what had happened. It was shocking enough for Samanca, but Virginia and Alison had only recently survived the bushfire. They hoped discussing the evening's event would help them rationalise their reactions. The fact that Leitch was dead meant the threat he had posed was gone. The women gradually relaxed. Virginia had suggested they all stay for the night. Eventually fatigue overtook them and they retired.

When Kufanu and Darke were left on their own, Darke breathed a sigh of relief. 'There go three very resilient women.'

The Superintendent nodded. 'We breed them tough in Kwazania.'

'And in Scotland,' Darke added with a smile.

Kufanu went to liaise with the investigation team. Darke walked out into the cool night air. He stood at the opposite end of the veranda to the scene of the evening's events. There was a half-moon. He breathed in the eucalyptus scented air and relaxed. A slight movement caught his eye. He turned to see Virginia by the door. She had been watching him.

'I didn't mean to disturb you. You seemed far away,' she said, moving to his side.

'Just winding down, listening to the cicadas.'

'You'll be leaving soon?'

'He half turned towards her before saying, 'I can't stay longer, I have a house to rebuild and a business to run.' He paused before continuing, 'It has been barely three weeks since we met. So much has happened; good and bad. It's difficult to realise you and I have spent less than two days alone together. That is no basis for beginning a relationship, is it?'

'If you say so.' She said quietly. Then, 'I'm planning to go to London in December, to see Mr. Tanwick about setting up a charity with the money.' She paused again, 'Alison has invited me to spend Christmas with her, in Scotland?'

He smiled to himself, before saying, 'Somehow that doesn't surprise me.'

Should I accept?

He drew her into his arms, before answering, 'I think that's a very good idea.'

Epilogue

It was refreshingly cool as usual, in the Superintendent's office. They sat on opposite sides of the large mahogany leather-topped desk.

The bigger man grinned. 'Well, it is no exaggeration to say you bear the responsibility for having stirred up quite a hornet's nest, since you arrived.'

Darke pulled a face. 'Yes,' he said, 'I guess you're right. I had just intended to put right the verdict on Lewis Bodell's death.'

'And to bring the threat of Leitch, to you and Alison, to a conclusion,' said Kufanu.

'That's true,' admitted Darke, with a wry grin.

Darke leaned forward. 'One thing intrigues me. How do you think Leitch knew we were all at Mount Muzindi farm?'

Kufanu paused to look at the ceiling, before answering, 'I was not going to mention it at this moment, but having raised the issue, I think you deserve to know. However, what I am about to tell you must go no further, for the time being.'

Intrigued, Darke nodded his agreement.

'A scrap of paper was found on Leitch's body. It had on it, in a hastily scribbled hand, "*THURSDAY EVENING, MOUNT MUZINDI FARM*". It was written on a page from a notebook, of the type used by the police. The three written "M's", in the message, are notable because the two diagonal lines at the top-centre of the "M's", extend too far down, so that they cross over each other, at the bottom of the vee, like a short-legged "X". It came as a shock, because I had seen that characteristic letter format written before. It was quite familiar to me: it reminded me of Inspector Desabi's memos.' He waved a hand regretfully. 'It is not pleasant having to admit to an informer on the Force.'

'Desabi? Really? Has he said anything?'

'Yes, after a while he admitted everything. Unfortunately, his expensive tastes were not confined to designer suits. It turns out he liked the best restaurants, expensive watches, the ladies and was also hooked on gambling. He was feeding information to Leitch via a dead letter drop, in the local park. The better the information, the more money he made. He has been charged with treason, and aiding an enemy of the state.'

'It occurs to me', Darke said, 'that he could have sabotaged the whole case by indicating the fingerprint he checked in the beginning, was not a match with the quaich I brought from Scotland. That would have let Leitch of the hook.'

'I questioned him about that. He said he couldn't bring himself to do it.'

'What will happen to him?'

'That's up to the court. We still have the death penalty for treason. He'll be lucky to get away with his life.'

Kufanu changed the subject. 'As it turned out, your actions triggered a series of events, that led to the thwarting of the KAPU raid on Fort Albert. God knows how much damage they would have done, and what would have happened thereafter.' Kufanu opened a drawer in his desk and withdrew an envelope before continuing, 'Even more important is the demise of KAPU. They were virtually a spent force, until Leitch came along. The loss of funding from the Russians had seriously affected their operations. Had they succeeded in a large-scale attack on the town, they could have gained a new lease of life and convinced the Russians to continue financing them.'

The Superintendent stood up and placed the envelope on the desk in front of Darke. 'There would normally be a ceremony of some kind to present this to you. However, the powers-that-be felt, for your safety, it would be wise not to advertise your part, in recent events, in case some aggrieved party might wish to seek revenge.' He paused, giving a rueful smile before continuing, 'Reading between the lines, I think the government has been embarrassed by the raid and does not want to give it more publicity than it has to. The letter is from King Tagaweyi, thanking you for your service to the nation. It also confirms that you are now an honorary citizen of Kwazania. Enclosed is your Kwazanian passport.'

Surprised, Darke answered, 'This is an unexpected honour, please convey my thanks to His Majesty and all concerned. I trust that your part was also recognised.'

'Yes, it hasn't been gazetted yet, but my promotion has been brought forward.'

'Congratulations, Chief Superintendent Kufanu.' Darke grinned, rose from the chair and stretching across the desk, shook the other man's hand. 'I'm not sure I would have survived that river, if it had not been for you, so I say, "very well deserved".'

'It's fair to say, you returned the favour at Muzindi Farm the other evening. So, I guess we're even.'

Darke changed the conversation and asked, 'Any news of Rifleman Aaron.'

'Yes. He's in the local hospital having a minor wound treated. He managed to climb into a tree when the tidal wave hit. When it subsided, he killed a KAPU man and took his uniform and put it on over his own. He re-boarded the Princess and came down river with her. When the Princess reached Fort Albert, Aaron went ashore with the landing units and kept to the right flank and disappeared into the trees. Discarding his KAPU uniform, he began picking off KAPU men, as they moved towards the town. Eventually he made contact with our counter attacking units. He has been marked for promotion. As for Sergeant Cheruwa, he is due to become CSM at the end of the year.'

'Good for them. Well, I'm glad they have received recognition. They both deserve it.'

Kufanu continued, 'Major Abumi has been congratulated from on high, for a successful operation. I took the liberty of giving him your regards. I think he feels a sense of responsibility for the loss of the helicopter and his men. I impressed on him that the situation was unforeseeable. It was sheer bad luck, that the first burst of fire from the ground brought down the helicopter. In fact, if we hadn't crashed and been captured, it's unlikely we would have discovered the KAPU plan to attack Fort Albert. He is at a top-level conference in Umbaka. Something to do with improving the security of our borders. Above my pay grade, I'm glad to say.'

'The weight of command, eh,' Darke replied.

The Chief Superintendent agreed and said, 'All KAPU prisoners have been interrogated by Special Branch, but there is little additional information about Leitch, or his henchman, Carl Brogan. Brogan seems not to have been involved, at any point with KAPU, except during the capture of the three of you, at Mount Muzindi Farm. There is no evidence of him being connected with the planning, or attack on Fort Albert. The consensus is, that his activities were confined to the growing and distribution of the marijuana. A warrant has been issued for his arrest, for his part in your abduction and attempted murder. In reality we have very little information on him, which will make apprehending him difficult.'

THE END

Printed in Great Britain
by Amazon

57548497R00145